Quixotic Ambitions

Pamela Lake

A Bright Pen Book

British Library Cataloguing Publication Data.
A catalogue record for this book is available from the British Library

ISBN 978-0-7552-1521-8

Authors OnLine Ltd
19 The Cinques
Gamlingay, Sandy
Bedfordshire SG19 3NU
England

This book is also available in e-book format, details of which are available at www.authorsonline.co.uk

For Gregor Dallas

Chapter 1

A jar of marmalade, old shoes, a half dead plant, a box of chocolates and a pile of books lay under the glass topped coffee table and papers and magazines were stacked on all the chairs. There was a mountain of clothes on the bedroom floor and other garments were draped over chairs or suspended on hooks on the doors. The kitchen work surface and the cooker were cluttered with pots of jam, chutney and honey. Katy surveyed the familiar scene wearily.

'God, what a mess! I must clear it up this weekend,' she said and was about to shut the front door when her next door neigbour, Mrs Bloch, appeared on the landing.

'A woman was here this afternoon looking for you. I met her on the stairs,' she said, her pointed nose twitching like a rabbit's.

Katy was suspicious. There had been several robberies in the district recently. 'It must be a mistake. I'm not expecting anyone,' she said.

'She's going to phone you this evening,' said Mrs Bloch, craning her neck to get a glimpse of the untidy flat through the half open door.

'What kind of woman was she?' said Katy. She disliked Mrs Bloch who was known to be a busybody.

'About seventy and elegantly dressed. She had a strong foreign accent.'

Katy gripped the door handle hard and managed to suppress the feeling of panic that threatened to overwhelm her. 'Thank you for letting me know,' she said abruptly and shut the door.

She flopped on the sofa exhausted. A foreign accent! Supposing this woman was in some way connected with her father? But her father had died years ago. Why would anyone want to get in touch with her about him now? It was ridiculous. She told herself it was undoubtedly a misunderstanding. If the woman did phone, she'd tell her she'd got the wrong number. End of story. She flung her raincoat on a chair and fetched a bottle of white wine and a packet of peanuts from the kitchen.

She looked out of the window. Disraeli Road was more than usually depressing that evening. The heavy November rain had stripped the trees, carpeting the pavements with sodden leaves and many of the Victorian terrace houses had 'For Sale' signs in their tiny front gardens. Why on earth had she decided to buy a flat in such a dismal street and why had she let it get in such a mess?

She went back to the sofa and turned on the television. She tried several channels but as there wasn't anything worth watching she switched it off again. As she was doing so, the phone rang. She picked it up, fearing that it was the call from the mysterious foreign lady. Instead she heard a familiar male voice.

'Hullo Katy, it's Richard.'

'For God's sake, stop ringing me? It's over!'

'I'll get a divorce.'

'You've been saying that for the past three years! You'll never get a divorce and anyway I couldn't care less what you do.'

'But I want you in my life!'

'All you've ever wanted was for me to be available when you needed some sex on the side! And don't give me that old story about not having had sex with your wife for years. How many other women have you said that to? I know one at least!'

'Katy, that's unfair. It was nothing. It's finished.'

'Unfair! It's the truth. You don't care about me. You were never there for me when I needed you.'

'Please Katy!'

'Don't ring again! Goodbye!'

She slammed the phone down on the coffee table. She turned the television on again and tried to watch a soap opera but she couldn't concentrate on the complicated love lives of the characters - infidelity, broken marriages, battered wives. Happiness didn't make good drama, misery did. She sometimes wondered, when she thought about her own friends, how many of them were genuinely happy when they were in love. But they seemed to think that an unsuitable man in their life was better than none at all, whereas she was fed up with the angst, the endless waiting for calls that never came, the analyzing of every remark. The men she'd been involved with had either been drifters who'd dropped out of university or couldn't hold down a job, or, like Richard, they'd been middle aged, married, and looking for an affair with a younger woman. She'd finally come to the conclusion that men were all selfish and out for what they could get.

She went into the kitchen and put a frozen shepherd's pie in the microwave, reflecting that she was much happier when there wasn't anyone in her life. With Richard out of the way she was free to be creative again and she'd started classes in oil painting at the Putney School of Art which was near her flat. It was a pleasure to mix the rich buttery paints on her palette - a pleasure that, unlike her love affair, didn't bring uncertainty and regret in its wake.

She took the pie out of the microwave and sat down at the kitchen table. She had just begun to eat when the phone rang again and this time it was a woman's voice with an unmistakable Slav accent.

'Miss Brennan? This is the Countess Elena Slobovna speaking. I am staying at the Maloslavian Embassy and I would like to meet you. I have something important to ask you.'

Katy caught her breath. So she'd been right about the woman after all!

'I don't want to get involved in anything to do with Maloslavia,' she said. 'I've never been there and I don't intend to after what happened to my father. I'm British.'

'That is not true and you cannot ignore the fact. Will you at least have lunch with me?'

Katy hunted desperately for an excuse. 'It's difficult. I'm working and I haven't much time for lunch.'

'I promise it will not take long. There is a pleasant Polish restaurant in the Old Brompton Road. Can you meet me there tomorrow at twelve thirty?'

Katy hesitated. The prospect of having a good lunch for once was attractive. After all, matters need go no further. She'd see what the Countess wanted and if she didn't agree she would be firm and say 'No.'

'Very well. I'll do my best but I might be a bit late.'

'Then it is settled. I will see you tomorrow. Good night.'

* * *

'Oh shit! It's eight o'clock already!' Katy jumped out of bed and went into the kitchen. She hadn't heard her alarm and she was going to be late again. She gulped down a bowl of cornflakes, had a quick shower and flung on the first clothes that came to hand. She ran all the way to East Putney station, gasping for breath as she hurtled on to the platform only to wait for twenty minutes before a train arrived. Why was her journey so slow and why did she never allow herself enough time to complete it? 'Late again,' she thought as she finally crept into the office. Jean wouldn't be pleased.

She worked for a monthly magazine called *The English Countrywoman*. It had a small circulation and was directed at the kind of affluent middle-aged woman who lives in a large country house with a husband who commutes to the City, wears Barbour jackets and green wellies and owns a four-wheeled drive and a Labrador. The all-female staff in the editorial office were under constant pressure which led to petty feuds, backbiting and occasional floods of tears. Katy worked in the section that dealt with readers' letters, headed by Jean Briggs, a bossy woman in her forties. Most of the readers wanted answers to questions concerning home-making, pets and gardening and Katy was part of the team who researched the solutions to the queries and drafted suitable replies. She shared an office with two teenagers, Sharon and Margaret, who were supposed to type these letters while she dealt with the next batch of problems. Unfortunately she had very little control over them and they spent much of their time discussing clubbing, gigs and their latest boyfriends.

'Ooh, you're for it!' Sharon said when Katy arrived. 'Jean Briggs wants you. It's the third time you've been late this week and she's furious.'

' That's all I need,' said Katy. She hung up her coat and knocked on the door of the adjoining office. Jean Briggs, a sallow, flat-chested woman in a beige twin set, looked up from the proofs that she was correcting.

'You're late again. This can't go on. You hardly ever arrive on time and your output last week was way below average. There's an enormous backlog of unanswered readers' letters.'

'I'm sorry. I didn't hear my alarm. It won't happen again.'

'It had better not. We expect staff to be punctual at *The Countrywoman* and to meet deadlines. I'll give you one last chance, but if you can't manage to be on time you'll have to look for another job.'

Katy returned to her desk and did her best to catch up on the morning's work but there were several interruptions. It was difficult to get away from the office to meet Countess Elena and it was already twelve forty when she arrived at the Polish restaurant. It was small and decorated with folk art - brightly coloured paper cut-outs of birds, flowers and horsemen - and there was a large oil painting on one wall of a procession of cavalry. The place looked shabby and the red-and-white checked tablecloths were plastic, but there was a glass case near the entrance with an impressive selection of Viennese pastries. The customers were mainly elderly Central Europeans, drinking tea and reading Polish or Czech newspapers.

A blonde at the cash desk looked at Katy and said something in Polish. Katy asked whether Countess Elena Slobovna was there and was directed to a table in a corner at the back of the restaurant.

A tall, elderly woman with an aquiline nose and piercing dark eyes greeted her with a critical stare. 'It is a pity that you do not look more like your father. Red hair like yours is most uncommon in Maloslavia and then there are these - these brown marks on your skin. I do not know the English word for them.'

'You mean freckles. My mother was Irish. I take after her.'

There was an uncomfortable silence. The waitress brought the menu and the Countess glanced at it quickly.

'The Beef Stroganoff is good here. You will have that? And perhaps some Barszcz to begin? It is Polish beetroot soup like the Russian Borscht. You will drink something? Polish beer is good.'

'Yes, that sounds fine, thank you.'

The Countess gave the order to the waitress and turned to Katy.

'Now I have to tell you the reason I wished to see you. But it is difficult for me to speak in English. Do you speak French?'

'Yes. I spent a year in Paris as an *au pair* when I left school.'

The Countess began to explain the reason for her visit in a carefully rehearsed speech in fluent French.

'When Communism collapsed in Maloslavia in 1990 the people were full of hope. Unfortunately, their hopes have not been realized. Many former Communists changed their allegiance and called themselves Social Democrats whilst using unscrupulous methods to amass huge fortunes. Capitalism has resulted in massive corruption and created a society where there are a few millionaires but the majority of the population live in extreme poverty.'

'Here we go! A political lecture,' thought Katy.

The Countess droned on: 'The country has been governed by a series of weak coalitions in which the two main parties are the right-wing Maloslavian Front and the left-wing People's Struggle. The Prime Minister, Ivan Petrovitch, has great difficulty in preventing his government from collapsing. Moreover, the President, Igor Grobov, is eighty-five and rapidly becoming senile. The people are restless and angry and there have been many strikes.'

'I've read something about it in the papers,' said Katy, helping herself to the soup which had just arrived, 'but I really don't see what it has to do with me.'

'A great deal! The Prime Minister thinks that it is necessary to have a young, dynamic Head of State who will bring hope of change to the country and it is for this reason that he has decided to hold a referendum for the re-establishment of the monarchy.' The Countess paused and looked intently at Katy.

'Katerina Bogdanova, I know that you have been brought up in

Britain and that you consider yourself British, but your father was King of Maloslavia. You are the rightful heir to the throne. Will you return to your country and take part in the referendum?'

Katy gulped a spoonful of soup and looked at her in astonishment.

'You mean a referendum to become Queen? Are you serious?'

'Of course.'

'But my life and friends are here. And why should I help the country that murdered my father?'

'It has never been proved that Maloslavia was responsible for his death. In any case, the Communist régime that forced him to abdicate no longer exists. Now you have an opportunity to honour his memory by serving his country.'

'But I haven't been prepared for such a role.'

'Of course you will have to undergo a period of training. It is now November and we propose that you go to Maloslavia in March. In the next few months you will have lessons in the Maloslavian language and also receive instruction for reception into the Orthodox Church.'

'I was brought up a Catholic.'

'Orthodoxy is the state religion of Maloslavia and since the Communist régime came to an end there has been a great spiritual revival. The monarch must be a member of the Orthodox Church.'

'Would I have to make speeches and appear in public?'

'Of course. And so we will have to do something about your appearance. You will need a more sophisticated hairstyle and elegant clothes. You will also have to lose some weight. But we have four months in which to make the changes.'

Katy was indignant. 'There's nothing wrong with my appearance and people admire my hair.'

'You cannot have long hair falling over your shoulders. It is important that you make a good impression on the people. You will accept?'

Katy's first instinct was to say 'No' but then she hesitated. 'Give me a couple of days to think it over.'

'I need a quick reply. You will telephone me at the Embassy? Yes?'

* * *

Katy returned to the office but found it impossible to concentrate on her work. She rang her closest friend, Emma, who worked in a City bank and was the only person, apart from her aunt in Ireland, who knew about her Maloslavian background.

'Something very important's come up and I must talk to you. Can we meet this evening for a pizza?'

'It's very short notice. I've got a singing lesson tonight.' Emma spent much of her free time rehearsing with an early music group.

'Couldn't you possibly cancel it for once? It's something that could change my whole life and I have to make a quick decision. I'd do the same for you if you had a problem.'

'It sounds very mysterious. Okay. I'll meet you at that pizzeria we went to once before - the *Vesuvio*.'

Katy and Emma had been friends since they were at a convent school together. Katy was untidy and disorganized and Emma, who was practical, had frequently helped her avoid getting into trouble. Their friendship had continued after they left school. They both spent a year in Paris in *au pair* jobs and would meet to complain about their host families. Afterwards, although Emma went on to university and Katy didn't because of poor A Level results, they kept in touch. Since Emma's return to London they had been meeting regularly, each knowing she could trust the other with any secret she revealed.

Emma had already found a table when Katy arrived at the restaurant. They ordered two *pizze pescatore* and a carafe of red wine and Katy related the story of her lunch with the Countess.

' I don't know what to do.'

'Well, I think you should go for it,' said Emma firmly. 'After all, what have you got to lose? You've just ended a messy relationship with Richard and you hate your job. And let's face it, you're like a fish out of water in that office.'

'But I'd have to become Orthodox and I don't think I believe in God.'

'Oh, come on! It's only for political reasons and because it's the state religion,' said Emma who hadn't been near a church since she left school. 'I shouldn't think Vladimir Putin believes in God but he's always turning up at official religious ceremonies looking smug.'

'But I'm not Vladimir Putin.'

'You might be converted! And it would be nice to have a complete make-over - new hair style, designer clothes, a slim figure!'

'I'm happy the way I am.'

' It's such a pity you don't make the best of yourself - you're only twenty-six and your red hair and green eyes are really striking. Okay, you're slightly overweight but it doesn't matter because you're tall. You've got a shapely, well-proportioned body, so be proud of it and stop hiding it under those baggy sweaters!'

'Perhaps I should go,' said Katy doubtfully. 'I ought to do what I can for Maloslavia in memory of my father.'

'Did they ever find out who murdered him?'

'No. He was taken ill after meeting two visitors from Maloslavia who claimed to be monarchists. Tests showed he'd been poisoned, probably on the orders of the KGB. But they've never been able to prove who actually did it. I don't remember him because I was only two when it happened and my mother always refused to talk about it to me.'

'Why?' asked Emma.

'She wanted to protect me from everything connected with Maloslavia and to be completely British. That's why I took her maiden name - Brennan - and I've always been called Katy although I was baptized Katerina. Nobody apart from you and my aunt in Ireland knows my real background.'

'But you're really Princess Katerina?'

'Yes, but it doesn't mean anything to me and I've always refused to think about that side of my family. If I go ahead with this, it will be on condition that nobody knows about it until I'm in Maloslavia. I don't want to be hounded by the press here and I don't want bodyguards shadowing me. Nobody knows who I am in London so it isn't necessary.'

'You'll have to put up with a lot of publicity and police protection when you get to Maloslavia. Do you think you'll be in danger? After all, if they poisoned your father...'

'I don't know. The Countess says there's no risk because the Communist régime doesn't exist any more. And she pretends there's no proof it was responsible but I don't believe that. Anyway, I'll have bodyguards. I just want to be left in peace while I'm still here.'

The food arrived but Katy wasn't hungry and couldn't finish her enormous pizza - the seafood topping consisted mainly of pieces of tough squid and the dough itself was chewy and hard to swallow. They ate in silence, but over coffee they tried to chat about their jobs, films and books. It was useless; Katy's mind was elsewhere, so they paid the bill and left.

When they parted Emma said, 'Go for it! It'll be a new experience and at least you'll have the chance to see your father's country. But make sure they pay you a generous allowance for the months you'll spend in London after you've left your job. You've got to have something to live on!'

* * *

Katy couldn't sleep. She kept turning the day's events over in her mind. She remembered reading somewhere that Maloslavia was one of the poorest and most unstable countries in Europe. Did she really want to get involved in its troubles? She told herself firmly that it was a new beginning - a definitive break with Richard - and in the morning she phoned Countess Elena to tell her she'd decided to take part in the referendum.

In the evening she went to the Maloslavian Embassy which was situated in an Edwardian mansion in Holland Park. The black and purple Maloslavian flag hung over the door which was manned by a guard in uniform. When Katy explained who she was he stared at her in amazement, bowed obsequeously and made a quick telephone call, saying something which sounded like '*Katerina Bogdanova zdyes.*' A minute later a secretary in a well-cut black suit appeared, gave her a contemptuous look and escorted her to an elegantly furnished office. The Countess was already there, seated on a Louis

XV chair. The Ambassador, a thick set man with small eyes set too close together, rose and bowed to Katy.

'It is an honour to meet you, Your Royal Highness,' he said smiling.

'Please don't call me that yet! I'm not used to it!'

'But now you will have to get used to it.'

'Only if I agree to your proposals,' said Katy sitting down. 'I've always considered myself to be British and I've chosen to ignore my Maloslavian background. I'm known by my mother's name of Brennan and I'd like to remain so for the time being.'

'That would be very unusual,' said the Countess.

'Perhaps, but I'm only prepared to do what you ask of me if you agree to my conditions.'

'And what are they?' asked the Ambassador.

'I'm willing to undertake the training programme you've devised for me - learning Maloslavian, being received into the Orthodox Church, changing my appearance and so on - but only if I'm allowed to continue my normal life. My aunt in Ireland and one close friend are the only people who are aware of my history, so I'm in no danger in London. Nobody needs to know anything about your plan. When I go to Maloslavia, you are free to tell the press and I accept that from then on I will have to have bodyguards, but not before.'

'I am not sure whether we can agree to this.'

'Then I refuse to have anything to do with your scheme.'

The Ambassador looked at the Countess as if seeking advice. She shook her head and pursed her lips and they were both silent. At last he said, 'Is this your final decision?'

'Yes.'

'This referendum is extremely important for the restructuring of our country, so I am afraid we will have to agree to your conditions. But your training programme must start as soon as possible. I understand that you work for a magazine. When would you be able to leave your post?'

'I need to give a month's notice, but as we're at the very beginning of November I could leave at the end of the month.'

'Then please give in your notice tomorrow. I will inform our government that you have agreed to take part in the referendum and that you will arrive in Maloslavia at the beginning of March. If you will now go with Countess Elena to the library, she will inform you of the plans that have been made for your training.'

'There is one other matter,' said Katy. 'If I leave my job at the end of November, I'll need an allowance to cover my living expenses until I go to Maloslavia.'

'That has already been arranged. £2000 will be paid into your bank account at the beginning of each month until you leave London. And, of course, the cost of language lessons, clothes, hairdressers and any other items connected with your training will be borne by the Government.'

Katy tried to hide her astonishment. The sum mentioned was considerably more than she earned at *The English Countrywoman.*

The Ambassador kissed Katy's hand and she left with the Countess who explained to her the arrangements she had made. At the beginning of December, after she had left her job, Katy would attend classes every Wednesday afternoon at the Maloslavian church of St Nicolas to prepare her for reception into the Orthodox Church. On Monday and Friday mornings she would have lessons in Maloslavian language and history with a retired lecturer in Maloslavian from the School of Slavonic and East European Studies of London University. On the first Tuesday in December, she would visit a specialist in weight loss in Harley Street who would prescribe an appropriate diet and exercise plan and there would be follow-up appointments to check her progress. On Thursday mornings she would attend a gym and there would also be trips with the Countess to couture houses, hairdressers and beauty salons.

'But won't it look bad to appear in expensive designer clothes in a country where there is so much poverty?' Katy protested.

'The people need a symbol that they can admire and respect,' said the Countess. ' Now there is one other matter. You must begin attending the Maloslavian Orthodox Church as from next Sunday. I know you will not be starting your instruction until December but it is important that you familiarize yourself with the Liturgy beforehand. Unfortunately, I shall be unable to accompany you but please do not be late. The service begins at ten o'clock.'

* * *

The next morning when Katy arrived at the office she went to see the Managing Editor to hand in her notice. Mrs Cartwright was in her late fifties - a hard faced woman with a mouth that was a thin scarlet line. The staff always knew when she was approaching because the overpowering aroma of Dior's '*Poison*' heralded her arrival.

Katy knocked and entered.

'What is it Miss Brennan?' (Mrs Cartwright refused to adopt the modern fashion of calling staff by their first names.)

'I've come to hand in my notice. I'll be leaving at the end of the month.'

Mrs Cartwright gave no indication that Katy should sit down, so she remained standing like a naughty schoolgirl.

'Well, I'm not surprised. It was bound to happen sooner or later. You've clearly not been happy here. It might have been better if you had been able to share an office with girls of your own class.'

'Oh, no! I get on very well with Sharon and Margaret,' stammered Katy.

'I suppose you'll want a reference? It's difficult to know what to say. Your performance here hasn't been very satisfactory. Your timekeeping has been appalling and you have continually let your private life interfere with your work.'

'I don't need a reference, thank you. I'm going abroad.'

'Really? Well, I don't know where you intend to go but I would have thought that you would still need a reference. You will find it very difficult to get another post without one. But still, it's your decision. If you should change your mind, let me know and we'll see if we can think of something. Is there anything else?'

'No, thank you,' said Katy and went out, feeling as if she had been given the sack.

In the evening she decided that she must telephone her aunt with her news. There was nobody else who needed to know as Aunt

Bridget, her mother's sister, was her only living relative. She was a gaunt, bitter woman who lived in a village in Connemara where she was housekeeper to Father O'Flaherty, the parish priest of St Philomena's. She disapproved of Katy whom she considered to be in mortal sin and they hadn't spoken since her visit to London three years ago when she discovered Katy was having an affair with a married man and hadn't been attending mass. There had been a colossal row and Bridget had returned to Ireland, declaring she would say a novena for Katy's return to the Church and an end to her adulterous relationship.

Katy found her aunt's excessive piety irritating but she was sorry their last meeting had ended badly and wanted to put matters right. She rang the presbytery.

'St Philomena's.'

'It's Katy.'

'Oh, so at last you've decided to get in touch. I hope this is an answer to my prayers for you.'

'My affair with Richard is over if that's what you mean.'

'Thank God! And have you started going to mass and confession?'

'I shall be going to mass again but it won't be Catholic. And I'll have to make a confession soon because I'm going to be received into the Orthodox church.'

'Your mother gave you a good Catholic education and you repay her like this?'

'Yes, but you forget my *father* was Orthodox. I'm about to go to Maloslavia. It seems I'm the only heir to the throne and the government want me to take part in a referendum for the restoration of the monarchy. If the majority vote 'Yes' I'll be Queen. That's why I have to become Orthodox and I must also learn Maloslavian.'

'I always thought you were wild and wilful, not to speak of your morals, but this is madness. Your mother made a terrible mistake in marrying your father and when he died she did everything she could to protect you from your Maloslavian roots. She must be turning in her grave!'

'I'm sorry that's the way you feel, but this is something I want to do in memory of my father. I never knew him, my mother wouldn't talk about him and it's for his sake I'm going to Maloslavia. Anyway, my life here is going nowhere. This is my chance to do something worthwhile.'

'Well, I only hope it does turn out to be worthwhile. And what will you be doing if the people vote '"No"?'

'I'll face that if it comes.'

'I can see you've made up your mind so there's nothing I can do except pray for you. I'll ask Father O'Flaherty to offer a mass for your intentions.'

'Goodbye then,' said Katy, thoroughly exasperated.

* * *

She looked out of the window. Another wet day! Church was the last place she wanted to be but she'd promised Countess Elena that she would attend the liturgy at St Nicolas and she was going to be late. It was nearly nine o'clock already. She drank a cup of strong Nescafé and hunted in her meagre wardrobe for something suitable to wear. In the end she put on her trench coat over a pair of black trousers and a black sweater and left the house as quickly as she could.

Katy considered herself an agnostic. Her convent school education with its novenas, rosaries, retreats and daily masses had completely turned her off religion. After she left school, she had occasionally gone to mass to please her mother, but since her death six years ago she hadn't been near a church and she felt uneasy attending an unfamiliar service.

The Maloslavian Orthodox Church was about five minutes walk from Earls Court station in a blind alley. It had formerly been a Wesleyan Methodist chapel but had been given to the small Maloslavian community in the 1930s. From the outside it was an ugly nineteenth century red brick building which couldn't hide its Non-Conformist origins in spite of the bright blue onion dome perched incongruously on the roof.

A group of old women in headscarves stood blocking the doorway and frowned at Katy as she approached, indicating that she should cover her head. She hunted in her pocket for a plastic rain hat which was all she had and put it on. She forced her way into the little church and entered an unfamiliar world. People pushed and shoved, wandered around, buying candles, kissing icons and continually bowing and crossing themselves. There were no chairs or pews, only some seats along the walls occupied by a few old ladies and a saintly-faced, bearded young man holding a pair of crutches. A constant flow of sound - deep sombre voices - came from behind the iconostasis, a shimmering golden wall which glowed in the dim light. Gradually Katy distinguished the faces of saints and prophets, a sorrowful Virgin and a stern Christ. Then the central doors in the iconostasis were flung open and a priest in a gem-studded brocade chasuble emerged with a deacon and an acolyte and stood at a lectern. Amid clouds of incense, he chanted a passage from the Gospels in a bass voice. Katy, who had expected to be bored, was moved. How beautiful it was! Perhaps God really existed? In this mystical atmosphere it was easy to believe that He did. To her surprise, she found herself praying that she would have the strength to carry out her duties in Maloslavia. And when she came out of the church, she felt a strange sense of peace and tranquillity.

Chapter 2

It was Katy's last day at *The English Countrywoman* and Jean Briggs organized a small farewell get-together in her office. She invited the six girls in the Readers' Letters Department and also asked a few people from Features to drop in if they were free. Katy hadn't wanted a party because she knew Jean didn't like her but as it was the custom she reluctantly accepted. When anyone left *The Countrywoman*, a collection was made to buy drinks, cocktail nibbles and a present, but Katy's party was a low key affair as so few people had contributed to it. There was very little cash left to buy a gift and it was decided that a book would be the best solution. Then Margaret remembered that Katy liked Russian literature so they bought her a copy of Chekhov's short stories.

At five thirty they gathered in Jean Briggs' office. All traces of work had been removed from her desk and replaced by paper cups, bottles of sherry, white wine and fruit juice and dishes of peanuts and crisps. Everybody stood in an embarrassed silence wondering what to say. Occasionally someone made a fatuous remark about work or the fact that it would soon be Christmas and they looked curiously at Katy, secretly wondering why she was leaving and where she was going. To all their previous questions she had simply said she was 'going abroad' and they couldn't understand why she wasn't more specific. When they tried to find out what country she was visiting, she replied that she hadn't made up her mind yet but that she wanted time to travel. The more malicious among them whispered that she'd probably got the sack. After all, she was so unconventional - not really *English*

Countrywoman material. She didn't seem to care what she looked like or what she said and her desk was always a complete mess. It was a mystery to them why she had chosen to work for a magazine that was devoted to upholding the traditional values of the Establishment.

After about ten minutes, when it was clear that nobody else was coming, Jean tapped on a bottle with a knife and called for silence. She made a short speech in which she attempted to be witty but only succeeded in sounding spiteful.

'Katy has been with us for two years now and I am sure we have all benefitted from her lively presence, her plain speaking and her original ideas. She is a free spirit and it would be wrong of us to imprison her any longer in an office or to subject her to our harsh rules on timekeeping. She tells us she is going "abroad" and of course we are intrigued. We hope that she will be happier than she has been here and that she will have a life free from the restrictions she so clearly dislikes. Katy, I would like to give you this small present with our best wishes for the future.'

Fighting back angry tears, Katy took the gift and unwrapped it. She was glad to see that it was Chekhov's short stories but her pleasure was marred by Jean's malicious words. She forced herself to make a brief reply.

'Thank you all very much. It was clever of you to remember my love of Russian literature and I know I'm going to enjoy reading this book. I do appreciate your coming here tonight, especially as I'm afraid I've not always been true to the ideals that *The English Countrywoman* represents. May they continue to flourish through your devotion and loyalty!'

There was some fairly enthusiastic applause. She'd meant the last two sentences ironically but they were taken seriously and the small gathering appeared delighted. Venetia Brown, who was in charge of the Country Fashion section of the Features department, came up to Katy smiling her bright, social smile.

'Katy darling, thank you for what you said! That was *so* sweet of you! We're going to miss you, you know! You brought such a refreshing breath of eccentricity into our dreary lives. When are you going abroad?'

'Not for several months yet,' said Katy, trying to get away.

'Oh, really? I thought you were leaving immediately?'

'No, I've got to plan my itinerary and organize visas and things like that.'

'What a bore! That's the downside of travel isn't it? All the bureaucracy and deciding what to take. Well, wherever you decide to go I do hope it will be worthwhile.'

'Thank you very much,' said Katy who had noticed that people were already leaving. She decided to make her escape and went to say goodbye to Jean Briggs.

'Thank you so much for organizing this party Jean and also for the book. I'm delighted with it.'

Jean gave her a peck on the cheek. 'Goodbye, Katy. I don't know what your plans are, but I wish you every success and I hope you find what you're looking for.'

Katy smiled and moved across to Sharon and Margaret.

'I do envy you, going abroad like that. It's going to be very dull without you!' said Sharon.

Katy gave her a hug. 'Goodbye, and thanks for everything,' she said and left the room, waving her farewells to those that were still there.

She returned to her office and collected her belongings. She had emptied her desk drawers earlier in the day and it only remained for her to put on her coat and go. For the last time she looked at the Philodendron whose branches trailed across the wall behind Sharon's desk, and at the dusty collection of holiday postcards that adorned the door of the stationery cupboard. Then, with a sigh of relief, she went home.

* * *

Katy had four days of leisure before Wednesday when her training programme would begin with her first lesson on Orthodoxy. She decided to make the most of this free time and on Saturday, after writing and posting her Christmas cards, she had a walk in the park, followed by lunch in an Indian restaurant and a visit to the cinema.

On Sunday she attended the service at St Nicolas and went to a Beethoven concert with Emma and Monday was spent painting at the Putney School of Art. She wondered if she'd ever have time to spend on such simple pleasures again. For the next few months, her training would keep her fully occupied and when she arrived in Maloslavia her life wouldn't be her own.

On Tuesday Richard rang but Katy told him that she was going abroad 'travelling' and cut him off. She sat in the kitchen, drinking tea, feeling glad that his calls no longer had the power to throw her into an emotional turmoil.

She had met him when she worked for a small publishing company in Fleet Street. He was one of the directors and she was his secretary. He was forty-five, tall and athletic, with a smile that oozed charm and a gift for making women feel special. Although she didn't know it at the time, he had already had affairs with other members of the staff and before long she too became more than a secretary. She was rather naïve and thought he was one of the most cultured and attractive men she'd ever met. They were soon spending long lunch hours in a hotel bedroom and she enjoyed them, for he was a skilful lover who knew how to give a woman pleasure; until then she'd endured clumsy unsatisfying episodes with a couple of younger boyfriends and wondered why everyone made such a fuss about sex. Inevitably she fell in love with him and he kept her happy by taking her to dinner in expensive restaurants after phoning his wife to say that he was working late. He even promised that he would find her a post as a sub-editor, for she longed to get away from being a secretary. No such job existed, so he decided to create one for her although there was insufficient work to justify it. The sub-editors protested and Richard's liaison became public knowledge. He had to back down and told her it would be better if she left the company, assuring her they'd be able to continue their affair in peace. It was then that she found the post with *The English Countrywoman* but she still saw him frequently and he promised to get a divorce. Their liaison continued for two years, until by chance she met somebody from his office who told her that he'd been sleeping with a secretary who had just joined the company. When Katy confronted him, he denied it but she ended their affair immediately.

'What on earth did I see in him?' she asked herself, rinsing her teacup.

* * *

Katy set off for her first meeting with Father Serge on Wednesday afternoon feeling nervous. How would he react when she told him that she was a lapsed Catholic who hadn't been to mass for six years and doubted the existence of God? She wanted to be honest with him, but when he knew the facts would he agree to receive her into the Orthodox faith? And did she want to be received? Totally confused, she rang the bell of the house adjoining the church. The door was opened by Fr Serge's wife, a stout, elderly woman who led her down a corridor to his study.

The small sombre room was decorated in Victorian Gothic style. There was a dado of dark wood panelling and above it the walls were covered with a heavily patterned William Morris paper. One wall, however, was completely hidden by shelves of theological books. The window was half concealed by dark green velvet curtains which prevented much daylight from penetrating. In a corner, a lamp burned before an icon of the Virgin and close to it, behind a mahogany desk, sat Father Serge, a tall bearded man who reminded Katy of a figure in an El Greco painting. Sitting near him she was surprised to see the young man with crutches whom she had noticed in the church every Sunday.

Fr Serge rose and greeted Katy warmly. Then he said 'I would like to introduce you to Vladimir Grodno.'

Vladimir smiled and was going to stand up but Katy motioned for him to remain seated and they shook hands.

'Vladimir is one of the younger members of our congregation and he is studying theology with me,' continued Father Serge. 'I asked him if he could take the afternoon off and come to our first meeting so that you could make his acquaintance. He is a brilliant student and you can discuss with him any difficulties you may have in understanding our beliefs and liturgy. Please sit down. Countess Elena has explained to me why you are going to convert to Orthodoxy but I understand that you have been brought up as a Roman Catholic?'

'Yes, my mother was an Irish Catholic and I had a convent education.'

'Well then, you have been baptized and you have a Christian background. There are many differences between Orthodoxy and Catholicism but you will find also that there are a number of things which will be familiar to you.'

'Before we go any further, I've got a problem.' And Katy began to speak very fast, anxious to unburden herself.

'You see, I had a very strict education in the convent school and I rebelled against it. I didn't like having to go to mass every day, and the retreats and the novenas and rosaries. After I left school I only went to church to please my mother and when she died six years ago, I stopped going altogether.'

'This is because you received a religious education that was wrong for you and which did more harm than good. You will find Orthodox spirituality is very different.'

'But I'm not sure I believe in God any more. I'm an agnostic.'

'We all of us doubt from time to time, even the saints, but you must remember that there is a little of God in each and every one of us. How else can we know Him? And His Holy Spirit dwells within us when we receive the sacraments and strengthens us for our journey. Are you prepared to let me be your spiritual guide?'

'I'm willing to try.' Katy was surprised to hear herself saying this. She had expected that she would put up some resistance to Father Serge but he was unlike any of the priests she had known and his humility and gentleness had almost won her over.

'It is not my intention to make you learn large portions of the catechism as you have undoubtedly had to study the Catholic catechism. Instead, we will examine the differences between Orthodoxy and Catholicism. I will explain our liturgy to you and show you some methods of prayer and meditation which may help you. After two or three months, when you are ready, you will make a confession of your sins and then, as you have already been baptized, you will be received into the Church by chrismation - that is by anointing with the holy oils. Now, let us begin.'

And Fr Serge began explaining how the Roman Catholic Church had always placed great value on human reason and its theology had developed over the centuries in the light of new ideas and new developments in philosophy. Orthodoxy, on the other hand, was true to the Scriptures and the traditions of the early Fathers of the Church and it did not try to make its teaching consistent with the results of human thought and science although if these results lent support to the teachings of the Church it did not refute them.

All this was new to Katy and she was surprised to find herself listening with interest, although she couldn't help thinking that Orthodoxy risked becoming fossilized by blind adherence to the teachings of the early Fathers of the Church. In fact, she had never heard of the Fathers of the Church before but didn't like to say so.

After about half-an-hour Father Serge said 'That will do for today. We will continue next Wednesday but please make sure you attend the Divine Liturgy each Sunday.'

Katy and Vladimir said goodbye and were escorted to the door by Father Serge's wife.

'Shall we have some tea?' said Vladimir as they were leaving.

'That would be nice,' said Katy.

They set off for a nearby café and she found that she was able to walk with him at almost her usual pace for he swung himself along on his crutches with surprising speed. They found a table near the window and ordered tea and toast. Katy suddenly felt shy. With his blonde hair and beard and clear blue eyes, Vladimir was so like one of the saints on the icons she had seen in the church that she was lost for words. Finally she said, 'Are you from Maloslavia?' and was relieved when he answered in a matter-of-fact voice, dispelling any air of saintliness.

'Yes, but I don't remember it because I came to London when I was only two. I've always spoken Maloslavian at home though and I'm completely bilingual. I should be! I've lived here for twenty-one years!'

'Why did you come to England?'

'I had polio when I was two. It was very common then in Maloslavia because there wasn't a proper vaccination campaign and if you got the disease the treatment was very basic and the hospitals had poor equipment. If I'd stayed there I'd never have learnt to walk. But I was lucky because there was a scheme to bring disabled children to England for treatment and I was one of those chosen.'

'What about your parents?'

'They came too. My father was a university lecturer in Svyatograd but he found work as a translator for the BBC World Service and my mother who is a nurse also found a job. So in the end we were allowed to stay. But that's enough about me. Why are you converting to Orthodoxy?'

'It's an odd story and I don't usually talk about it,' said Katy, pouring the tea. 'My father was King of Maloslavia for a short time but he was thrown out of the country by the Communists when he was only twenty-one.'

Vladimir looked at her in amazement. 'What happened?'

'He came to England. He studied law and then he joined a legal firm in Gray's Inn. My mother, who was Irish, worked there as a secretary and they fell in love and got married. When I was born, my father was determined I should be completely British and although my full name is Katerina I've always been known as Katy. He was also quite happy that I should be brought up in my mother's religion as a Catholic. I don't remember him because he died when I was only two in mysterious circumstances. He was suddenly taken ill and all the tests seemed to prove that he was poisoned, probably on the orders of the KGB.'

'I'm not surprised!' said Vladimir, savagely cutting his toast in half.

'Until a few weeks ago I'd had nothing to do with Maloslavia and then, out of the blue, a Countess called Elena Slobovna phoned me and asked me to meet her.'

'Who on earth is she?'

'She's here on behalf of the Maloslavian government. They want me, as the only heir to the throne, to stand as candidate in a referendum for the restoration of the monarchy. But I must be received into the Orthodox religion and learn Maloslavian.'

'How crazy!' said Vladimir indignantly, spilling his tea. 'Become Orthodox if you feel it's your way to God, but being Queen of that corrupt little country won't do anything to improve the conditions there and your life will be impossible. You'll just be a puppet of the government. And imagine having to go everywhere surrounded by bodyguards!'

'I know. At first I wanted to refuse. Then I thought "Why not?" I'm twenty-six and my life recently has been rather a mess. This is a chance to make a fresh start.'

'But is this the right fresh start for you?' said Vladimir. 'I don't know what mess you've been in but you could land up in a worse one!'

'I'm going to give it a try.'

'Well, it's your decision, but I think you're very brave!'

'I feel a sham becoming Orthodox, though. I don't want to convert just for political reasons. I want to be sincere about it and the trouble is that I've really lost my faith in God.'

Vladimir looked at her sympathetically. 'Don't be so hard on yourself. Everyone has doubts. What good is a faith if you don't question it and put it to the test?'

'I hadn't thought of it like that,' said Katy, helping herself to another piece of toast.

'I had no faith and I refused to go to church from the age of twelve until quite recently. I'll tell you about it one day.'

'I'm also a bit worried about learning Maloslavian. Starting next week, I'm to have private lessons with a retired lecturer from the School of Slavonic and East European Studies.'

Vladimir thought for a moment and said, 'I can help you with your homework if you want me to.'

'Thank you. I'd like that,' said Katy.

'Well then, why don't we meet here after church next Sunday and you can tell me all about your first lesson?'

'That's fine for me. I'll look forward to it,' said Katy.

It was getting late. They paid the bill and went out. As Vladimir struggled to his feet, supporting himself with his crutches, she said 'Does it hurt to walk?' and then was afraid she'd been tactless. He didn't appear to mind and said 'Sometimes the muscles in my legs are painful if I've walked a lot but you just have to get on with it!'

* * *

The next day Katy went to the gym for the first time and was handed over to her personal trainer, Damon, a powerfully built young man with a blond pony tail, earrings, and piercings on his nose and chin. He devised a programme for her involving weights, a treadmill and several other instruments of torture. She had always been bad at games and gym when she was at school and had avoided sport ever since, so she didn't enjoy her session and felt exhausted when it was over. Damon, however, said that she had 'made a good start' and promised that he would get her 'into shape'. Unlike Father Serge, he was unaware of the Maloslavian project and thought that she simply wanted to get fit. She saw no reason to tell him the real reason she had to work out, so she thanked him and went home feeling ravenous.

Her Maloslavian lesson on Friday was much more enjoyable. Her teacher, Olga Semyonova, was a tiny, bird-like woman in her seventies who lived in a shabbily furnished ground floor flat in Camden Town. Faded photographs and some oil paintings in poor condition hung on the walls and a large samovar stood on a table covered with a dark blue cloth. As in Father Serge's study, there was an icon of the Virgin beneath which a lamp burned and on the sofa a large grey cat was curled up asleep amidst a pile of cushions.

Olga Semyonova put some textbooks on the table and asked Katy to sit down.

'Before we start, would you like some tea?' she asked.

'Yes, thank you.'

'I am afraid the samovar is only for decoration. It is too complicated to use it, what with finding the charcoal to heat it and then lighting it. Modern samovars are electric but this is an antique. I shall make the tea in the kitchen in the usual way.'

She left the room and Katy glanced at the photos on the walls and decided they must be pictures of Olga Semyonova in her youth in Maloslavia - a little girl in a frilly party dress and a striking young woman sitting by a lake with a background of mountains. There was also a tall man with a huge moustache and a boy in military uniform.

Mme Semyonova returned and poured tea into two glasses in silver holders. She passed one to Katy and gave her a slice of a rich, moist chocolate cake.

'Countess Slobovna has explained to me why you have to learn Maloslavian,' said Olga Semyonova. 'I shall be very happy to teach you, but I must point out that it is a difficult language and you will only be able to acquire a basic knowledge in the three months we have at our disposal. Are you good at languages?'

'I speak French fairly well because I spent a year as an *au pair* in Paris and I did Latin at school but I wasn't very good at it.'

'Latin will help you to understand the declension system. There are six cases in Maloslavian just as there are in Latin. But first you must learn the Cyrillic alphabet. Everyone thinks it is difficult but in fact it is quite easy and very logical. Then we will concentrate on pronunciation and some basic grammar. I think that for you the most important thing will be to memorize some useful everyday phrases that you can use in polite conversation.'

They worked for two hours and although it was hard, Katy found it interesting. She was surprised how quickly she mastered the alphabet and by the end of the lesson she had also learnt quite a few words.

When they had finished, Olga Semyonova said 'You can call me by my patronymic - Olga Vassilyevna - it is less formal than "Mme Semyonova" and in Maloslavia it is the usual way for a pupil to address a teacher. My father's name was Vassily, so I am Olga Vassilyevna - daughter of Vassily. Your father's name was Boris, so you are Katerina Borisovna.'

'Now I understand why the names in Russian novels are so complicated.'

'Maloslavian is one of the Slav languages closest to Russian and if you learn to speak it well you will have no difficulty in mastering Russian. But it is a pity that you are only having two lessons a week. If you are to make any progress that is not enough. Do you know someone with whom you can practise what you have studied with me?'

'I know someone who goes to St Nicolas Church - Vladimir Grodno,' said Katy.

'I sometimes go to that church and I know Vladimir Grodno. He is a very clever young man and he will be glad to help you.'

'He's already offered.'

'Good! It's such a pity that he didn't want to go to university. His parents were very disappointed.'

'Why didn't he want to go?' asked Katy.

' I believe at school he was ignored by his classmates because of his disability. Children can be so cruel. Perhaps he was afraid the same thing would happen at university. He works in a bookshop.'

They went into the hall and Olga Vassilyevna said, 'I have never been back to Maloslavia since I left in 1951 when I was twenty-one.'

'Wouldn't you like to go back?'

'Not now. I am too old and I do not wish to see what the country has become. I think you may find life there very difficult, but you are young and energetic and perhaps you will be able to do some good.'

She kissed Katy on the cheek and waved goodbye to her as she went down the path to the gate.

* * *

Katy began seeing Vladimir once or twice a week when he finished work and also on Sunday afternoons. Sometimes they met in the little garden near the church, but more often in a café. They went through Katy's homework and Vladimir corrected her pronunciation and helped her to understand the mysteries of Maloslavian grammar. Afterwards they often talked for two or three hours and she found it a refreshing change to be able to have a serious discussion with a man without sex rearing its head. Not that she didn't find Vladimir attractive, for he was very good looking with his fine features and large blue eyes and she didn't have the impression that he was gay; it was simply that he had an inner calm and when he talked about his Orthodox faith his face shone with a kind of Dostoievskian spirituality. But apart from religion, they talked about all kinds of subjects; Katy discovered they both loved the music of Beethoven and Mahler and that he shared her passion for nineteenth century Russian literature. They had heated arguments on Tolstoy, although this inevitably led them back to Orthodoxy. She approved of Tolstoy's heretical religious views, but Vladimir was strongly opposed to them, although he agreed to differ with no hard feelings.

One afternoon she explained to him why her life had been in a mess and told him about her affair with Richard. He listened sympathetically and said that even if she thought she didn't believe in God, it was certainly He who had guided her to end the relationship. Katy was doubtful about this but said nothing.

The following day, when they were in their favourite café, Vladimir told Katy more about his own life. He had gone to the one remaining grammar school in his district and done well, with top grades in his A levels, but although he hadn't been actually bullied, the other pupils had avoided him.

'I think they were embarrassed by my callipers and crutches and were afraid to talk to me.'

'How stupid and unkind!' said Katy.

'Well, I suppose they were shy and didn't know what to say. They didn't understand that I was a normal human being who just wanted their friendship. I was lonely and unhappy and I blamed God for my disability. When my parents tried to get me to go to church I refused and they were very upset. Then I began drinking heavily. I was only fourteen, so I was under-age.'

'How did you manage to get hold of alcohol?'

'It all started because a boy in my class sold me some bottles of wine. He hadn't taken any notice of me before but he was very pleased to have a customer. Then I found one or two places that were willing to sell me beer even though they knew it was illegal. I used to drink in my bedroom with the door locked when my parents thought I was doing my homework. I often turned up in class with a splitting headache and red eyes, but somehow I managed to keep up with the lessons and as I was always by myself during break, nobody noticed I'd got a hangover.'

'How long did this go on?' asked Katy, pouring him some tea.

'It was thanks to Sofia that I stopped. She was a new pupil from Romania - full of life and very warm-hearted. She was beautiful too, but because her English wasn't good when she arrived, she was ignored by her classmates just as I was. She spoke French well though, which was more than they did. We were both looked on as outsiders and this drew us together. We became very close and of course we fell in love. When I left school, my parents wanted me to go to university but I was afraid of being treated as an outcast again. Instead, Sofia and I rented a tiny flat and moved in together. She got a job in a florist's shop and I was taken on by the bookshop where I still work. Then about a year ago she told me that she'd met someone else - a music student from Bucarest called Ion - and that she was going to marry him and return to Romania.'

'That must have been a shock.'

' I wasn't really surprised and in a way I was relieved. For some time I'd had the feeling that she'd stayed with me more out of pity than love and I didn't want that. She was always fussing over me and treating me as though I was an invalid. I know she meant to be kind but she made me feel very conscious of my disability. We didn't really have much in common either. She hadn't any opinions of her own - she didn't argue with me like you do.'

Katy smiled. 'Do I argue?'

'You've got very strong opinions but I like that even if I don't always agree with you. Sofia always agreed with everything I said. If I'd married her, it would have been a big mistake. We parted good friends and I had a letter from her recently telling me that she's now married to Ion.'

'I'm sorry it didn't work out.'

'There's no need to be sorry. It was for the best. Anyway, shortly after we split up, I started going to church again. I hadn't been since I was about twelve and as a child I used to get very bored during the long services. But now I found I was overwhelmed by the beauty and majesty of the liturgy. For the first time, I felt a great need for God. I started repeating the Jesus Prayer frequently - *Lord Jesus Christ, Son of God, have mercy on me a sinner* - and gradually I began to accept my disability. I was always saying "Why did this happen to me?" But now I saw that it was my cross which I had to bear cheerfully and that in a way it was a privilege to be chosen to carry it.'

'But it must be quite a heavy cross.'

'The books I read on Orthodox spirituality and monasticism helped me a lot. Then it suddenly occurred to me that perhaps my vocation was to be a monk. So that's why I'm studying theology with Father Serge and I'm in the process of applying to be accepted as a novice in a monastery on Mount Athos.'

Katy nearly dropped her cup, 'You want to be a...*monk*!'

'I want to try to serve God in a positive way. Monasteries are the powerhouses of prayer that give spiritual energy to the world!'

'Yes, but if you must be a monk, surely there are monasteries that aren't quite so inaccessible?'

Vladimir's eyes shone. 'Mount Athos is the most beautiful place - I've seen photos of it. It's at the very centre of Orthodox monasticism. If I'm going to be a monk then I want to do it at a deep level.'

'But if Sofia hadn't broken up with you, you wouldn't have decided to enter a monastery at all, would you?'

'Possibly not, but my decision was made some months after we split up. It hasn't anything to do with her.'

'But you can serve God in the world.'

'It's much harder to do that. You see, a monk dies in order to live, he forgets himself in order to find his real self in God.'

'I don't think much of God if He expects such a sacrifice from you.'

'St Paul said the celibate life is a higher calling than marriage.'

'Oh come on! Orthodox *priests* marry! And by the way, I read somewhere that there haven't been any women or female animals on Mount Athos since the tenth century!'

Vladimir laughed and handed her a slice of cake. 'Women would be a temptation!'

'But not goats and chickens? How can you spend your whole life cooped up in a monastery on a rock?'

'I don't want to spend the rest of my days working in a bookshop!'

'You could go to university. You said you had good exam results.'

'I could, but I have a feeling that God is calling me to serve Him in a life of prayer, whether I like it or not.'

Katy was exasperated. 'I'm sorry, but I can't help thinking that if there is a God, the best way of perceiving Him is by seeing Him in other people - loving them and being loved by them - not by making pointless sacrifices!'

Vladimir sighed. 'You don't understand and I'm not going to make you try. In any case, I may not be able to go to Mount Athos.'

There was a sadness in his eyes that Katy hadn't seen before. 'Why not?' she asked.

'It's quite primitive. Until recently there were no roads at all - just rough mountain paths between the monasteries which are often twenty miles apart. I couldn't walk that distance, especially in those conditions. But there's a paved road now to one of the monasteries and the monks drive a small van, so they could fetch me from the harbour. They're worried though that I wouldn't be able to cope.'

'Why?'

'When you begin your novitiate you are expected to do hard physical labour - digging the garden and working in the kitchen. But I could do a lot of kitchen jobs, like preparing vegetables, sitting down. Then, when I'd taken my vows, I could work in the library.' He brightened at the thought of it.

'What does Father Serge think about your decision?'

'He would have preferred me to wait for a year or two. He's afraid I may change my mind. But in the end he's agreed to try and persuade the monastery to let me try my vocation.'

When they parted at Earls Court station, Vladimir said 'Thank you for listening.'

'Well, I don't understand your decision but if it's what you really want, I hope it works out for you.'

He laughed and set off for his flat which was quite near. Katy watched him go, puzzled. She found it hard to believe in his vocation and, although he denied it, she couldn't help thinking that his decision to become a monk stemmed partly from his break-up with Sophia.

Chapter 3

Katy spent the first half of December in a whirl of activity - classes in Orthodoxy, workouts at the gym, Maloslavian lessons with Olga Vassilyevna and frequent meetings with Vladimir to practise the phrases and grammar she'd learned. She visited a Harley Street dietician and an exclusive hairdresser who created an elaborate chignon for her long red hair. The Countess took her to the couture house of a young Italian designer where she chose a few simple but elegant outfits - Chanel-style suits, a black cashmere coat, silk shirts and a slim-fitting evening dress in dark blue satin. If she didn't become Queen she would at least have enough clothes to last her for many years.

She had no idea what she would be doing for Christmas but it looked as though she would be alone. It was always a difficult time for her. Until she was twenty she had spent Christmas with her mother, and as a child often wished she was part of a big family with a father, brothers and sisters. It was supposed to be a festive season but it felt very bleak when there were only two people to celebrate it. After her mother's death she'd had Christmas dinner with Emma and her parents on two occasions, feeling rather an outsider, and for the last three years she'd been alone in her flat, refusing invitations in the hope that Richard might be able to get away from his wife to spend a few hours with her. This never happened and it had taken her a long time to realize what a fool she'd been.

One evening, when they were meeting in their usual café, Vladimir asked her if she had any plans for Christmas?'

'I'm not sure yet,' she said, not wanting him to think that she had none.

'I usually go to my parents, but this year, as it may be my last Christmas before I enter the monastery, I've decided to organize my own celebration. I like cooking and I want to try my hand at a Christmas dinner. I've invited some friends of mine - a couple from the church, Kiril and Marina - and I wondered if you'd like to come too.'

Katy's face lit up. 'I'd love to!'

'I'm going to cook a goose and stuff it with apples and prunes. It's what they eat in Maloslavia, served with red cabbage. We'll have it in the evening on Christmas Day.'

'Would you like me to bring a Christmas pudding? I'm not up to making it but I can buy a good one at Harrods or Fortnum's and I'll make the brandy butter to go with it.'

'That would be great! I'll get smoked salmon as a starter and Kiril's offered to bring the wine. It's a good thing Maloslavians celebrate Orthodox Christmas on December 25th. The Russians don't celebrate until January 7th.'

'How will you manage to carry all the shopping? I could come with you and help.'

'Don't worry,' said Vladimir abruptly. 'I'm used to it. I'll put everything in a rucksack.'

Katy persisted. 'Yes, but Christmas shopping is a bit different. The goose will be heavy and so will the red cabbage and the other vegetables. And I don't know whether you want to get a tree, holly and mistletoe.'

She was so insistent that he relented and smiled. 'Well, I'm sure I could cope, but it would be much more fun to go shopping with someone. Thanks for offering.'

* * *

On Monday morning, two days before Christmas, Katy met Vladimir at his flat which was on the ground floor of a shabby Victorian house near Earls Court station. It was his day off and he was waiting for her, wearing a Soviet army fur hat that a friend had brought back from St Petersburg. It suited him and instead of looking like a saint on an icon, she decided he now resembled a character in a Chekhov play. He laughed.

'Thanks for the compliment! Look, I've got a big rucksack for the goose.'

'I've got two large bags and I've also brought the Christmas pudding,' said Katy, handing it to him.

They left the pudding in the kitchen and headed for a street which had a number of small shops about five minutes walk from the flat. Vladimir was scornful of Katy's idea of buying everything in a supermarket and had ordered the goose from a poulterer who had been recommended to him. It was ready for collection and he had an earnest discussion with the assistant about the cooking time for the bird and asked him to check whether the giblets were inside it. 'I need them for the stock,' he explained to Katy who knew nothing about giblets or stock.

It was a big goose, weighing nearly nine pounds. Vladimir put it in his rucksack and Katy said she would carry the vegetables. These were loaded into one of her bags and smoked salmon from a delicatessen was added to the rucksack along with a few groceries.

Vladimir smiled at Katy.

'We've got everything!'

'Shouldn't we buy a small tree and some holly? They can go in my other bag.'

'If you think you can carry them.'

They found a tree about three feet high and a bunch of holly and bought lights in an old-fashioned ironmonger's. Katy put the lights into the bag with the vegetables and Vladimir crammed the holly into his rucksack. She looked at him doubtfully. She could see that it was difficult for him to carry a heavy load on his back whilst hauling himself along on his crutches, but she knew he was very independent and would refuse assistance. Although outwardly he always seemed cheerful, she sensed that he suffered because he felt he was different from other people. She wanted to help him but she said nothing and tucked the Christmas tree under her arm, threatening to poke any passer-by who came too close.

After a few minutes Vladimir suddenly stopped.

'Katy, can you do something about this holly? It's scratching the back of my neck!'

She put the tree down on the pavement and examined his rucksack. Most of the holly was sticking up out of it and she managed to force it down and close the zip, pricking her hands as she did so.

'I've pushed it down into the bag, but it's lost most of its berries.'

'It didn't have many in the first place!'

Katy picked up the tree again and it shed most of its needles all over the pavement. They looked at one another and burst out laughing. Then she plucked up courage and said, 'Are you sure you can manage?'

'Of course I can! My legs may not be much use but my arms and back are very strong.'

When they reached the flat, Vladimir collapsed on the sofa, happy but exhausted.

'It's the first time I've done Christmas shopping on this scale and I really enjoyed it,' he said.

'I did too!' said Katy, and she had the feeling that this was going to be the best Christmas she'd ever had.

They unloaded the shopping and she fixed the lights on the tree while Vladimir sat at the table chopping vegetables and giblets for the goose stock and shredding red cabbage. He looked up at her, grinning, and she was surprised at the pleasure he derived from a job that she would have considered a tedious chore.

When she left, he said, 'I'll see you at St Nicolas on Christmas morning. Come and sit with me in church.'

'But I'm supposed to stand.'

'If you're with me it won't matter if you sit. You can stand part of the time and sit down occasionally. It's very tiring standing throughout the service when you're not used to it. And thank you for coming shopping with me. You were right. I couldn't have managed without you!'

* * *

Although Katy was looking forward to the festivities, she couldn't forget that this might be the last Christmas she would spend in England. At this time next year she would probably be in Maloslavia and Vladimir would be shut away on Mount Athos. She was confused when she thought about him. He was devout and observed the many periods of fasting of the Orthodox Church, but she couldn't see him as a monk and the better she knew him, the more she felt this. He wasn't at all pious - he was funny, full of life, and when he wasn't fasting he loved cooking and good food . But perhaps it was people like him who made the best monks.

She didn't know what to give him for a Christmas present. It was the first time she'd had a purely platonic friendship with a man and she couldn't give a future monk the kind of gift that she'd give a boyfriend - after-shave, cologne or a tie. She decided a book would be the best choice and, as she knew he liked Russian literature and could read it in the original language, she bought him a volume of Pushkin's poems in Russian in an attractive binding, wishing she was capable of understanding it herself. After much thought, she wrote a conventional greeting on the flyleaf:

'To Vladimir. With every good wish for Christmas and the New Year from Katy.'

On Christmas Day the church wasn't as crowded as she had expected because many people had gone to the long Vigil liturgy the night before. Vladimir hadn't attended it and had told Katy that, as she was unfamiliar with the service, she would find it very exhausting and it would be better to come in the morning.

He was waiting for her by the door and they went into the church together. He sat on the bench which ran round the walls and Katy stood beside him. From time to time she sat down and he whispered explanations which made the ritual clearer to her. He had brought an English translation of the liturgy and with its help she began to appreciate the significance of what was happening. She was moved by the grandeur of the words and music and remembered how the emissaries of a Russian prince had said of the Orthodox liturgy, 'We knew not whether we were in heaven or earth.' She glanced quickly at Vladimir. His face shone with belief and she prayed that she might have a faith like his.

The moment came to receive communion and he rose to join the line of people waiting. Katy felt sorry that she couldn't accompany him. She watched how each communicant received the sacrament from a spoon and afterwards kissed the chalice. She liked the way the priest said their names - '*The servant of God, Vladimir, partakes of the precious and holy Body and Blood of our Lord and God and Saviour Jesus Christ unto forgiveness of his sins and unto life eternal.*' In the midst of the splendour and mystery of the Eucharist, it was something human and personal.

The service lasted two-and-a-half hours but to Katy's surprise she didn't find it too long. When they came out of the church, she handed Vladimir his present and watched him anxiously, wondering how he would react.

'It's a book. I hope you haven't got it already.'

He opened it and smiled at her. 'Pushkin! The greatest Russian poet! No, I haven't got it. Thank you so much! I've got something for you too.'

He gave her a small parcel and she was pleased to find it was also a book of Russian poetry - the poems of Anna Akhmatova, translated into English.

'Thank you very much! I don't know Akhmatova's poems and I'll look forward to reading them.'

They said goodbye andVladimir told her to be at his flat at seven. In the Tube, Katy looked at her present and saw that on the flyleaf he had written 'To Katy from Vladimir. From one lover of Russian literature to another. Happy Christmas!' 'My greeting to him was too formal,' she thought.

In the afternoon she went through her wardrobe looking for something suitable to wear for the dinner. She had lost a considerable amount of weight and found she could fit into a pair of black velvet trousers that she hadn't worn for some time. She teamed them with a green silk top and chose her favourite malachite pendant as her only jewellery. Then she gathered her long titian hair into a graceful coil at the nape of her neck and was pleased with the effect. She knew she wasn't pretty - her mouth was too wide and her snub nose was lightly powdered with freckles, but her clear green eyes, were lively and expressive.

She was greeted by the smell of cooking goose when she arrived at Vladimir's flat. He opened the door, wearing a striped butcher's apron and took her through to the living room. It was small and simply furnished but he had created a real feeling of Christmas. The lighted tree stood on a corner cupboard and he had covered the dinner table with a dark green cloth and arranged a circle of red candles as a centre piece, surrounded by holly. As an afterthought, he had bought some gold and silver crackers and put two on each place setting. Maloslavian carols were playing softly in the background.

'It's lovely,' said Katy, looking round, admiring everything. As she was removing her coat, Marina and Kiril arrived and Vladimir introduced her. They were London correspondents for a Maloslavian newspaper in their thirties and spoke perfect English. Kiril was a tall, heavily built man with an impressive moustache and Marina was small, with dark hair cropped like a boy's. With her permission, Vladimir had told them Katy's history because he knew they would be discreet and would be able to give her some useful information about Maloslavia. He served them glasses of mulled wine and disappeared into the kitchen.

'We've heard a lot about you,' said Kiril. 'Are you looking forward to this Maloslavian adventure?'

'I've got mixed feelings,' said Katy. 'I can't help wondering whether I'm being foolish and going into a dangerous situation with my eyes wide open.'

'Maloslavia is having a difficult time,' said Kiril. 'The passage from Communism to Capitalism has been too abrupt and most people are very poor. There's a lot of unrest and crime and Ivan Petrovitch's government doesn't seem able to control the situation. I suppose he's thinking of restoring the monarchy as a sop to the population, but in my opinion it won't change things. Perhaps a few old people will be pleased but the monarchy wasn't all that popular.'

'Why?'

'I shouldn't say this to you, but your grandfather doesn't have a good reputation. It's widely believed that during the Second World War he collaborated with the Nazis. The government before the war was very right-wing, bordering on a Fascist dictatorship, and probably because of that the country was never occupied. It was Maloslavian police, not Germans, who rounded up Jews and handed them over for transportation to concentration camps. Probably your grandfather couldn't have done anything to stop it but he certainly didn't speak out against it.'

'For goodness sake, Kiril!' said Marina. 'It's Christmas! Katy doesn't want to hear all this. It isn't her fault!'

'No, of course it isn't. But I think it's only fair to put her in the picture and show her why people may not welcome the monarchy with open arms. Though I've never heard any criticism of your father. He was just sixteen when he came to the throne in 1945 and he was only king for five years. People know he's completely innocent.'

' I'm glad to hear that,' said Katy. 'But it looks as though I may lose the referendum and if I do, I shan't be sorry. I'll have done what I could and I'll be glad to come back here!'

'One other thing. Your Countess Elena Slobovna is a very shady lady. It's known that she belonged to a Fascist youth movement before the war and it's rumoured that at the age of seventeen she was the mistress of a Nazi general who had headquarters in Svyatograd. When the Communists came to power, she quickly changed her political colour and succeeded in keeping in with the régime by relying heavily on her beauty and sex appeal. Of course, that's all finished now - she's eighty, I believe. But be careful of her. She's cold and cunning.'

'That's enough,' said Marina. 'You've told Katy all she needs to know. Now let's enjoy ourselves.'

At this point Vladimir came in and said that dinner was served. He lit the candles and they sat down to eat the smoked salmon. The conversation turned to cooking and the difference between Christmas food in Maloslavia and England.

'In Maloslavia,' said Kiril, 'we celebrate on Christmas Eve before the midnight service so there's no meat or poultry - only fish and vegetable dishes and some special sweets.'

'But people eat goose or duck on Christmas Day,' interrupted Marina and then added, 'If they can afford it.'

'I don't remember Christmas in Maloslavia because I was only two when I left, but my parents told me there were a lot of shortages,' said Vladimir, returning to the kitchen. He checked that the goose was cooked and called out, 'Can you carry the food in for me? I don't think I can manage by myself.'

Kiril got the bird out of the oven, set it on a large platter and brought it to the table, while Katy and Marina carried in the wine and dishes of red cabbage and roast potatoes. Vladimir carved generous portions of goose for everyone with prune and apple stuffing and Katy served the vegetables. Marina made a sauce with Vladimir's homemade stock and Kiril poured the wine he had brought - a rich, full-bodied St Emilion.

Vladimir's cooking was delicious. The goose was tender and full of flavour and the red cabbage, prunes and apples made a perfect accompaniment. Warmed by the wine and good food, the conversation flowed easily. Kiril told some unkind but amusing anecdotes about the aged president of Maloslavia, a former Communist, whom he described as 'a mummy wheeled out for special occasions' and Katy made them laugh when she related her experiences at *The English Counrywoman*.

'You should become a chef, not a monk,' said Kiril as Vladimir served him a second helping of goose.

Vladimir laughed. 'It's not quite the same thing!'

'No, but you're someone who clearly enjoys good food and wine and you're an excellent cook. It doesn't make sense. What do your parents think about your going to Mount Athos?'

Vladimir looked guilty. 'I haven't told them yet.'

'What!'

'I know they won't like it and I don't want to upset them unnecessarily. I'll wait until I know that the monastery will accept me. They may reject my application because of my disability.'

'Thank goodness you haven't told your parents. They'd be

heartbroken and I hope the monastery does refuse your application! You're too talented to be walled up on Mount Athos. It would be such a waste.'

'Can we stop this, please!' cried Marina. 'Kiril, I think you should propose a toast.'

'Yes,' said Kiril standing up. 'I'd like to propose a toast to Vladimir for cooking this wonderful Christmas dinner for us and I wish him every success whatever he decides even if I don't agree with him.'

Katy and Marina rose and the three of them drank his health. Then Vladimir got up and raised his glass.

'Thank you. And now I want to propose a toast to Katy and to thank her for all the help she gave me with the shopping for this meal. I couldn't have done it without her. Katy!'

They drank to her and she blushed with embarrassment. 'I enjoyed it!' she said.

'We haven't had the pudding yet,' said Vladimir. Katy brought it in and he poured a generous quantity of rum over it and put a match to it. Blue flames shot up but the blaze fizzled out after a few seconds, leaving a pool of alcohol. He began serving lavish helpings of pudding while she fetched the brandy butter from the fridge and put it on the table.

'Christmas Pudding is terribly filling,' said Marina. 'I've eaten so much food already. I know it's the custom here but it's an odd thing to have after a big dinner of goose or turkey.'

' I like the brandy butter best,' said Vladimir.

'I could eat a whole bowlful if I was alone,' said Katy.

They sat in the flickering candle light, drinking small glasses of a Maloslavian apricot liqueur and listening to the carols sung by a children's choir while Vladimir went to make coffee. When he came back, Katy got up to help him with the tray of cups.

'It was a lovely meal,' she said. 'That's the way Christmas ought to be.'

Vladimir smiled. 'I agree,' he said.

* * *

Early in January Katy received a telephone call from Countess Elena.

'You are invited to Count Konstantin Fedorovitch's annual New Year reception next Tuesday at his Hampstead home. He is the doyen of the exiled Maloslavian aristocrats in London and it is important that you attend. It will give you the opportunity of talking to members of several noble families who would like to meet their potential queen. It will be a useful learning experience for you. A car from the Embassy will call for you at seven o'clock.'

Katy's heart sank. She was beginning to realize what lay in store for her when she arrived in Maloslavia - an endless round of visits, receptions and talks with pompous officials, always being careful to say the right thing. It wasn't her style; she was too outspoken and knew she would have difficulty in holding her tongue. If she became Queen, she would insist on seeing the people who couldn't afford to eat properly and lived in wretched conditions but she was afraid it would be a struggle to get her own way.

On Tuesday she went to the hairdresser and in the evening she put on her new blue satin evening dress which had been delivered the day before. She owned very little jewellery and most of it was the cheap costume variety, so she wore the malachite pendant and dressed her hair in a chignon again. When the car arrived, she was sorry to see the Countess was there, elegant in black velvet with a mink wrap. She studied Katy critically as she took her place beside her, then nodded and said 'Very nice.'

There was very little traffic and they were soon in Hampstead. The driver stopped before a large red-brick Lutyens house facing the Heath and they got out of the car and walked through a formal garden to the portico which was supported on Doric columns. There they were greeted by Count Fedorovitch, a man of around eighty, with a long thin nose and a white pointed beard, wearing full evening dress. He bowed and kissed Katy's hand.

'Your Royal Highness, this is indeed an honour,' he said.

Although she was embarrassed, she rose to the occasion and said with as much enthusiasm as she could muster, 'It is a great pleasure for me to be here tonight, Count Konstantin.'

The Count turned and greeted Countess Elena.

'Dear Countess, it has been such a long time since we met. You must tell me the latest news from Svyatograd. I have not visited Maloslavia for many years and now unfortunately my health does not permit me to travel far.'

The Countess gave him a chilly smile and, accompanied by Katy, went into the large reception room furnished in First Empire style. A small crowd had gathered round a long buffet table resplendent with crystal and silver and Katy glanced quickly at the guests who were all elderly. Many of them appeared to be over eighty and one was in a wheelchair. The women were dressed in long evening gowns which might have been fashionable in the nineteen thirties and forties and their wrinkled skins were encrusted in heavy make-up. They were lavishly bedecked with jewellery and some of them wore tiaras. The men were in shabby tailcoats, adorned with rows of medals and the ribbons of various orders. There was an air of dusty, faded grandeur about them. 'They're like something in a museum,' she thought.

As Katy approached, they all clapped. Count Konstantin raised his hand for silence and said 'We are proud and happy to have with us tonight Her Royal Highness, the Princess Katerina Borisovna, daughter of our beloved and much lamented King Boris. Let us pray, that with God's help, she will become Queen of our great country, Maloslavia!'

There was more clapping and then the assembled guests burst into the national anthem in cracked voices. Olga Vassilyevna had taught Katy the words in Maloslavian and she forced herself to join in singing the banal little verses which sounded even worse when translated into English:

O Blessed Maloslavia,
Thou land of heroes brave,
Who fought the Turkish tyrant
The poor and weak to save.
Thy blood still cries for vengeance.
We'll fight and kill our foes.
The day of victory beckons,
The end of all our woes.

Everyone looked at Katy expectantly and the Countess, who was standing behind her, leaned forward and hissed in her ear 'They are all waiting for you to say something!'

Katy's mind went blank and at the same time she struggled to stifle the urge to laugh at this bizarre Ruritanian circus. She quickly pulled herself together and blurted out a few words of thanks.

'It is a great privilege for me to be with you all tonight and I am very touched by Count Konstantin's welcome. I er..I. never had any intention of becoming Queen and I did not want to but, er... if the Maloslavian people choose me, then I will do my best to serve them and improve their miserable living conditions. Thank you all.'

Her little speech sounded awkward and unprofessional and she realized that it was probably not what these mummified aristocrats wanted to hear. Looking at them, she had the feeling that they probably didn't care much about the poverty of the Maloslavian population, that they hadn't been near the country for years and that they spent their declining years dreaming of the days when they lived on their estates, waited on by peasant servants. 'Anyway, I don't care what they think,' she said to herself.

The guests began to move towards the buffet table and Katy followed them, hoping none of them would engage her in conversation. She was bad at small talk and had no idea what she would say to them. She took a plate, helped herself to blinis with red caviar and was just starting to eat when Count Konstantin approached her, accompanied by a tall gangling young man with protuberant eyes behind horned-rimmed glasses and thick lips. Apart from Katy, he appeared to be the only person under the age of seventy in the room.

'Your Royal Highness, allow me to introduce my grandson to you, Count Stefan Fedorovitch. He is an investment banker in the City,' said Count Konstantin.

Count Stefan bowed and kissed Katy's hand. She suppressed a strong desire to snatch it away and a feeling of revulsion swept over her as his slobbery mouth touched her skin. He gave her an ingratiating smile.

'Princess, it's such a pleasure to make your acquaintance. I wonder why we've not met before? Where have you been hiding all these years? I've not seen you at any of my grandfather's soirées.'

Katy avoided his gaze and looked down in embarrassment.

'Well, I'm only half Maloslavian, you know. My mother was Irish, living in England, and after my father died she brought me up to be completely British.'

'But you're not completely British are you? And now you may become Queen of Maloslavia? That must be very exciting for you!'

'It's not, actually. It's turned my whole life upside down and I've only agreed to do it because I never really knew my father and I felt I owed it to his memory.'

'How very noble of you! What work were you doing before this momentous event in your life occurred?'

'I had a job with a women's magazine.'

'How amusing! If you become Queen, you'll be able to sell them your story! Or you could write a monthly column for them - a sort of "Queen's Diary"!'

'I know you're joking, but I don't think it's particularly funny. Of course I wouldn't dream of doing such a thing and anyway, it's not that kind of magazine.' She was becoming angry with this odious young man.

'Have you ever been to Maloslavia?'

'No.'

'Well, I'm one hundred per cent Maloslavian but I've never set foot in the country. It's terribly poor and run down so I'm told and I'm much too busy here enjoying the good life to think about it. My father goes there all the time - he's trying to persuade the Government to give back our estate - the Communists turned it into an orphanage, but since their régime collapsed it's being run by nuns.'

'Perhaps there isn't anywhere else for the orphanage to go.'

'But it's our inheritance! There was very good hunting there too, apparently. I shall see it one day I suppose. If you become Queen, I hope that I may have the privilege of paying you a visit?'

Katy froze. 'I think it highly unlikely that the people will vote in favour of a return of the monarchy.'

'In any case, it would be delightful to see you again before you leave London.'

'I'm afraid that won't be possible. I have so much to do before I go.'

The sound of a Strauss waltz wafted from the adjoining room and Count Stefan took her arm and led her in. A quartet - two violinists, a cellist and a pianist - were playing on a small platform. They were angular, lugubrious women of the type that used to be seen playing in tea rooms in seaside resorts. The more able-bodied guests were already shuffling round the floor, probably dreaming of the Viennese balls of their youth. Once again Katy had to suppress an urge to laugh.

'May I have the pleasure?' said Count Stefan.

Katy's amusement turned to horror. She could think of nothing more disagreeable than having to waltz with this unpleasant man, but it was difficult to refuse. She was a bad dancer and he turned out to be little better. They stumbled around, treading on one another's toes, and she felt sickened by his clammy hands and alcoholic breath. He held her very close, pressing his body against hers and then suddenly deposited a wet kiss on the back of her neck. She angrily turned her head away.

'I'm sorry,' he said.

She remained silent, wishing she could walk away, but realized it would not do to make a scene. A minute or two later the quartet stopped playing and they went back into the dining room. She looked round desperately, trying to think of a way to get rid of Count Stefan, and then fortunately a number of other guests approached her. They began telling her about Maloslavia in the old days before the Second World War - the balls, the bear hunts and the country estates. Some of their stories were interesting, especially those told by the lady in the wheelchair who was ninety-eight and very deaf. At the age of three, she had sat on the knee of the Emperor Franz Joseph and tugged on his moustache when he paid a state visit to Maloslavia in 1912.

The evening dragged on and Katy longed to go home. At last she managed to catch Countess Elena's eye and indicated that she would like to leave. The Countess nodded her agreement. They thanked Count Konstantin for his hospitality and got into the waiting car.

As they drove back, the Countess said 'Count Stefan is a charming young man don't you think? He would be a very suitable friend for you.'

'Is she trying to marry me off to that slobbering wimp,' thought Katy, but aloud she said 'He may be charming but unfortunately I'm afraid that we have very little in common.'

* * *

The following day, Katy phoned Vladimir.

'I had a ghastly evening at a reception with a bunch of aged Maloslavian aristocrats and I can't wait to tell you about it.'

'Sounds interesting!'

'Instead of meeting after church, why don't you come to supper on Sunday evening at my flat? Say around seven?'

'Thanks! I'd like that very much.'

'There's one problem though. I live on the first floor without a lift. Can you manage the stairs?'

'I'm sure I can but it'll take me some time. Will you help me?'

'Of course.'

Over the next three days Katy rushed around tidying and cleaning the flat. Some of the clutter she stuffed into bin bags and threw out and piles of shoes and clothes were pushed into cupboards. When she had finished the place looked quite presentable and she was able to give her attention to the meal. She wanted it to be a success because she'd enjoyed Vladimir's Christmas dinner so much, but knowing that she wasn't a great cook she decided to keep it simple. She bought the first course and the dessert in a delicatessen and found the ingredients for the main course, which was to be Spaghetti Bolognese, in the supermarket. She prepared the sauce in advance from an Italian cookery book and grated some Parmesan.

On Sunday evening, she set the table with a lace-edged Irish linen cloth and napkins that had belonged to her mother and placed a vase of anemones in the centre. It was a long time since the flat had looked so attractive.

Promptly at seven the bell rang and Katy ran downstairs to open the front door. Vladimir entered and it suddenly struck her what a wonderful smile he had; it illumined his whole face as he greeted her. He removed his rucksack and handed it to her with his crutches.

'I'm going up the stairs sideways, holding on to the bannister with both hands,' he said. 'Can you hold the bag and the crutches and come up behind me so you can catch me if I slip?'

Clutching the bannister, Vladimir swung his right leg on to each step and then brought the left leg up to join it. Katy could see the struggle this was for him because he couldn't bend his knees. She suggested that he undo the hinge on one of his callipers but he was afraid that his leg would give way. Half way up he stopped to rest, grinning at her. 'Do you know, you're the first person I've ever asked to help me like this?'

'But I'm not helping. You're doing it by yourself. Anyway, I'm sure Sofia helped you.'

'I wouldn't let her. She fussed too much. You don't fuss and you can take that as a compliment!'

Now that he was familiar with the height of the steps, he continued the ascent with less difficulty. He reached the landing and, letting go of the bannister, put his arms round Katy and hugged her. 'Thanks!' he said.

'What are you thanking me for?'

He laughed. 'Well, for inviting me of course!'

'I'm glad you could come,' she said, handing him the crutches.

They went into the living room and he looked round approvingly. 'It's very cosy,' he said, taking his rucksack from her and sitting on the sofa. She smiled, wondering what he would think if he could see what it usually looked like.

He pulled a bottle of Valpolicella out of his bag and gave it to her. 'A contribution to the meal.'

'Thank you! How did you guess we were going to eat Italian?'

'I didn't! But it's a wine I like.'

'I'll get the corkscrew.' She fetched it, together with dishes of nuts and crisps and put them on the coffee table. He opened the bottle and poured the wine. She was going to sit next to him on the sofa but then, suddenly remembering he was going to be a monk, she felt shy and took the armchair opposite him.

When they were settled with their drinks, he said 'Now tell me about your soirée with the Maloslavian aristocracy.'

Katy gave him a lively account of the evening at Count Konstantin's house and he laughed at her description of the guests, the dancing and the string quartet.

'I suppose it's rather sad really. They're exiles who've never fitted in here and they just live with their dreams of the past,' she said.

'They could have fitted in if they'd wanted to make the effort but they'd been used to a life of luxury and didn't know how to work. They've tried to go on living in the same old way but most of them are short of money. That's why they wear shabby tail coats and evening dresses that were fashionable in the nineteen thirties.'

'Some of them had diamond tiaras though.'

'They may end up having to sell them if they have to go into a home for the aged! Of course, the second generation who were born here are quite different. They've studied and got jobs.'

'Count Stefan is an investment banker.'

'I've heard about him,' said Vladimir. 'Kiril and Marina met him once. He's rather a nasty character. Some of his dealings in the City are a bit shady and he drinks heavily and gambles too.'

'He reeked of alcohol when I had the misfortune to dance with him.'

'Do you like dancing?'

'No, I'm very bad at it, I don't enjoy it and with him it was torture,' Katy said emphatically and wondered why she was so anxious to let him know that she hated dancing; even if he had been able to dance, he wouldn't have done so because he was going to be a monk. Then she added 'Count Stefan was the only man under seventy in the room and I had the feeling that he'd been brought there for my benefit. Countess Elena said he would be a suitable friend for me!'

'And what did you say?'

'I told her firmly that we had absolutely nothing in common.'

She was surprised to see a look of relief on his face. She smiled at him and said they could have the first course while she heated the water for the spaghetti. She brought the hors d'oeuvres from the kitchen, after putting the pasta pan on a burner, and they began to eat Parma ham and red pepper salad.

'This is delicious,' said Vladimir, helping himself to more salad, and Katy decided not to tell him that she hadn't made it herself. Instead she said 'Have you had any more news from the monastery?'

He was silent for a moment and then said 'No, but it takes a long time. There are a lot of things to be considered.'

She rose. 'The water must be boiling by now. I'll cook the spaghetti.'

She went into the kitchen and put the spaghetti in the pan, sensing he didn't want to talk about the monastery. But when she returned to the dinner table, she couldn't stop herself from saying what was on her mind.

'Hasn't it ever occurred to you that we're both of us being Quixotic - tilting at windmills? After all, in the twenty-first century it's rather unusual to apply to be a monk in a remote place like Mount Athos or to try to become queen of a run-down Balkan country.'

Vladimir frowned. 'They're not quite the same thing. The people of Maloslavia will decide whether or not you become Queen. God will decide whether or not I become a monk.'

'Ultimately, yes. But the monastery has to decide first.'

'The monastery will decide with God's help. The monks will pray and ask for His guidance. If I go to Mount Athos it will be because it's part of God's plan for me.'

'But do *you* think it's God's plan for you? And is it what *you* want?'

Vladimir sighed. 'I don't know, Katy. I thought I did and now I'm not sure. But I feel that God loves me and I must do what He wants for me. If He calls me to be a monk, I must obey. If He doesn't, then so be it. But please don't let's talk about it any more. We don't want to spoil this lovely dinner!'

She felt ashamed. 'I'm sorry. I shouldn't interrogate you like this.'

'It's all right. I wouldn't take it from most people, but with you I don't mind.'

She laughed. 'Is that another compliment?' she said and went to drain the pasta. She tipped it into a bowl and put it on the table with the sauce and the Parmesan cheese.

'I thought you said you couldn't cook,' said Vladimir, refilling their glasses with the Valpolicella. 'This is excellent.'

'Well, any fool can boil spaghetti and the sauce wasn't difficult to make.'

As they enjoyed their food and wine, the conversation became less serious. They talked about films, music and cooking and Katy tried to speak Maloslavian to Vladimir's amusement. After they had eaten the dessert, she made coffee while he inspected her video and DVD collection.

'I see you've got *The Best of Monty Python*. I'm a great Python fan. I'd love to look at some of it'

'Of course! I'm a Python fan too.'

She put the video in the machine and this time had no hesitation in settling herself on the sofa beside him. In any case, it was the only place from which to see the television screen. They sat drinking their coffee and roaring with laughter at *The All England Summarizing Proust Competition.*

When the video came to an end, Vladimir began looking at Katy's CDs and found one of a recital by Kathleen Ferrier.

'You said you liked Mahler. Do you know this song?' he asked.

'*Um Mitternacht*? It's one of my favourites.'

They listened to it, following both the German text and the English translation in the CD's booklet. After the anguish of the first part of the song, in the final verse, the singer and the orchestra burst into an outpouring of joy and faith. Katy turned to Vladimir.

'When I hear that great cry, *In deine Hand gegeben,* I do believe God exists!'

'I feel the same way,' he said smiling.

It was time for him to leave and she accompanied him down the stairs. When he reached the front door, he held her by the shoulders and looking at her intently said 'Thank you. It was a wonderful evening. I enjoyed myself very much.'

'I'm so glad. I enjoyed it too.'

She went back upstairs and sat on the sofa, remembering the events of the evening. Vladimir was such a delightful companion and she'd felt so happy with him. If only he'd kissed her when he left! Then she remembered he was going to be a monk and punched a cushion in frustration.

'Oh, why does he have to go to Mount Athos and why do I have to go to Maloslavia? There's no sense in it!'

* * *

A few days later Katy had lunch with Emma in their favourite Chinese restaurant in Soho. They hadn't seen one another for some time and Emma wanted to hear the latest news about Katy's preparations for Maloslavia.

'Well, I've worked out regularly at the gym, I've lost some weight and had a new wardrobe of designer clothes made, I'm soon to be received into the Orthodox Church and I've acquired a basic knowledge of Maloslavian.'

'Impressive! Is Maloslavian difficult?'

'It is rather. If it hadn't been for Vladimir, I wouldn't have got on as well as I have.'

Emma was curious. 'You mentioned him the last time I spoke to you. How did you meet him?'

'Father Serge introduced him to me. He goes to the Maloslavian church and he's thinking of becoming a monk.'

'Good gracious! How old is he?' said Emma laughing.

'He's twenty-three and he works in a bookshop. He's very clever and interesting and he's got a wonderful sense of humour.'

'And you told me he looks like a cross between a saint on a Russian icon and a character in a Chekhov play! Really, Katy!'

She blushed. 'Well, he's very good looking.'

'Didn't you say he was disabled?'

'He had polio as a child in Maloslavia. He walks with crutches.'

'And he wants to be a monk?'

'He's applied to join a monastery on Mount Athos but they may not accept him because of his disability. He says that if it's God's will for him to be a monk, he'll obey.'

'Now look here Katy, you're not falling in love with him are you?' Emma looked at her severely through her horn-rimmed glasses.

Katy was indignant. 'No, of course not! He's a very good friend and I enjoy his company. That's all.'

'I hope so, because I know you. You lose your heart far too easily and there's no future in falling in love with a prospective monk. Besides you'll soon be going away yourself.'

'I know,' said Katy dejectedly. 'I wish I wasn't.'

'It's only natural to feel like that. Just before my holiday in India, I didn't want to go and then when I got there I was fine.'

'Yes, but you were coming back. I may never come back!'

Chapter 4

Katy's classes with Fr Serge were over. She was ready to be received into the Orthodox Church by chrismation but first she had to make a general confession of her sins and she was dreading it.

Vladimir laughed at her. 'You're not the only person who's had a relationship with a married man. We're all sinners and priests hear that sort of thing every day. In fact they find sin rather boring!'

Over the past three months, with Vladimir's help, Katy had come to see that she was on a spiritual journey and it was better to question God's existence, to seek Him and pray for the gift of faith, than to accept Him without reflection. Nevertheless, she couldn't help being frightened when she considered what it meant to be a sincere member of the Orthodox Church. Father Serge had said that it was a religion with no place for the half-hearted and she was horrified by the number of periods of fasting in a year - Wednesdays and Fridays, Lent, Advent, before the feast of Saints Peter and Paul, before the Dormition (Falling Asleep of the Virgin), and Holy Cross Day. Moreover, if one intended to receive Communion it was necessary to go to confession first and to be fasting from midnight - not even a glass of water was allowed. Vladimir told her not to worry - the most important thing was not fanatical adherence to the rules for fasting, but to have a loving heart.

Her confession took place in the church on the Saturday before the chrismation ceremony. She stood in front of the icon which was on the lectern and Father Serge said *'Behold, my child, Christ stands here invisibly receiving your confession. Do not be ashamed and do not fear, and do not withhold anything from me; but without doubt tell all you have done and receive forgiveness from the Lord Jesus Christ.'*

Katy crossed herself, kissed the crucifix and the Gospels as she had been taught and began her confession. Once she had started she stopped worrying and recited her list of sins calmly, leaving her affair with Richard until last. `

'Have you ended this relationship?' asked Father Serge, when she had finished.

'Yes, Father.'

'Whatever sins you have committed are forgiven if you are truly penitent. Your past experiences are not wasted and they can influence how you behave from this day forward on your spiritual journey. Now you must look to the future and pray daily for guidance.'

Father Serge covered her head with his stole and said the prayer of absolution. Then she rose, kissed the cross and the Gospels again and, after receiving a blessing, left the church thankful that her ordeal was over.

She arrived early at St Nicolas on Sunday morning. She had fasted from midnight because after her chrismation she was to make her First Communion. Vladimir and Olga Vassilyevna, who was to be her sponsor, were waiting for her at the church with Marina and Kiril and a rather reluctant Emma. Katy knew that Countess Elena would not attend as she had had to return suddenly to Svyatograd, but there was nobody present from the Embassy either. She whispered to Vladimir,

'I'm surprised there isn't anyone from the Embassy here. I can't help feeling that, as ex-Communists, they insisted I convert to Orthodoxy as a formality to please the devout Maloslavian population.'

Vladimir smiled. 'It doesn't matter whether they're here or not. All that matters is that you're being received into the Church.'

Katy put on a long white robe which the sub-deacon brought for her and the Liturgy began. She felt very nervous and it seemed to her as though the vesting of the deacon and priest, the lengthy entrance prayers, litanies and the preparation of the holy bread would never come to an end. At last, after a short sermon, Father Serge asked her to step forward with Olga Vassilyevna. She recited the Creed and read a long statement of belief in the teachings of the Orthodox Church which included accepting the seven sacraments of the New Testament. Then Father Serge anointed her with holy oil, saying *'The seal of the gift of the Holy Spirit'* and the congregation replied *'The seal!'* There was a final prayer, she received a kiss of welcome to the Church from Father Serge, the sub-deacon and her sponsor and the Eucharist continued.

The singing of the choir seemed even more beautiful than usual to Katy and when with Vladimir she received her First Communion, she felt supported by his prayers and smiled at him. At the end of the service he kissed her on the forehead and said 'Welcome to our Church!'

Father Serge and his wife had arranged a celebration buffet lunch in their house and had invited Olga Vassilyevna, Vladimir, Kiril, Marina and Emma. They congratulated Katy and presented her with gifts - a prayer book with the liturgies of St John Chrysostom and St Basil in English from Fr Serge and an icon of her patron saint, St Catherine, from Olga Vassilyevna. She also received an icon of Christ from Vladimir and one of the Virgin from Kiril and Marina. Emma, who seemed rather overwhelmed by the occasion and stood silently to one side, had not known what to give her. In the end she had decided on a book on Russian religious art and she handed it to Katy, looking awkward.

Katy thanked her and took her to meet Vladimir. 'This is Emma, one of my oldest friends,' she said. 'We were at school together.'

'I've heard a lot about you,' said Emma.

Katy blushed but Vladimir laughed. 'Only good, I hope!'

Olga Vassilyevna approached and Katy left Vladimir to talk to Emma, feeling slightly worried that she might air her views on religion too freely.

'I was touched that you asked me to be your sponsor,' said Olga Vassilevna.

'Thank you for supporting me and also for all your help in teaching me Maloslavian. I think I've got a good basic knowledge now.'

'You worked very hard. I hope all goes well for you in Maloslavia but remember that you are still a British citizen and if things become difficult you can always come back. Nobody can force you to become Queen.'

'I'll certainly remember that,' said Katy, helping herself to some stuffed cabbage.

'Life was very pleasant in Svyatograd when I was a child,' said Olga Vassilyevna. 'My father was a doctor and we had a comfortable apartment, but that privileged life was only for the few. The peasants were desperately poor. Now *everyone* is poor and the country is ruined. Only the corrupt ministers and the Mafia are rich.'

Father Serge, with his wife, Marfa Andreevna, had been listening and joined the conversation. He turned to Katy.

'You have a difficult task ahead of you,' he said, handing her a glass of wine.

'Everyone keeps telling me how difficult it's going to be and, to be honest, I wish I wasn't going. But I'm glad to have been received into the Orthodox Church and I want to thank you for your guidance.'

'I will remember you in my prayers. Try to find something positive that you can do for the country and this will help you face the difficulties of life there.'

'You could visit some of the Maloslavian orphanages,' said Marfa Andreevna. 'The conditions in them are terrible. Many of the children are not orphans at all but have been abandoned by their parents, often because they are handicapped. But you will have to insist on going because government officials will certainly try to stop you. They don't want people to know the real situation.'

'I've heard of one orphanage, run by nuns, which is housed on the estate of an exiled aristocrat. He's trying to get the Government to give the property back to him because the hunting is good. The estate was seized by the Communists and it's in a very bad condition.'

'I hope you can help, but you must tread carefully,' said Father Serge.

Marfa Andreevna fetched the dessert, which was a cream filled cake, and began slicing it. Katy put several pieces on a plate and moved over to Emma and Vladimir who were deep in conversation.

Vladimir grinned. 'I've been hearing about the things you got up to at school. You certainly gave the nuns a hard time!'

'I suppose I did. I rebelled against a lot of their rules and I always seemed to be in trouble but Emma usually got me out of it.'

Kiril and Marina came up to them and Katy passed round the plate of cake.

'We occasionally go to Svyatograd to visit the head office of our paper,' said Kiril. 'We'll try to get in touch with you next time we're there.'

'I'd like that very much, but I hope they'll allow you to see me and that I won't be surrounded by a wall of security guards.'

'We've got press passes. We're journalists and we'll say we want to interview you.'

Everyone had finished eating and it was time to leave. Katy said her farewells, thanked Father Serge and his wife and was putting on her coat when Vladimir came up to her.

'There's a concert by the London Symphony Orchestra at the Barbican next week, two days before you leave. Valery Gergiev is conducting and they're playing Mahler's Symphony No. 2, *The Resurrection*. I know you like Mahler and I thought it would be fun if we could go. We could have something to eat first.'

' I'd love to!'

' I'll book the tickets. We can meet at Earls Court and take the Tube.'

* * *

'For God's sake, stop whinging!' Katy told herself on the day of the concert. She'd finished her packing, tidied the flat, given a set of keys to a friend who was renting it, said goodbye to everyone except Vladimir and she was feeling miserable. She didn't want to go on this crazy expedition to Maloslavia and couldn't understand why she'd agreed to it. She hated the thought of leaving her friends and her familiar surroundings, possibly never to return, and above all she hated the thought of leaving Vladimir.

'But I'm not going to let anything stop me from enjoying this evening,' she decided as she set out to meet him. He was waiting for her at the Underground entrance and his face lit up when he saw her.

'Hi! It's good to see you again,' he said, handing her his crutches and he began to descend the stairs sideways very slowly, holding on to the handrail. It was the rush hour and he was constantly being jostled by impatient commuters but he kept going, unperturbed by the crowds.

'I'm slow aren't I?' he said, smiling.

Katy felt a lump in her throat. 'No, you're not!' she said, suppressing her fear that he would fall.

By six o'clock they were at the Barbican station and Vladimir suggested they went to the Jaipur Palace, an Indian restaurant nearby which had been recommended to him. They found it easily because the entrance was guarded by two large gilded elephants and they were immediately swept inside by the manager who escorted them to a table and handed them the menu. As it was early and they were the only customers, they were the object of constant attention from the waiters who surrounded them and would not leave them in peace to decide what they wanted to eat.

'May I recommend the Roghan Josh, Sir?'

'Perhaps some Tandoori Chicken to start?'

'What would Sir like to drink? Will you have an apéritif?'

'Please could you leave us for a minute,' said Vladimir. 'We haven't decided yet.'

'Very good, Sir.' They took a few steps back but still hovered in the background.

Katy whispered to Vladimir 'They're often like this in Indian restaurants!'

He grinned. 'We'll order when we're ready and not before!'

They decided on lamb korma and a cauliflower curry accompanied by Indian beer. Vladimir summoned one of the waiters and gave the order.

'I'm looking forward to this concert,' said Katy.

'So am I. I've never been to a Mahler concert before. I've only listened to his symphonies on CDs.'

'Do you know, I once played the choral finale of the *Resurrection* symphony to a friend who laughed at me and said it was sentimental kitsch worthy of the Hollywood Bowl! I was really hurt.' (She didn't mention that the friend was Richard.)

'You shouldn't be hurt. Anyone who thinks that must be really insensitive.' He smiled at her and she thought 'How kind his eyes are!'

The waiter brought the first course and the beer and stood looking at them until they had finished eating. He took their plates and disappeared to the kitchen.

'The way they keep hovering is making me nervous,' said Katy. 'I feel as though we're animals in a zoo. They'll be putting the food in our mouths next!'

Vladimir laughed. 'Well, I suppose it's better than bad service.'

The waiter returned with the lamb korma and cauliflower curry. He served the food and stood by the table again. They found it difficult to talk as he kept interrupting them, asking whether everything was all right or whether they wanted anything else. In the end, Vladimir became exasperated and said 'Look, everything's fine, but we're trying to have a conversation. Do you think you could leave us alone for a bit?'

The waiter retreated looking offended.

They began talking about Katy's conversion to Orthodoxy.

'I think it's going to be difficult for me to stick to all the rules of the Church in Maloslavia. I know they insisted I convert, but I don't think the people I'll be dealing with are particularly religious. They were brought up to be atheists.'

'The Church doesn't expect the impossible. If there's a genuine reason why you can't do something, then you don't do it.'

The waiter reappeared with coffee and dessert. 'Gulab Jaman, Sir. On the house,' he said.

'What's this?' asked Vladimir, tasting the sticky sweetmeats.

'Balls of curd cheese poached in syrup,' said Katy.

'Not bad, but a bit too sweet for my taste.'

The bill arrived and Vladimir took out his wallet. Katy felt uncomfortable. She guessed that he didn't earn very much but he clearly intended to treat her and as she didn't want to hurt his pride by offering to pay her share she simply said 'Thank you very much for a lovely meal. I did enjoy it and I'm really looking forward to the concert.'

'My pleasure,' said Vladimir.

They were escorted to the door by the manager who smiled effusively. Once outside they looked at one another and laughed.

'They're incapable of letting people eat in peace,' said Katy. 'It must be something in their genes.'

'The food was good though. Where's the Barbican Centre?'

'In Silk Street. There's a short cut but it involves a lot of steps. Let's take the other route. It isn't much further.'

They arrived at the concert hall and took their seats just before the orchestra started tuning up. Vladimir gave a quick look at the programme.

'They've got a lot of extra instruments - ten horns, eight trumpets, a tuba, not to mention cymbals, triangles, glockenspiel, harps and the organ! And the choir's huge too.'

'Mahler always did things on a colossal scale,' said Katy.

Valery Gergiev, accompanied by the soprano and contralto soloists, came on to the platform to loud applause. He raised his hand and with a terrifying crash from the percussion, the first movement of the symphony began in a great cry of despair. It was as if it echoed Katy's sadness at her departure and she felt she was drowning in a whirlpool of angry sound. It swept over her - a sombre funeral march, then loud calls on the French horns and trumpets. Occasionally it would become sweet and gentle, but almost immediately the percussion would come thundering back. The fourth movement was a calm, beautiful soprano solo, but the fifth began with another crash on the drums, heralding the Day of Judgement. For a long time the music was dark and ominous and then suddenly there was a trumpet call followed by an eerie silence. Very faintly the choir began to sing. The singing and the playing of the orchestra grew louder and the soprano soloist joined in, followed by the contralto. They reached a crescendo - an apocalyptic outburst of love and joy which seemed as though it would never end. The effect on Katy was so powerful that tears started pouring down her cheeks and Vladimir put his arm round her. The choir sang '*What thou has fought for shall lead thee to God*' and with drum rolls and an earth-shattering volume of sound the symphony came to an end amid tumultuous applause. Katy wiped her eyes and turned to Vladimir.

'I'm sorry to cry like that. It was wonderful.'

'You wouldn't be normal if it didn't move you!' he said and she saw a tear on his cheek.

They were both in a state of euphoria after the symphony but it was quickly dispelled when they came out of the concert hall and saw that it was raining hard.

'I haven't got an umbrella,' said Katy dejectedly.

'And I can't hold one anyway with my crutches.'

'Let's get a taxi. It would be much simpler. You can get out at Earls Court and I'll go on to Putney.'

Vladimir hesitated. 'Taxis are expensive.'

'It doesn't matter. With my living allowance from the Maloslavian Government, I can afford to pay.'

Vladimir gave her a grateful smile. 'Well, thank you! A taxi would certainly make things easier.'

'Thank *you* for suggesting the concert and getting the tickets,' said Katy.

They waited for a taxi, only partly protected from the rain which dampened their spirits as well as their clothes. The realization that she would probably never see Vladimir again suddenly hit her like a sledgehammer. 'It's going to be so hard to say goodbye to him,' she thought, 'and the worst of it is that, as he's going to be a monk, I can't really suggest writing to him.'

After about ten minutes, a vacant taxi arrived and they got in. They sat in an awkward silence until finally Katy said, trying to sound cheerful 'I'll come back here if I don't win the referendum. But I expect you'll be on Mount Athos by then?'

'Perhaps. I don't know.' His voice was devoid of expression.

They were silent again. Then she said timidly 'It was a wonderful evening. I enjoyed it so much.'

'I did too.'

They didn't speak until the taxi drew up outside Vladimir's flat. He took her face in his hands and kissed her on the forehead. 'God bless you, Katy,' he said softly. 'You, too!' she said in a choked voice. He got out of the taxi and bent down, turning towards her. She leaned forward and handed him his crutches. For a brief moment their eyes met, then he straightened himself and went slowly towards the front door.

Katy gave the taxi driver her address and sank back in her seat. 'Well, at least we didn't actually say "Goodbye",' she thought.

Chapter 5

Katy watched the fields and towns of southern England recede until the Austrian Airlines Airbus burst through the clouds into a limitless blue sky. Then she sat back and relaxed, enjoying the luxury of travelling in Business Class for the first time. Now that she was at last on her way to Svyatograd, her fears of the previous week had diminished and she was determined to face her stay in Maloslavia philosophically. She was going to miss Vladimir, but she comforted herself with the thought that he'd said 'Everything is in God's hands.' If they were destined to meet again, they would.

She started to read the book of Akhmatova's poems that he'd given her for Christmas but was conscious of being watched by Yurek, her bodyguard. He had been in the Embassy car which came to take her to Heathrow and from now on he would accompany her everywhere. Her first impressions were not encouraging. He was a swarthy, thickset young man with bushy black brows and a snub nose on a face that appeared to wear a permanent scowl. So far there had been little communication between them because his English was almost non-existent and her Maloslavian was still at the elementary stage. He was sitting immediately behind her and although she told herself she was being ridiculous, she had the impression that he was following every word she read. She tried to ignore his presence and concentrate on the poems but without much success until she came to one with the opening lines '*I dream of him more rarely now, thank God. No longer do I imagine that I see him everywhere.*' 'How well Akhmatova understands me!' she thought.

Her reading was interrupted by the arrival of lunch which was elegantly served and very different from the unimaginative food she'd had on budget holiday flights. There was venison in a wild prune sauce and then a delicious apple strudel. She could hear Yurek eating noisily behind her, making slurping sounds as he drank his beer. Occasionally he would blow his nose loudly or sneeze explosively and she decided he must have some kind of allergy. 'I'm surprised they didn't give me a bodyguard with better table manners,' she thought, 'but perhaps most Maloslavians eat like that.'

They hardly had time to finish their meal before the plane began its descent to Vienna's Schwechat Airport. As they disembarked, Yurek said in English 'Here we go change. Get on Maloslavian plane.'

'Yes,' said Katy. 'We must go to the transfer section.'

While they were waiting in the departure hall for the gate to be announced for the flight to Svyatograd, she tried to have a conversation with Yurek and came to the conclusion that he was in fact quite good natured in spite of his apparent scowl. He simply lacked the words to communicate effectively in English and, in any case, he didn't have much to say. She asked him where he came from in Maloslavia and he said 'Village' and grinned at her. His grin was almost more disconcerting than his scowl because it revealed a set of gleaming stainless steel dentures which gave him a robot-like appearance. She persevered and said 'Do you like being a bodyguard?'

He gave a loud laugh. 'No! I like watch my father's cows, but no money in village. So I come to Svyatograd. Now am bodyguard! But don't like big town. Like country.'

Katy gave up her attempt to talk to him and passed the time by reading a Maloslavian tourist leaflet until they were called to board the plane to Svyatograd which turned out to be an old Soviet turboprop Ilyushin with 'Maloslavian Airlines' painted on the side. The so-called Business Class was separated from Economy by a curtain, but the shabby uncomfortable seats were much the same in both classes. The two stewardesses who greeted them wore their long hair in a thick plait down the back and were dressed in linen smocks in the Maloslavian colours - purple with black embroidery round the neck and on the sleeves. Yurek smiled proudly. 'National costume!'

he said. They were the first to get on the plane and after them the other passengers, who were all Maloslavian, began boarding and Katy had a good look at them. The men were dark and thin, but many of the older women were overweight, some of them obese, and they had puffy sallow faces. A number of them wore the same type of stainless steel dentures as Yurek. 'They must have had terrible teeth to end up like that,' she thought. They were laden with an odd collection of plastic bags and cardboard boxes tied with string and they pushed their way down the aisle aggressively, struggling to get the best seats because there was no reservation system. Finally, after much shouting and arguing, they settled down and the plane took off.

As the Business Class section was very small on this flight, Yurek had to sit next to Katy and she was unpleasantly aware that deodorants were unknown to him. He quickly fell asleep, snoring loudly, and his head kept dropping forward and threatening to fall on her shoulder. In these conditions reading was impossible and she began studying the only other passenger in Business Class - a plump, well-groomed man in an expensive looking suit whose flashy gold watch and other jewellery made her wonder if he was a member of the Mafia. He had his own supply of food and spent the flight stuffing himself with caviar, smoked salmon, cold roast chicken and chocolate cake, washed down with a bottle of Chablis. He refused the refreshments the stewardess brought with an imperious wave of the hand and Katy understood why. She was offered a choice of fizzy mineral water or a carton of a bright pink juice called 'Shquip' with a small packet of biscuits. She took the juice and immediately regretted it; it was sickly sweet with a synthetic taste and she only managed to drink half of it. Yurek woke up and wisely chose the mineral water which he gulped down straight from the bottle.

An hour-and-a-half elapsed and then the pilot announced in Maloslavian and bad English that they were about to land at Svyatograd. The plane shot rapidly down from the heavens at a sharp angle and hit the ground with an alarming bump. Katy was terrified but Yurek just laughed. 'Old Soviet plane!' he said by way of explanation. 'No money to buy new planes.'

They were the first to disembark and, as there was no bus, they walked the short distance to the tiny airport building. Because Katy was considered to be a distinguished visitor they were greeted by smiling officials who escorted them through Immigration and Customs to the entrance hall where a piece of red carpet had been laid down. Countess Elena was waiting for them with the Prime Minister, Ivan Petrovitch, and a few cameramen who began frenziedly filming. A little girl was pushed forward and timidly handed Katy a bunch of carnations. She wasn't expecting this and for a moment she stood in a daze, unable to respond. Then instinctively she bent down and kissed the child. '*Spasob*,' she said, which was the Maloslavian for 'Thank you' and the small crowd that had gathered started clapping. The Prime Minister, a nervous-looking little man, kissed her hand.

'Welcome to Maloslavia, Your Royal Highness,' he said. 'This is a great day for our country.'

Katy couldn't see that it was a particularly great day but she managed what she hoped was a gracious smile.

'We will go now,' said Countess Elena. 'Your luggage will be collected and brought to you later.'

They went outside, pursued by the photographers. A black Volga limousine was parked in front of the main entrance and Katy got in with the Countess, Ivan Petrovitch and Yurek. They drove off and Katy looked out of the window, curious to have a glimpse of her new country.

'It is not a good idea to look out of the window,' said the Countess. 'We do not want people to see you until the appropriate time.' She leaned over Katy and drew the thick curtain, blocking the view and most of the light.

'But I want to see the countryside,' protested Katy. 'What harm is there in that? In any case, people have already seen me at the airport!'

'That is not quite the same thing. It could be dangerous to look out of the window.'

'It is understandable, Countess, that Her Royal Highness should wish to see her country,' said Ivan Petrovitch. 'If she wants to look out of the window, we should let her. We have an armed guard with us and I do not think there is any risk.'

Katy drew back the curtain, fixed the Countess with a stony stare and then studied the landscape all the way into Svyatograd.

The city was only twenty kilometres from the airport but the journey took a long time because of the heavy traffic on the narrow, potholed road and the air was thick with diesel fumes created by the long queue of monster lorries. 'Malovitchis' - small private cars similar to a Fiat 500 - dodged in and out between them, hooting ferociously, and the situation was made worse by peasants, in horse-drawn carts or driving herds of goats, suddenly emerging from side lanes and fearlessly inserting themselves into the line of vehicles.

The road was bordered by flat fields of dried up grass but on the horizon a range of jagged mountains rose abruptly from the plain. The only human beings Katy saw in this desolate landscape were a man struggling to till the soil with a primitive horse-drawn wooden plough and an old woman, bent nearly double, hobbling along the footpath that ran beside the road, leading a cow on a rope. There were a few villages, each consisting of a single street bordered by ugly concrete huts and older Turkish-style timbered houses in which the upper storey overhung the ground floor. One village had a delapidated church and a little shop which optimistically bore a sign showing a laughing mother with a fat child on one arm and a basket laden with shopping on the other. As the Volga crawled nearer to the city, a number of factories appeared, none of which seemed to be working, and then came suburbs of the endless shoddy housing estates to be found in every ex-Communist country. Graffiti decorated their walls, washing hung from their tiny balconies and children played in the muddy area that separated the apartment blocks from the road. A long line of people were boarding a battered yellow bus watched by a group of youths in jeans and leather blousons drinking from bottles or beer cans. After these endless suburban districts the city centre was small, consisting of several wide avenues of nineteenth century buildings in the Hapsburg Empire style and an area of older lanes surrounding an ancient Byzantine church. Finally Liberation Square came into view. On the west side of it stood the new Svyatograd Hilton and opposite it was the Hotel Franz Joseph, built before the First World War. To the north was the Royal Palace facing the long, tree-lined Avenue of Heroes on the southern side, which led to the railway station.

'If you become Queen you will of course live in the Royal Palace,' said Ivan Petrovitch, 'but for the time being it is the home of the President, Igor Grobov, so we have reserved a suite of rooms for you in the Hotel Franz Joseph. It is a historic Maloslavian hotel and more appropriate than the American Hilton. Your bodyguard and a maid will live with you and all your meals will be brought up from the hotel kitchens and served in your private dining room.'

The Volga stopped in front of the hotel. They got out and were greeted by the manager who bowed, kissed Katy's hand and led her towards the lift. Ivan Petrovitch and the Countess took their leave, after informing her that the following morning she would be visited by a member of the Maloslavian Front who was responsible for the referendum campaign.

'Permit me to accompany you to your rooms, Your Royal Highness,' said the manager with an unctuous smile. 'We have reserved a delightful suite for you on the sixth floor where you will not be disturbed.'

They entered the lift, leaving behind a bewildered Yurek.

'What about my bodyguard?' asked Katy.

'He and your maid will use the servants' entrance to the suite. They will have their own quarters. Your maid is already waiting for you and your bodyguard will bring your luggage as soon as the porter returns with it from the airport.'

The manager unlocked the large mahogany doors of the suite. Katy went in and saw a small, thin girl of about sixteen dusting the furniture. She looked at Katy with frightened eyes and spoke Maloslavian rapidly in a voice that was little more than a whisper. Then she began to cry. The manager was annoyed.

'This is Boyana. She has been employed in the hotel kitchen and as she was a good worker we decided to promote her to be your maid. But now she is afraid she will not be able to please you.'

'What nonsense! I'm sure she'll be fine,' said Katy and she put her arms round the girl and hugged her. Boyana looked surprised, but then a big grin spread over her face. The manager, who clearly disapproved of Katy's spontaneous behaviour, spoke to Boyana in a stern voice and she nodded her head.

'I have told her that if she cannot do the work she will have to return to the kitchen. If you have any trouble with her, please let me know.'

'I think we'll get along very well, thank you,' said Katy. 'Perhaps you can leave us alone now.' The manager bowed and went out.

She began to inspect her new home. It was shabby, but spacious, and had an air of faded grandeur. The decoration had clearly not been changed since the hotel was built in 1912 in celebration of the state visit of the Emperor Franz Joseph. The mahogany furniture was massive and ugly with an abundance of crimson velvet upholstery some of which was threadbare. There was a dining room with an enormous dinner table, a sitting room which contained an ancient looking television and a gloomy bedroom with a double bed covered by a hideous purple and gold brocade counterpane. The large en-suite bathroom was tiled from floor to ceiling with dingy white tiles reminiscent of a public lavatory. When Katy turned on the tap over the washbasin the water that emerged was brown and when she flushed the WC the light went out. There was a big, old-fashioned kitchen adjoining the dining room and from there a door led to the bathroom and the bedrooms for Boyana and Yurek. 'What a depressing dump this is!' she thought. 'I'd have been better off at the Hilton even if it isn't typical of Maloslavia!'

Doors from the sitting room and the dining room led on to a narrow balcony and she went out and looked down. It was six o'clock in the evening and Liberation Square was full of people hurrying home from work. There were also a number of beggars - gypsies with small children, a legless man on a little trolley, drunken tramps - and a man with a pathetic, sickly bear on a chain who had attracted a small crowd. Outside the Royal Palace there were two sentry boxes and a couple of guards were goose-stepping to and fro in front of them. They wore nineteenth century hussar style uniforms - blue tunic with black froggings, scarlet breeches, black riding boots and a shako - but they looked as if they had been kitted out by a theatrical costumier.

'Well, if I'm bored I can at least admire the view,' she said to herself.

She went back into the dining room. Boyana was trying to explain something to her.

'*Opasna peet vodoo! Nada peet mineralnoo vodoo,*' she said emphatically.

Katy understood and nodded. 'It's dangerous to drink the water. I must drink mineral water?'

She had no intention of drinking the evil brown fluid she had seen coming out of the bathroom tap. Boyana went to the refrigerator in the kitchen and came back with a bottle of the same fizzy mineral water that had been served on the plane. She mimed cleaning her teeth.

'*Tosha da zoobee,*' she said.

'Okay,' said Katy, 'I'll clean my teeth in mineral water.'

By this time Yurek had arrived with the luggage and Boyana began to unpack it, uttering cries of delight when she saw the silk shirts, cashmere sweaters and the blue satin evening dress. Although it was chilly in the room, she was wearing a thin rayon dress which hung loosely on her bony body and she looked cold. There were six sweaters and Katy knew she would never wear all of them. She picked up a red polo-necked pullover and gave it to her.

'*Da vas.* For you,' she said.

Boyana couldn't believe it. She stroked the soft cashmere and then she put the sweater on and looked at herself in the mirror. '*Spasob! Spasob!*' she cried and rushed up to Katy and kissed her.

Yurek was watching the scene with interest and laughed. 'Now she very beautiful!' he said.

At seven o'clock a waiter brought the dinner on a trolley and left it with Boyana. She served Katy in the dining room while she and Yurek had their meal in the kitchen. Katy found the watery vegetable soup and the tough shish kebabs unappetizing, but the baklava for dessert was better. She was bored, eating alone at the long mahogany table, and after chewing on the kebabs for a while she picked up her plate and went into the sitting room where she finished her meal in front of the television. She was curious to see what programmes were on offer but found that there was a depressing choice between quiz shows and very old dubbed American films. Presumably for reasons of cost the individual actors' voices were not dubbed. Instead, a narrator gave a running commentary in Maloslavian on what was happening - 'Now he is telling her that he loves her, but she says she cannot leave her husband and children,' and so on. Katy was rapidly becoming fed up with this when Boyana came in looking shocked. She clearly felt it was un-royal to eat in front of the television but said nothing and took the remains of the meal to the kitchen.

'*Spasob*,' said Katy. She sensed that she was not living up to Boyana's expectations of how a future queen should behave. 'But if I'm going to be Queen, I'll do it my way,' she decided, 'and I don't care what any of them think.'

It had been a long day and she was drowsy. She placed Vladimir's icon on the table by the bed and slipped under the heavy quilt with the book of Akhmatova's poems. But she had only read a few lines before she fell asleep.

* * *

The following morning, after breakfast, Dimitar Stoev, a member of the Maloslavian Front, came to see Katy. He was young and seemed unsure of himself. His English was excellent but he spoke very quietly and kept blinking behind his steel rimmed spectacles.

'Your Royal Highness, I am here to inform you of the plans we have made for the referendum campaign,' he said, nervously clearing his throat.

'What have you in mind?' asked Katy.

'We propose to hold the referendum during the last week of June, which gives us nearly four months to introduce you to the Maloslavian people.'

'Wouldn't it be better to have a shorter campaign?'

'No! There has to be time to re-educate the people so that they are ready to accept the idea of a monarchy. Meetings will be held to explain what the referendum means and how they should vote. There will also be radio and television interviews and as from next week posters will appear all over the country. Leaflets will be distributed in every town and village and you will have to make public appearances. During March you will confine your visits to Svyatograd but during April, May and June you will travel to various parts of the country. You will be accompanied by me as interpreter and by your bodyguard.'

'What kind of accommodation will be provided for me on these visits?'

'Er,' he cleared his throat again, 'Accommodation outside Svyatograd is not of a very high standard and it would not be suitable for you. We have decided it would be better for you to make day trips from the city. The distances are not great: the longest journey will be to the village of Shkrapova in the Pivtsoi Mountains which is 150 kms away, but by leaving early in the morning that should be feasible.'

'Will I have to make speeches in these places?'

'Of course! You will have to speak in Maloslavian. But do not worry. I will write the speeches for you and you will read them.'

'I would like to be free to walk round Svyatograd by myself and see its museums and churches. Is that possible?'

Dimitar blinked frantically and coughed. 'No!' he said, horrified. 'That would be extremely dangerous. The People's Struggle Party is strongly opposed to the restoration of the monarchy and your life could be at risk. However, tomorrow I will arrange for you to visit the city on foot with Yurek and an extra bodyguard. I will also accompany you as your guide.'

Katy protested. 'If I'm protected by three people it will attract a lot of attention!'

'Not if we are all dressed plainly and melt into the background. We will plan the excursion for tomorrow morning. But this afternoon I have organized a meeting for you with President Igor Grobov in the Royal Palace.'

'Will he want to see me since I may be going to depose him?'

'It is a courtesy visit. He will probably not understand who you are because his memory has almost gone He is eighty-five, senile and confined to a wheelchair. If he does realize that you may become queen it will not bother him.'

'But where will he go if the monarchy is restored?'

'He will live in a comfortable villa in the country with a nurse and a resident doctor. It will be better for him. Now I have to leave you but the car will take you to the palace at three o'clock.'

' I can walk! I've only got to cross the square.'

'It will be safer and more appropriate to go by car, Your Royal Highness. I will see you at three.'

* * *

At three o'clock, having had her photo taken for the campaign poster, Katy, with Yurek, went down to the foyer where several girls in mini skirts and thigh-length boots were lounging on a sofa, laughing and talking loudly. Yurek's eyes gleamed. 'Tarts!' he said. 'For tourists. Too expensive for me!'

'But there aren't any tourists,' said Katy.

'Not yet,' said Yurek. 'People too frightened. But they will come soon.'

'I hope so,' said Katy and they went outside to the Volga where Dimitar Stoev was waiting. They got in and drove the short distance across the square to the Palace. The gates swung open and they entered the courtyard where an official opened the car door. He bowed deeply as Katy alighted.

The palace had been built in the Austro-Hungarian style in the late ninteenth century after Maloslavia's liberation from the Turks. There were cracks in the dirty grey facade, but when they entered the hallway Katy gasped in astonishment. There was gold leaf on every available surface. The mouldings on the doors, walls and ceiling glistened and there was an abundance of fat golden cherubs.

'When Igor Grobov became President fifteen years ago, he had the interior of the palace completely restored. It has been redecorated in the style of Versailles. No expense has been spared,' said Dimitar Stoev in reverential tones. 'Everywhere there is gold and just look at the wonderful frescoes on the walls and ceiling. They depict Igor Grobov when he was a younger man with his wife, who unfortunately has now passed on.'

Katy wanted to laugh. The frescoes showed a fat middle-aged man, with an equally fat middle-aged lady, floating on a pink cloud supported by cupids. They were naked, apart from a piece of cloth which artistically concealed their private parts, and the man was holding out his arm towards another younger lady, also naked, who was drifting towards him on a separate cloud.'

'Who is the other woman?' asked Katy.

'That is Igor Grobov's former mistress,' said Dimitar Stoev. 'The President wished this fresco to be a memorial to her. He wanted to be portrayed like Louis XIV, the Sun King, with the women in his life.'

'But isn't it rather embarrassing for his mistress to be on display in such a public place?'

'Not at all. Nobody sees the frescoes apart from the Palace staff and members of the Government and they all knew about her anyway. The public never set foot in here. Now we will go to the President's apartments. Since the decline in his health he never leaves his rooms except when he is wheeled on to the balcony for state occasions.'

They began to climb a wide marble staircase and Dimitar said in a solemn whisper, 'President Grobov's bed is an exact copy of Marie Antoinette's bed in Versailles. It was made specially for him in France and shipped here.'

Katy didn't answer. She was appalled by the vulgar and extravagant way in which the Palace had been decorated and knew that she could never live there.

They entered a large reception room which was as opulent as the hall below. Katy and Dimitar sat on small gilded chairs and Yurek remained standing by the door. After about five minutes another door, which apparently led to the bedroom, opened and a nurse appeared with President Grobov in his wheelchair. She pushed the chair so that he was facing Katy and went out.

The President was grossly overweight. His face was red and bloated and his little eyes were sunk deep in pouches of fat. He wore carpet slippers and a brocade dressing gown which had fallen open revealing a bare chest and an enormous stomach which bulged over the top of his silk pyjama trousers. He stared vacantly at Katy.

'President Grobov,' said Dimitar, '*Vot Konageena Katerina Borisovna.*'

The President smiled vaguely. '*Koto?*' he asked.

'*Konageena Katerina Borisovna. Ya vam shkazal shto ana preeyaydyet.* I told you she was coming!'

Igor Grobov didn't reply. It was obvious that he didn't understand who Katy was, but he stretched out a pudgy hand and she shook it. Then he leaned forward and peered at her more closely for some time. Finally he spoke.

'*Oo yayoh krasseevy krassnee vollosee!*'

'He says you have beautiful red hair,' translated Dimitar Stoev.

Katy laughed. '*Spasob,*' she said.

The President whispered something to Dimitar who shook his head and turned to Katy in despair.

'It's hopeless. He has recently had two strokes and he doesn't understand who you are, although we have explained to him many times. He has just asked me if you are here to milk the cows! I think we should leave.'

They rang the bell for the nurse to come, shook the President's hand and departed. When they were back in the car, Dimitar said to Katy,

'Well, at least you have been able to see what a beautiful palace you will live in if you become Queen.'

Katy exploded. 'If I ever become Queen I shall certainly not live there. It's outrageous to think of the colossal amount of public money that has been spent on that vulgar monstrosity. I shall live somewhere simple and I'll have all that hideous decoration ripped out and turn the place into a hospital or a school!'

Dimitar Stoev laughed cynically. 'But of course you may never become Queen!'

When she returned to her suite of rooms, Katy found Boyana in tears. Sobbing loudly, she poured out her troubles and Yurek translated.

'She say Manager think she thief. He think she stole sweater. He take sweater away.'

Katy was furious. She phoned the reception desk. 'Would you kindly send the manager to me at once!'

The manager arrived a few minutes later, smiling obsequeously.

'Is something wrong, Your Royal Highness.'

'How dare you accuse this poor girl of stealing! I *gave* her the sweater because she was cold and she has nothing warm to wear. Kindly have it returned here immediately!'

'As you wish, Your Royal Highness. I will give the necessary instructions. But I must warn you that many girls of this sort turn out to be thieves.'

'Where I come from,' said Katy, 'people are considered innocent until proved guilty. You may go.'

The manager looked uncomfortable. Bowing very low, he left the room. A few minutes later a chambermaid arrived with the red sweater. Boyana gave a joyful cry and put it on.

'*Ya nyay vor*!' she said.

Katy put her arm round her. 'I know you're not a thief,' she said. 'Don't worry. Everything's going to be all right!'

Chapter 6

The following morning Katy set out with Dimitar on the promised walking tour of Svyatograd. They were accompanied by Yurek and an extra bodyguard, Slavomir. The four of them wore jeans and anoraks and nobody took any notice of them as they pushed their way along the narrow crowded pavements.

'First we are visiting the historic old city and here you see architecture from the days of the Turkish occupation,' said Dimitar as they turned into a cobbled alley.

The 'architecture' consisted of a number of wooden houses with a projecting upper storey in various stages of decay. Some of them appeared about to collapse but they were all inhabited. Washing hung from their windows and on the doorstep of one of them a woman, with her head wrapped in a scarf, was sitting peeling vegetables. A small girl, whose head was also covered, stood beside her stroking a scrawny kitten.

'They are Muslims,' explained Dimitar. 'We have a small Muslim minority in Maloslavia, dating from Turkish times. We also have many problems with Jews in Svyatograd.'

'What problems?' said Katy.

'The usual ones. They take the best jobs.'

'Well, Jews are usually very intelligent and they know how to work hard,' said Katy in a frosty tone.

Dimitar ignored this remark and pointed to a small mosque at the end of the alley.

'That is the only mosque in Svyatograd and opposite it is the church of St Bogomil.'

They had come out into an attractive little square bordered by trees. There was a fountain in the middle and at the far end was the tiny Byzantine church that Katy had seen from the car on the day she arrived. It faced the mosque and on a bench outside it several old women in black were sitting enjoying the early spring sunshine.

'The church of St Bogomil is one of the oldest in Maloslavia,' said Dimitar. 'The remains of the saint are buried here. Did you know that he was one of your ancestors?'

Katy did know because Olga Vassilyevna had told her. Bogomil had been one of the first kings of Maloslavia in the tenth century and had been murdered by robbers while hunting in the forest.

'There is a legend about him,' continued Dimitar. 'When members of the court discovered his body, which had been hacked to pieces with an axe, they brought his remains back here and buried them. They built this church over the grave and people made pilgrimages to it. One day a blind beggar was praying at the tomb and his sight was miraculously restored. That is why Bogomil was canonized. Did you know this story?'

'No, I didn't. Thank you for telling me.'

'How does it make you feel, having a saint for an ancestor?'

'Well, it's rather a lot to take in,' said Katy smiling. 'Can we visit the church now?'

They went in. It was very dark, but she could see that the iconstasis was a beautiful example of Byzantine art in a remarkable state of preservation. The tomb of St Bogomil was on the left-hand side of the church and next to it, on a lectern, was an ancient icon of the saint which glowed in the light of the many votive candles that had been placed on a stand in front of it.

'I'm going to get a candle,' said Katy and she bought one from the nun in charge of a stall near the door and fixed it on the stand. She stood for a moment in front of the icon and said a prayer for Vladimir. Dimitar had been watching with an amused expression on his face. 'Are you religious?' he asked.

' I was recently received into the Orthodox Church.'

Dimitar gave a cynical laugh. 'Well, I have been baptized and I am Orthodox but I don't go to church. Church is for old ladies who are afraid of dying!'

Katy was beginning to dislike Dimitar but she knew she had to get on with him so she said nothing. They left the church and went down another narrow lane which led to the market square. There were stalls piled high with vegetables and others with bowls of yoghourt, sour cream and cottage cheese which the saleswomen ladled out into small pots. One stall had some rather dubious looking hunks of meat on sale and another specialized in sticky Turkish pastries. Cheap clothes, kitchen utensils, brooms and buckets were also on offer.

'Very dirty here,' said Yurek. 'In summer many flies. Better to shop at Tesco.'

Katy laughed. 'Is there a Tesco here?'

'Of course!' said Yurek. 'Very big one!'

They turned into another alley which took them out of the old town and into the nineteenth century Boulevard Victoria.

'Here we will visit the National Museum,' said Dimitar.

The museum turned out to be a vast, gloomy building with a disappointing collection of exhibits. Room after room displayed costumes from the different regions of Maloslavia - endless embroidered sheepskin jackets, layer upon layer of women's starched petticoats, countless pairs of men's linen trousers bound with leather thongs, pile upon pile of long scarlet boots - all of them dusty and neglected. Other rooms contained the skulls of prehistoric men and women found near Svyatograd and a variety of stuffed animals. There were a few bad nineteenth century paintings - dark, depressing landscapes with cracks in the paintwork and stiff, ugly portraits. Katy was bored.

'Aren't there any icons here?' she asked.

'Only bad nineteenth century ones,' said Dimitar. 'Most of the valuable ones were smuggled out of the country for dollars. Now the Government has put a stop to it but it is too late. Much of our cultural heritage has gone.'

They continued their walk down the boulevard and she was surprised to see that there were some elegant shops displaying clothes by Dior and Versace and others that had expensive cosmetics and perfumes.

'Who can afford to buy these things?'

'Only a few members of the Mafia. Of course, if any Japanese or American tourists come here they will buy them too.'

They had now arrived at the Cathedral of the Redeemer which had been built after the liberation from the Turks. It was large and ostentatious and its iconostastis was adorned with sentimental works of art painted in a Western European style completely out of keeping with the Orthodox tradition. It lacked the simplicity and beauty of the little church of St Bogomil and after a quick look round Katy, who was beginning to feel tired, suggested they move on.

Next to the Cathedral was the railway station which was similar to those built on a grand scale in many European capitals in the mid-nineteenth century. It resembled the Gare de l'Est in Paris but it had clearly seen better days and appeared to be deserted.

'Are there any trains?' Katy asked.

'There is a regular service to Poposlavsky in the south of Maloslavia. It is a slow train and it stops at many stations but we shall have to take it for some of your visits because it is safer than the roads. There are fewer accidents. Occasionally there are also trains to Bucarest and Vienna and sometimes even to Athens. I am not sure what the present schedule is,' said Dimitar vaguely. Then, apparently feeling embarrassed by the transport situation, he hurriedly pointed to a large modern building next to the station.

'Look! That is our new Tesco. You can buy anything there.'

The store, at the bottom of the Avenue of Heroes was an eyesore on a pleasant boulevard bordered on both sides by parkland.

'We have military parades down this avenue,' said Dimitar as they strolled back to the hotel. 'Independence Day is quite soon and there will be a parade. President Grobov will be wheeled on to the balcony to take the salute. It would be nice if you could be there with him.'

This idea didn't appeal to Katy but she smiled and remained silent.

On Friday morning Dimitar told Katy that in the afternoon she was to record a speech to the nation which would go out on television on Sunday night.

She was alarmed at this news. 'I've never done anything like this before.'

'It is very important that you speak to the people,' said Dimitar. 'It will mark the opening of the referendum campaign. As from Monday you will begin making visits in the Svyatograd area to schools, hospitals and other public places.'

'But where will this recording take place and what am I supposed to say?'

'You will be filmed in the main hall of the Palace, Your Royal Highness, and I have written your speech for you in Maloslavian. I propose that we now go through it and that I correct any errors in your pronunciation.'

'Very well,' said Katy, beginning to wish she'd never set foot in Maloslavia. 'but please would you call me "Katy" instead of "Your Royal Highness" and I'll call you "Dimitar". I think it'll make for a friendlier working relationship. I hate being called "Your Royal Highness" and I'm not used to it.'

Dimitar was shocked. 'But Your...er...This would be most inappropriate! You are heir to the throne of Maloslavia.'

'But I'm not Queen yet and, as you reminded me the other day, I probably never will be. In Britain and the United States it's very common now to use first names in working relationships.'

'Very well,' said Dimitar reluctantly. 'If that is what Your...I mean, if that is what you wish, er, Katy.'

'It is,' said Katy and they began working on the speech. It contained all the usual platitudes and promises found in this type of television broadcast - uniting the country, overcoming political differences, restoring the cultural heritage, looking towards a brighter future, working together, relieving poverty and suffering - promises that she felt would be very hard to fulfil. She read the speech aloud several times, struggling with her pronunciation but after correcting her stress on several words Dimitar was satisfied.

In the afternoon she put on a sage green Chanel-style suit with a cream silk shirt and, after Boyana had dressed her hair, she was once again driven across to the Royal Palace. A team of television cameramen and technicians were waiting in the great hall where cables trailed across the fine parquet floor, cameras stood on tripods and special lighting had been installed. Katy, who had never made a broadcast before, felt very nervous but although she didn't understand much of what she was saying, by some miracle she sounded as though she did. Dimitar and the crew said that the recording was '*harosh*' which meant 'good' and she began to look forward to seeing herself on television.

On Sunday morning she wanted to attend the church of St Bogomil. She couldn't see what danger there would be in doing this as the vast majority of the population wouldn't know what she looked like until they saw her on television that evening. She decided to go, dressed in her anorak, jeans and a headscarf. Yurek accompanied her but wasn't happy.

'Not good! Countess Slobovna and Dimitar Stoiev will be angry. You must do what they say!'

'I'm not a prisoner!' said Katy as they crossed the little square and entered the church. The liturgy had already begun and it was difficult to find somewhere to stand in the throng of worshippers. Eventually they found a place squashed between two obese women who were continually bowing and crossing themselves. Yurek was bored and occasionally gave a loud yawn but Katy was now sufficiently familiar with the service to follow what was happening and tried hard to concentrate. She thought of Vladimir who at this time would also be at church and wished she could tell him about St Bogomil and how different it was to St Nicolas; the congregation was much bigger and they sang with tremendous fervour and didn't rely on a choir for the music. There were many women with babies and small children and a little girl near Katy took hold of her hand and smiled at her. Katy smiled back and the child, who seemed afraid of being crushed in the crowd, clung to her until the end of the liturgy when the mother appeared and claimed her with a grateful look.

'You happy now?' said Yurek as they came out of church.

'Yes!' said Katy, feeling the service had done her good. She returned to the hotel for lunch but when she reached her rooms she found an angry Countess Slobovna waiting for her.

'I came to see how you were settling down and I find you have gone to church without asking our permission,' she said.

'It never occurred to me that I had to ask permission to go to church. Anyway, it was you who told me I must convert to the Orthodox church.'

'Only for political reasons.'

'I suppose it never crossed your mind that I might want to take my conversion seriously and try to follow the teachings of the Church?'

The Countess ignored this question and continued, 'This is a dangerous city. There is much crime. You are a public figure. Your life could have been at risk.'

'What utter nonsense! Very few people know who I am and they won't until they see the television broadcast tonight. I took my bodyguard with me and, as you can see, I'm wearing clothes that don't mark me out in a crowd.'

'Well, I suppose that is true but after today you will be known to the population and you will have to be more careful. In future you must ask Dimitar Stoev's approval for any visits you wish to make. He will see whether they clash with the official programme he has planned for you and whether they entail any risk to your life.'

'May I remind you,' said Katy 'that if you persist in treating me like a prisoner, I can go to the British Embassy and ask for their assistance in returning to London. In any case, I'm informing you now that I intend to go to church at Easter.'

'That is perfectly permissible. In fact, an official visit to an Easter service would be very appropriate and good publicity for the referendum campaign.'

Katy was speechless at this blatant hypocrisy. The Countess dropped a deep curtsey and swept out of the room, nearly colliding in the doorway with a waiter who was arriving with the lunch trolley.

Katy sank into an armchair in front of the television and Boyana, who was now used to this behaviour, served her meal. She ate it, watching the Maloslavian version of the Teletubbies and wondering how on earth she was going to spend the time until the broadcast of her speech at eight o'clock. There was really nothing to do except read and she was trying to avoid devouring too quickly the small stock of novels and biographies she had brought with her. When she had eaten, she decided to finish Olga Vassilyevna's *Short History of Maloslavia* before attacking another book and stretched out on the sofa with it.

She learned that she was descended from one of the oldest royal houses in Europe. Her ancestor, Rostik Bogdanov, became the first king of Maloslavia in the tenth century and his descendents had reigned peacefully until the Turkish invasion in 1395. During the lengthy occupation, the Bogdanovs survived, living quietly on a farm in the country until in 1880 Maloslavia regained its independence. The young Prince Stanimir ascended the throne and was succeeded by Todor II, Rostik IV and finally in 1945 by Katy's father, Boris III who was forced to abdicate in 1950.

She reached the end of the book and saw that it was already seven o'clock and time for another meal. Boyana had returned from an afternoon off at the cinema and brought her an omelette, salad and ice cream accompanied by a glass of rough red "Maloslavskaya Burgundaya". Katy finished her meal, switched on the television again and sat on the sofa waiting for the broadcast of her speech. She was half-heartedly looking at a game show and wondering why dreadful programmes of this kind were so popular the world over when, to her surprise, the door suddenly opened and Dimitar Stoiev appeared.

'Good evening, Dimitar. I wasn't expecting you,' she said.

Dimitar bowed and kissed her hand. He looked at her, blinking nervously.

'I thought I would watch the television broadcast with you, Katy. I wanted to see your reactions to it.'

Katy laughed. 'I'll probably be horrified! I've never seen myself on television before.'

Dimitar sat down beside her on the sofa. 'Oh no!' he said, 'You mustn't be shocked. You're...you're..' he stammered, 'You're a beautiful woman. You've got lovely red hair.'

She was irritated by his familiarity. 'I sometimes wish I hadn't got red hair! People go on about it all the time and I get fed up with it!'

He appeared crushed by this remark and they sat looking at the television in silence. At eight o'clock the Maloslavian flag came up on the screen to the accompaniment of the national anthem. Then the words *Konageena Katerina Borisovna* appeared, followed by Katy in the green Chanel suit. Her speech lasted five minutes and came over rather well but her pleasure in watching it was marred by Dimitar who was gradually sliding closer to her until at the end of the broadcast he succeeded in pressing his body against hers. She glared at him and edged away.

'You were very good. Are you pleased?' he asked, giving her a stupid smile.

'Yes, I suppose so,' she said in a cold voice, standing up.

Dimitar rose and stared at her. Then, looking down at the floor, he cleared his throat and said in a determined voice that sounded as if he was arranging a political meeting, 'Would you care for a little sexual activity?'

She wondered if she had heard him correctly. How could this fussy little bureaucrat, with his nervous mannerisms, pluck up the courage to suggest such a thing? She was annoyed but she also thought it was rather funny.

Trying to sound regal, she said 'I don't think that would be a good idea and I am surprised that you should even think of it.'

Dimitar was offended. 'I thought you were expecting it. You have a lover in England perhaps?'

'My private life is my own business,' said Katy.

'You asked me to call you "Katy" which was a most unusual request. Naturally I had the impression that you were lonely in this country and were waiting for me to...to..er, satisfy your needs,' he said angrily.

'In Britain and the United States, asking somebody to call you by your first name is simply an attempt to create a good working relationship; it is not an invitation to have sex,' said Katy. 'I am not looking for sex and even if I was, it would be highly inappropriate for me, as heir to the throne, to have it with you. In view of the effect that calling me Katy seems to have had upon you, I would be glad if you would kindly revert to calling me "Your Royal Highness"'.

She hated making this formal little speech and couldn't help feeling sorry for Dimitar who was now clearly worried about his behaviour. 'He's no older than me,' she thought. 'and he's very unsure of himself. I do wish he'd stop blinking all the time!'

Dimitar looked at Katy earnestly. 'I'm sorry, Your Royal Highness. Forgive me for misinterpreting your wishes. I trust I may rely on your discretion.'

Katy smiled. 'I won't say anything, but please never let this happen again.'

'Of course. Thank you, Your Royal Highness!' stammered Dimitar. He hurried out of the door and when he had gone Katy collapsed on the sofa in helpless laughter.

* * *

At nine o'clock the following morning Dimitar returned and neither he nor Katy mentioned the previous evening's events. He was his usual bureaucratic self and bowing low he said 'Good morning, Your Royal Highness. This morning we are visiting the First of May Primary School on the outskirts of Svyatograd. The car is already outside the hotel if you will be so kind as to accompany me.'

'He's deliberately being even more formal than usual,' she thought as, with Yurek, they went down to the waiting Volga. They left the city centre and drove through an attractive suburb with avenues shaded by trees and large villas surrounded by gardens. Police stood on guard outside some of the houses.

'Who lives here?' she asked.

'Members of the Government, foreign diplomats, a few rich people.'

'*Are* there any rich people here?'

'Not many, but they are *very* rich. Genuine millionaires!'

'Mafia!' Katy thought.

They arrived at the primary school, which was bright and modern with a large grassy playground, and entered a classroom. Twenty children, about eight years old, stood up and chorused in English, 'Good morning, Your Royal Highness!'

The girls were all dressed like Soviet primary school children in white frilly pinafores over black dresses. One of them, with long blond plaits, came up to Katy, curtseyed and presented her with a bunch of carnations.

'Thank you!' she said.

The teacher, a thin, tired-looking woman, also curtseyed.

'In this primary school,' she said, 'children are taught English from a very early age. The class have been practising an English song for you.' She went to the piano and the children sang 'Jack and Jill went up the hill' to a cheerful little tune which she had composed herself.

Katy smiled and clapped. 'Do all primary schools teach English?' she asked. The teacher looked embarrassed.

'No, for the time being this is the only one. The children at this school live near here and come from very good families. They are highly intelligent.'

'I see,' said Katy and she thought she saw only too well.

'Why do the girls still wear uniforms like Soviet primary school children?'

'These uniforms were abolished in Russia after the collapse of Communism but we have kept them in Maloslavia because we feel it gives the children a sense of pride in their school. Now I will show you some of the other rooms.'

The teacher took them to see several other classrooms which were decorated in bright colours with examples of the pupils' artwork on the walls. There was also a hall with a stage where concerts and plays were given, a gymnasium and a canteen where cooks were preparing lunch.

Katy was impressed. The school was modern, well equipped and the children seemed happy, but she had the feeling that she was not being given a true picture of Maloslavian primary education. In the car, driving back to the hotel, she said 'Are all the primary schools here similar to this?'

Dimitar blinked and cleared his throat vigorously. 'Er, well not *yet*. That school is a prototype.'

'You mean it's a school reserved for the children of the rich and privileged?'

'Er, well for the time being we...'

Katy interrupted him. 'Why do you take me to see a school designed for children of Government members and millionaires? I want to see a school where ordinary children go.'

'I'm afraid that may not be possible.'

'Well, please make it possible!' she said, getting out of the car. She stormed into the hotel and left Dimitar on the threshold wishing fervently that he had never been given the job of organizing her campaign.

Chapter 7

The Volga stopped in the courtyard of a flat-pack furniture factory a few miles from Svyatograd.

'This is the Maloslavian IKEA,' said Dimitar.

It was the first factory that Katy had visited, although over the past few weeks she'd been to hospitals, crêches and homes for the aged and even succeeded in seeing an ordinary school with dingy classrooms where forty or fifty pupils were crammed together. The hospitals were overcrowded, with large, old-fashioned wards and patients lying on beds in the corridors, and in one retirement home people sat all day in a small dark room with nobody to attend to their needs. The doctors and nurses were polite but indifferent to her and she sensed their lack of interest in her campaign. They were overworked and underpaid and what difference would it make to their lives to have a queen who would simply be a tool in the hands of a corrupt government?

Katy got out of the car to find herself facing a shrieking mob, brandishing red banners and singing the Internationale.

'What do they want?' she asked.

'They are protesters from the People's Struggle Party - Communists under a new name who are against the restoration of the monarchy. They are fighting for a return to a Socialist state and they can be violent. I am afraid they may try to stop us entering the building. It is a pity we have only one bodyguard.'

Katy was uneasy. She had seen several demonstrations by the People's Struggle Party from her balcony at the hotel but they had passed off peacefully. This one looked as though it could become very nasty. There were about a hundred protesters and many of them had truncheons and clubs. A member of the factory staff was leaning out of a first floor window shouting to them to disperse but they replied by throwing bricks and stones at the window and he quickly disappeared.

'Get back into the car,' said Dimitar and they got in and locked the doors. He rang the factory on his mobile. 'They have phoned for the riot police,' he said. 'We'll wait till they arrive and see what happens.'

After about five minutes, several vans of police armed with helmets, shields and batons arrived. When the crowd refused to disperse, they charged, firing tear gas and seizing and beating anyone they could lay their hands on. The protesters fought back, waving their clubs wildly. Suddenly one of them drew out a knife and plunged it into a policeman's stomach. He collapsed in a pool of blood, screaming. In a flash several other police fired at the attacker, killing him instantaneously and the rest of the crowd ran away.

The courtyard was a battlefield littered with torn banners, crumpled leaflets and pieces of brick. The pool of blood from the injured man spread until it mingled with the stream that gushed from his killer's multiple gunshot wounds. He was a heavily bearded young man and his face had been reduced to pulp by the bullets, one of which had shattered his right eye. Katy caught a glimpse of him through the car window and closed her eyes. She felt sick.

'I must see what's happening,' said Dimitar. He got out of the car and went over to the cluster of riot police surrounding the injured policeman. After a few minutes he came back looking grave.

'They have phoned for an ambulance but if it does not arrive soon it will be too late. He is bleeding to death and his pulse is very weak. I think we should leave.'

Although Katy wanted to get away as quickly as possible she said 'Surely we ought to wait and see whether this man's life can be saved? And couldn't the police have arrested the attacker instead of riddling him with bullets?'

'It would have been too dangerous.'

'But the police were armed to the teeth and there were plenty of them. They should have been able to seize him and put him in prison until he was brought to trial.'

'Even in your country it is a very bad crime to kill a policeman,' said Dimitar. 'It deserves death.'

'Well, we have abolished the death penalty in Britain and anyway we don't know yet whether the policeman will die. Perhaps he'll recover.'

'But it will still be a case of attempted murder.'

Katy couldn't deny this and she was revolted by what had happened. If a visit to a factory could end in such a blood bath what would happen when the referendum campaign really began to get under way? All her instincts told her to escape - to take the first available flight back to London - but she forced herself to remain outwardly calm.

'I'd like to see the injured man,' she said and got out of the car, followed by Dimitar. She went over to the group surrounding the policeman. A boy of about nineteen or twenty lay moaning softly, his pain-filled dark eyes wide open. Blood was spurting from a wound in his abdomen and the police stood looking at him helplessly. One of them had tried unsuccessfully to stop the bleeding with a pad made from a scarf. Katy knelt down beside the boy and he turned his head towards her. There was nothing she could say, but she took his hand. He smiled at her and very faintly said '*Spasob.*' Then he muttered something she couldn't understand.

'He says he is going to die,' said Dimitar.

'The ambulance will soon be here. Tell him to hold on a bit longer, then he will be taken to hospital and I will visit him there.'

Dimitar translated and the boy smiled. At that moment the ambulance arrived and he was carried into it on a stretcher and driven away. Katy asked his name and was told he was called Anatoly Hristov and he had only been in the police a year.

'Please keep me informed of his progress,' she said. 'I'd like to see him again.'

The three of them got into the Volga and were driven back to Svyatograd.

'Very bad business,' said Yurek. 'Campaign will be difficult and bloody.'

'No!' snapped Dimitar. 'This is an unfortunate incident, Your Royal Highness, but it is not typical. You must not distress yourself. Everything will be all right.'

'All right!' said Katy. 'Do you really expect me to believe that? I've just seen an attempted murder and a brutal killing by the police. I have the impression the people don't want a monarchy and if so I'm wasting my time here.'

'That demonstration was organized by the People's Struggle Party; they always behave like that. But do not worry. They are a small minority.'

'Well, they didn't look very small to me,' said Katy 'and please let me know if they manage to save Anatoly. I'll go to the hospital when he's fit to have visitors.'

* * *

'The young policeman is out of danger,' said Dimitar a week after the visit to the factory. 'He was given a massive blood transfusion and although he is still very weak he will make a full recovery. We can go to see him this afternoon.'

Anatoly was in a hospital in the residential suburb where Katy had visited the First of May Primary School. It was a small but modern establishment and Dimitar explained that it was usually reserved for private patients who could afford to pay. Anatoly had been taken there because his injuries had been caused by attempted murder and there was no other hospital in the city sufficiently well equipped to save his life. He was in a small room by himself, propped up by pillows and attached to various wires and tubes. His face broke into a broad smile when he saw Katy. He said something that she couldn't understand and Dimitar translated.

'He wants to thank you for staying with him when he was wounded and he says you are the only visitor he has had.'

'Aren't any of his family coming to see him?'

Dimitar asked him and said 'He doesn't have any family. His

mother died of cancer when he was six and his father was always drunk and used to beat him. He was taken away from him and put in an orphanage. A year ago, when he was eighteen, he joined the police because it was the only job open to him.

'*Vee hoteetye vernootsya v poleetz poslyay balneetsee?*' said Katy in bad Maloslavian, wanting to know if he meant to go back to the police when he recovered.

'*Nyay! Na shto delat?*' Anatoly replied emphatically.

'I quite understand that he doesn't want to go back to the police. Couldn't he be trained for some other kind of work?'

'His education is insufficent for the university and anyway there are very few places. Perhaps he could go to the technical college where he could train to be a baker or a plumber. I will ask him.'

Anatoly grinned. '*Ya hachoo beet boolochneek!*' he said.

Katy looked at Dimitar. 'He wants to be a baker. He's had a terrible life up till now. We must help him. Can a place be arranged for him in a technical school?'

'I will make enquiries. I think it will be possible.'

'*Ya boodoo vsyo delat shtobee vwee payaydyete v boolochnooyoo shkoly,*' she said to Anatoly. The poor kid deserved a chance and she was determined to do everything she could to help him train as a baker. His face lit up.

'*Spasob, spasob!*' he said and added something she couldn't understand.

'He says God has sent you,' Dimitar translated with a sneer and Katy blushed.

A nurse came in and said that they must leave as Anatoly was only allowed short visits until he was stronger. Katy bent over and kissed his cheek to Dimitar's disapproval and Yurek's surprise and they went back to the car.

* * *

Orthodox Easter was drawing near and Katy was determined to be at the great celebration of the Resurrection on the Saturday night. She was sorry she couldn't go to the Good Friday liturgy but she knew that difficulties would be put in her way and thought it would be best to concentrate on getting permission to attend the most important service of all. She asked Dimitar to make the necessary arrangements.

'I'd like to go to the Easter Vigil at St Bogomil.'

'That is impossible, Your Royal Highness,' said Dimitar. 'The church is very small, there will be huge crowds and we cannot guarantee your safety. As heir to the throne it is appropriate that you should make an official visit to the liturgy at the Cathedral of the Redeemer and everything has already been organized. There will be full television coverage and it will be very good publicity for the campaign.'

Katy was furious. 'Don't you understand? It's my first Easter service as a member of the Orthodox Church and I want to feel part of it like everyone else without having cameras and paparazzi following me!'

'The Easter Vigil at the Cathedral is always televised, Your Royal Highness. It has not been arranged specially for you but I will tell the cameramen to be discreet and not disturb your devotions,' said Dimitar smiling ironically.

There was nothing she could do but accept his arrangements and late on Saturday evening he accompanied her, with Yurek in attendance, to the cathedral. A cluster of photographers gathered round the car as she got out and she was annoyed to see that the area round the building had been cordoned off and police were holding back the crowds.

'Can't anyone attend the Vigil?'

'Not this year, for security reasons, Your Royal Highness. The cathedral is already full of people who have been carefully vetted and nobody else will be allowed to enter. Let us go in.'

They entered the building in darkness and were given candles. They held them, unlit, listening to the plaintive chanting of the choir. Then the clergy appeared. They went out of the cathedral, followed by the entire congregation and processed round the outside of the building three times in search of the risen Christ. The Bishop knocked on the cathedral door and they re-entered. The golden gates of the iconostasis were flung open, there was a blaze of light from the chandeliers and each person took a flame from another until all the candles were lit.

Katy had never been to such a dramatic Easter service before. She stood, holding her lighted candle as the Bishop cried out three times, '*Hristos voskryese!* Christ is risen!' and with the rest of the congregation she replied '*Voisteenoo voskryese*! He is risen indeed!'

A strange feeling came over her. For a brief moment she seemed to be in a state of heightened awareness which she could not have described - the light in the cathedral appeared unnaturally brilliant and her perception of the choir's singing was extraordinarily acute. It was as though for a few seconds she was in another dimension and then the sensation vanished as rapidly as it had appeared. For the first time in her life she was convinced that God existed. Although she had been moved when she was received into the Orthodox Church, her doubts had remained. Now suddenly she had faith.

The liturgy lasted for three hours. Dimitar was bored and wanted to leave but Katy meant to stay until the end. To her surprise, Yurek appeared to be enjoying himself and enthusiastically bowed and crossed himself. When it was over he smiled and said 'First time I come to Easter service. Very beautiful!'

They came out of the cathedral and saw a group of women standing behind tables laden with baskets of scarlet eggs and tall cylindrical loaves decorated with hundreds and thousands.

'These loaves are traditional Easter food,' said Dimitar. 'They are sweet and contain nuts and raisins. The women are waiting for the priest to come and bless the food.'

Katy would have liked to stop, but the cameramen were surrounding her again and Dimitar hurried her towards the waiting car. She couldn't help noticing that the members of the congregation they passed leaving the cathedral were all well dressed and looked prosperous.

'Who are the people who were allowed to come to the service?' she said.

'They were carefully selected. They all live in the suburb where you visited Anatoly in hospital.'

'So they are fairly wealthy?'

'Of course.'

'And in the past the Cathedral has been open to everyone at Easter?'

'Yes, but this year most people will have had to go to St Bogomil and other churches in the city.'

Katy was silent. It was sad to think that her attendance had prevented many worshippers from entering the Cathedral.

* * *

On Easter Sunday morning, Katy was eating a late breakfast when Boyana came in, very excited, and said that the Prime Minister, Ivan Petrovitch, wanted to see her.

Katy was surprised. 'Send him in,' she said.

Ivan Petrovitch entered and bowed. He looked grave.

'I have some sad news, Your Royal Highness. President Igor Grobov had another stroke last night and died early this morning.'

'I'm very sorry to hear that,' said Katy.

'It was to be expected. He had been in poor health for a long time and quite incapable of carrying out the duties of President. For him it is a merciful release but for us there will now be many serious problems.'

'Why?' asked Katy.

'President Grobov was the Leader of the People's Struggle Party. Of course, over the last few years he has been a leader in name only and Nikola Popnikov has deputized for him. He is only thirty-five and a fiery politician. He comes from a family of revolutionaries and has never made a secret of his devotion to Communist ideology. There is no doubt that he will now be elected Leader of the People's Struggle Party and he is also a member of parliament and, unfortunately, a minister in my coalition government.'

'Yes, but does this matter much?'

'Certainly it does! The People's Struggle Party are bitterly opposed to the restoration of the monarchy because they are all Communists hiding under another name. While President Grobov was alive I managed, with great difficulty, to persuade the members of their party who were in my coalition that it was better to have a young, healthy monarch than a sick, senile president. Even then, they wanted to replace Grobov by Popnikov rather than restore the monarchy. Now they will clamour for him to be President and for the referendum to be abandoned.'

'Well, perhaps it would be for the best.'

'No! Popnikov is ruthless and ambitious. If he became President he would quickly turn the country into a Communist dictatorship again. We need a constitutional monarchy like you have in Britain which is above politics.'

'What do you propose to do?'

'The people must be allowed to decide their own future and the campaign will continue as planned. I will try to pacify my government by suggesting that Popnikov is voted in as Acting President until the referendum takes place. However, I am afraid there may be some very violent demonstrations by members of the People's Struggle Party.'

'You know, I would be perfectly happy to return quietly to England,' said Katy. 'I've never been very keen on the idea of being Queen and I'm not convinced that it's the best thing for the country.'

'Your Royal Highness, I beg you not to give up. You have made a good impression on all the people you have met in hospitals and schools. They have never had anyone before who talked to them and listened to their problems. Everybody speaks warmly about what you did for that poor boy who was stabbed.'

'I really didn't do anything,' said Katy, feeling embarrassed.

'You gave him hope. Now, because of your intervention, we have made arrangements for him to train to be a baker which is what he wants.'

'You ought to have been able to do that without me!'

Ivan Petrovitch sighed. 'Perhaps. But in this country it is difficult to get such things done without pressure from someone like yourself who can cut through all the bureaucracy. This is where you have an important role to play.'

'Well, I'll continue for the time being,' she said but her voice lacked conviction.

'Good. And now we have to plan for President Grobov's funeral. Tomorrow and Tuesday he will lie in state in the Cathedral of the Redeemer. As heir to the throne you will be the first to file past his coffin, followed by members of the government and foreign leaders and diplomats. After that the public will be able to pay homage. Wednesday will be a day of national mourning and the funeral will take place in the Cathedral. Then there will be a procession to the cemetery in which you will participate.'

Ivan Petrovitch bowed and went out, leaving Katy with the feeling that her Easter Sunday had been completely shattered.

* * *

Katy ate her lunch watching the television news which was devoted entirely to President Grobov's death and included a film covering his whole life. There was footage of him as a young man, standing on a tractor waving a red flag and surrounded by cheering farm workers. Other shots showed him playing with his wife and children in his garden and on a bear hunt in the forest. In the final pictures, taken at the last Independence Day parade, he was sitting in his wheelchair on the palace balcony, with a vacant smile, waving feebly to the crowds. After the film Nikola Popnikov paid a tribute to the President. He was a big, broad-shouldered young man with a mass of untidy black hair and a fierce expression. He spoke with emotion, but also with a certain agressivity, praising Igor Grobov as a true hero of Socialism and urging the nation to remember him by continuing the struggle against Capitalism.

Katy switched off the television. She couldn't help thinking that the President's vulgar palace, dripping with gold leaf and plastered with frescoes of his mistress, was hardly compatible with a Socialist hero. She finished her meal and went out on the balcony. It was a beautiful spring day and lilacs were in bloom in the gardens that bordered the Avenue of Heroes. People were strolling in the sunlit square in front of the Palace and a few of them were laying wreaths and bunches of flowers against the railings. One old woman in black was sitting on a bench sobbing and a girl had her arm round her and was trying to comfort her. Katy was surprised at this outpouring of grief but told herself that she had only seen the President when he was senile. Whatever faults he may have had, he must have done some good when he was younger to inspire such emotion.

The brilliant sunshine, the flowers and the fresh green of the trees contrasted with her sombre mood. Igor Grobov's death would make her campaign more difficult and possibly dangerous and in any case she felt it was bound to fail. She longed to go home and wished she could talk to Vladimir who always saw things so clearly. Perhaps he was still in London? She suddenly had an irresistible urge to send him a letter and fetched a pad of paper from her bedroom. She sat at a table on the balcony and wrote rapidly.

Dear Vladimir,

I'm writing this letter in the hope that it will reach you before you leave for Mount Athos. Of course, you may already be there and if so you will probably never receive it. In any case, I hope that you're well and that things have turned out as you wanted.

It's been quite hard for me to adapt to life here but I'm getting used to it. I'm living in a suite of rooms in the Hotel Franz Josef, an old-fashioned hotel built before the First World War. I have a maid, Boyana, and a bodyguard, Yurek, who live with me. Boyana is only sixteen and a sweet girl. Yurek is a big strong peasant and very good hearted. I'm fond of them both and don't know what I'd do without them.

So far I've made a television broadcast and visited a number of hospitals, old people's homes and schools in Svyatograd and, now that Easter is over, I'll start making trips to places in other parts of the country. I've found it very rewarding talking to people about their difficulties and seeing if anything can be done to help them, but apart from that I sometimes wonder why I'm here. The People's Struggle Party are bitterly opposed to a monarchy and recently when I went to a factory there was a violent demonstration in which a young policeman was stabbed and his attacker was shot dead. Things will probably get worse now because, as you may have heard, Igor Grobov died early this morning and the

People's Struggle Party want the militant young Nikola Popnikov to be President rather than have me as Queen. I can see trouble ahead!

Last night I went to my first Orthodox Easter Vigil in the Cathedral of the Redeemer and it was wonderful. I prayed for you and wished that you could have been there with me.

I often think about all the discussions we had and the things we did together. I enjoyed them so much.

Affectionately,
Katy

She hesitated before deciding how to sign this letter. 'Yours sincerely' sounded too stiff and formal. 'With love' could mean absolutely nothing - she used it writing to girlfriends - but again, it could mean everything and embarrass him. 'With best wishes' was rather cold and so in the end she wrote 'affectionately'. Then she remembered the final lines of a Shakespeare sonnet she had learned at school and she added them after her signature:

But if the while I think on thee, dear friend,
All losses are restored and sorrows end.

Chapter 8

President Grobov's body lay in state in the Cathedral of the Redeemer. His coffin, which was open in accordance with Orthodox tradition, had been placed on a catafalque draped with the Maloslavian flag and four guards of honour stood on duty - one at each corner. It was Easter Monday and a long queue of people, mostly old and shabbily dressed, filed past. Many of them were in tears and a few left bunches of flowers. The President's face, once red and bloated, was now a greenish white and on the backs of his hands, which were crossed on his breast, were clusters of small brown warts. Katy approached the coffin apprehensively. The shrunken body brought back memories of her mother's death and how she had not wanted to visit the funeral home to pay her last respects. She would have preferred to remember her mother as she was in life, but Aunt Bridget had insisted that she go. She had never forgotten the wasted face, marked by the suffering that morphine had been unable to relieve and she looked at the President with a feeling of horror. The sight of the warts made her feel nauseous. Not knowing what to do, she made the sign of the cross, moved on quickly and thankfully left the cathedral.

When she woke on Wednesday, the day of the funeral, it was raining heavily. The fine spring weather had broken after a violent storm in the early hours of the morning. If the rain continued, the long walk in procession from the Cathedral to the cemetery would be extremely unpleasant and royal etiquette would prevent her from holding her own umbrella. Yurek would have to do it which wouldn't work very well; she'd probably be soaked by the time she returned to the hotel. She showered, dressed and breakfasted in a sombre mood.

In spite of the rain a large crowd had gathered to watch the arrival of government ministers, diplomats and representatives from a number of countries. Television cameras were focussed on Katy as she got out of the car and entered the Cathedral which was already full. She was escorted to a place next to the Prime Minister and Countess Elena who were standing close to the celebrating priests. The service began with the chanting of psalms, prayers and litanies. There were readings from scripture and a sermon in which the Bishop praised President Grobov's fortitude in the face of suffering. After the dismissal prayer, members of the family were invited to come forward to see the dead man. The President's daughter and three small grandchildren approached and kissed him, followed by other members of the congregation who simply bowed to the coffin and made the sign of the cross. A priest anointed the body with oil and earth and then all the people sang the hymn *Eternal Memory.*

Fortunately when they came out of the Cathedral the sun was shining and the procession to the cemetery began. First came the coffin, borne by army officers and draped with the Maloslavian flag on top of which lay a wreath of red roses. It was followed by a military band playing Beethoven's funeral march and the clergy carrying banners, icons and crosses. Behind them were the Maloslavian and foreign dignitaries. Katy walked with Countess Elena who wore a long black velvet coat, a hat with a veil and carried a silver-topped cane. She leaned on it occasionally but her head was held high, her back was straight and it was hard to believe that she was eighty. From time to time she cast a sidelong glance at Katy as if to check on her deportment but Katy looked straight ahead and tried to ignore her.

When they arrived at the grave, which was at the far end of the cemetery surrounded by trees, the priests chanted the final prayers and the President's family went to the coffin and said their last farewells. As the lid was about to be nailed down, a plump, elderly woman with long bleached hair rushed forward and flung herself on the body of the dead man. She kissed his face and caressed it, sobbing and murmuring '*Maya daragaya, maya daragaya!*' ('My darling.')

There was a shocked silence and then two detectives in plain-clothes approached her and pulled her away, still wailing hysterically.

'That is the President's mistress, Rosa Baleva,' whispered Dimitar in Katy's ear. 'His family forbade her to come to the funeral but somehow she has managed to get into the cemetery.'

Calm was restored and the burial service came to an end. The coffin was closed and the priests censed it before it was lowered into the grave. The band played the national anthem and a gun salute was fired. The crowd of mourners began to disperse and as Katy left, she passed close to Rosa Baleva who was still held firmly by the detectives. She had a clear view of her raddled face - wild-eyed and scarlet-lipped. She must have been in her sixties although the heavy make-up which clogged her wrinkles made her look older. But beneath the sagging flesh her bone structure was good and Katy thought that she must have been beautiful when she was younger. She felt sorry for this desperate woman who had thrown away her life on an extravagant, pleasure-loving man who had abused the power entrusted to him.

'What will happen to Rosa Baleva now?' she said as they drove back to the hotel.

'Nothing much. She will be taken to the police station and she might have to spend a night in prison. Then they will release her. She is half crazy but she is not dangerous. When the President became senile she was forced to leave the palace. She had no pension and nowhere to go. She lives in a small room in a slum district and her mind has been destroyed by drink.'

'Can't something be done for her?'

Dimitar gave a shrug. 'They could put her in an asylum perhaps, but she is probably better off as she is!'

* * *

The morning after the funeral Katy was surprised to receive a telephone call from Kiril.

'How lovely to hear from you! Where are you?'

'I'm here in Svyatograd with Marina. We came to report on

President Grobov's funeral and to do an article for *The Sunday Times* on the situation created by his death. Of course we want to interview you and we're going to take you out to dinner tonight!'

'I'd love that, but will you be allowed to see me?'

'It's all arranged! We've fixed it with the appropriate authorities and a table's been booked at the *Tziganka* for eight o'clock. It's one of the best restaurants in Svyatograd, though that's not saying much! But you'll like it. The food's quite good and they've got gypsy musicians.'

'It sounds great. I'll be glad to get out of this hotel for once. But I'll have to ask Dimitar's permission.'

'Who's Dimitar?'

'Dimitar Stoiev. He's my guide, interpreter and organizer of the referendum campaign. I'm supposed to tell him about any visits I want to make which aren't on my official schedule. I even got into trouble for going to church without letting him know!'

'How absurd! Well, you'd better tell him but I don't think he can make difficulties because we've received permission to talk to you from the Ministry of Information. We'll pick you up at the hotel.'

Katy rang Dimitar who sounded irritated to learn that she was meeting friends whom he had not approved personally, but raised no objections. She felt happier than she had done for a long time at the thought of seeing Kiril and Marina again and telling them about her experiences. She also hoped they might give her news of Vladimir but decided not to mention her letter to him although she was eager to know whether he was still in London and had received it.

They were waiting for her in the foyer when she came down at seven thirty and she rushed up to them and hugged them.

'It's so good to see you again,' she said.

Marina looked at her critically. 'You've lost weight and you look pale. Are you all right?'

'I'm pale because I'm shut up in this hotel far too much,' said Katy. 'I know I've lost weight, but that's probably because the food's not very good here. I don't like it and so I don't eat enough.'

'Well, you can eat as much as you like tonight,' said Kiril. 'The

Tziganka is run by Hungarians and Hungary has one of the world's great cuisines.'

They took a taxi to the restaurant and were ushered downstairs to a candle-lit dining room furnished like a Central European bistro with red-and-white check tablecloths. At one end there was loud music from a group of gypsy musicians playing Hungarian dance tunes. The manager bowed, kissed Katy's hand, and led them to a table which fortunately was some distance from the musicians. Yurek was placed by himself at a small table nearby.

The waiter brought the menu and on Kiril's recommendation they all decided on spinach soup and paprika chicken, followed by pancakes.

'Now tell me what's been happening to you,' said Kiril when he had given the order.

Katy related the events of the past few weeks - her meeting with President Grobov, her television broadcast and the violent demonstration at the factory. She told them about Boyana and the cashmere sweater episode and made them laugh at her story of Dimitar's reaction after she asked him to call her by her first name. When she described how the young policeman, Anatoly, had been stabbed, Kiril looked grave.

'When she had finished, he said 'It can't have been easy for you being thrust into this unfamiliar world, but it sounds as though you're doing a good job.'

Katy blushed. 'Do you really think so?'

'Of course! In your position the only useful thing you can do is to listen to people and try to see how they can be helped. I love the way you stood up for that poor kid Boyana and how you managed to get a place for Anatoly to train as a baker. This is the kind of role a monarch can play. Most presidents are just interested in hanging on to power.'

The waiter appeared with a tureen and served the spinach soup.

'Delicious! What a change from the hotel food!' said Katy as Kiril poured her some wine.

'I don't like the sound of the riot at the furniture factory,' said Marina. 'Do you think Katy's in danger?'

'Nikola Popnikov is a violent young man,' said Kiril. He's also ambitious and wants to be President. He'll try to stop the referendum taking place and there'll probably be strikes and demonstrations.'

'I think I should return to London,' said Katy.

'No! Surely you can see that it would be much better for the country to have you as Queen than Nikola Popnikov as President?'

'But I don't *want* to be Queen and anyway I'm going to lose the referendum.'

'Perhaps you will, perhaps you won't. Isn't it better to go through with it and have the satisfaction of knowing the result? If you lose, so be it. Then you can return to London knowing you've done your best. My advice is wait and see.'

'But be careful,' said Marina.

They had finished the soup and were now eating chicken, coated with a creamy pink paprika sauce.

'Watch out if you have to go on visits into the countryside,' said Kiril. 'It's very different from Svyatograd.'

'In fact,' said Katy, 'I'm taking my first trip outside the city next Monday, to a place called Shkrapova. We're going by train.'

'Good luck then! There's only a slow train that goes there and it stops at every station and wayside halt.'

The conversation turned to President Grobov's death and the appearance of his mistress at the cemetery.

'Rosa Baleva was a popular singer in a nightclub before she became Grobov's mistress,' said Kiril.

'Did she drink much then?'

'I don't think so. Grobov was an alcoholic and and it was because of him that she took to the bottle.'

'It's tragic,' said Katy and then, looking down at her plate, she said quickly 'Have you any news of Vladimir?'

'Not really. We've been very busy recently and we haven't been to St Nicolas at all apart from the Easter Vigil. We caught a glimpse of him then but there was such a huge crowd that we never got a chance to speak to him afterwards. Anyway, he's still in London.'

Katy was relieved. She realized he must have received her letter but she said nothing and quickly changed the subject.

The pancakes arrived, filled with chopped walnuts and topped with a chocolate and rum sauce. and Kiril ordered a bottle of Tokay to accompany them.

'Let's drink a toast,' he said. 'To Katy as Queen!'

'No!' said Katy. 'Let's drink to the referendum. May fate decide the outcome!' They drank the toast just as the musicians came up to their table wanting them to request a tune. They chose one of Brahms' Hungarian dances and it was a perfect end to the meal.

Kiril and Marina hailed a taxi to drive Katy and Yurek back to the Hotel Franz Josef and they set off down the Boulevard Victoria. It was late and there was no traffic, but they had not gone more than a few hundred yards before they heard shouting and the sound of breaking glass. Ahead of them a group of youths were hurling stones and beer bottles at shop windows and shrieking *'Popnikov, dla President! Nay referendum!'* Kiril asked the driver whether he could turn into a side street and translated his reply.

'He says there isn't a turning yet. We'll have to get much nearer to the rioters before we can get off the Boulevard.'

'Where are the police for heaven's sake?' said Marina.

'There are never many police around at this time. There's very little nightlife in Svyatograd and the city's usually completely dead by now.'

The taxi moved at snail's pace as the driver looked for an escape route and then stopped abruptly. The youths had overturned a car and set light to it, completely blocking the boulevard.

Kiril took out his mobile and called the police. They told him that they knew about the riot and were on their way.

'There's nothing we can do but sit tight until they come,' he said.

'Do you think these kids are members of the People's Struggle Party,' asked Katy, doing her best to appear calm.

'No! These are just drunken yobbos out for trouble. They may look frightening but they're not a threat to the referendum. You don't need to worry about them.'

'I hope you're right,' said Katy, 'but it's a bad omen. It shows there are some kids who don't want a monarchy; they want Popnikov.'

At last the police and the fire brigade arrived. They extinguished the flames and turned water-cannons on the mob. Some youths managed to run away but the majority were arrested, savagely beaten, pushed into vans and driven away. The wreckage of the burnt-out car remained in the middle of the boulevard and the road surface was carpeted with pieces of broken glass. The taxi driver edged his way carefully, trying to avoid damaging his tyres and, after what seemed a very long time they were able to turn off into a side road.

'We could have done without that little adventure,' said Marina as they approached the hotel.

'All that hitting and smacking,' said Yurek in his rudimentary English.

The remark eased the tension they were all feeling and they laughed. Yurek and Katy got out of the taxi and there were tears in her eyes as she kissed Kiril and Marina goodbye.

'It was lovely to see familiar faces from London. Thank you for a wonderful evening,' she said.

'I'm sorry it had such a dramatic end,' said Kiril. 'Try not to worry about it. Just keep going and things will sort themselves out.'

'I hope so,' she said, but there were tears in her eyes as she saw the taxi drive away.

* * *

The following Monday, after an early breakfast, Katy left the hotel with Yurek and Dimitar for the trip to Shkrapova. They arrived in good time to board the eight o'clock train and settled themselves in a reserved first class compartment but at eight fifteen they had still not left the station.

'How long does the journey take?' asked Katy.

'Three hours.'

'Well, why are we still here?'

Dimitar gave a shrug. 'Signals probably. It is always like this. But at least we are comfortable.'

At eight thirty the train finally departed. It crawled through the suburbs and out on to the plains that surrounded the city, stopping frequently at small stations to pick up passengers laden with boxes and baskets. After about half-an-hour the landscape began to change; there were slopes covered in thick forest on one side of the track and on the other, a stream of clear green water. Occasionally they passed villages of small wooden houses surrounded by blossoming fruit trees and from time to time they stopped at isolated halts without a platform, where elderly peasant women had difficulty in getting up the steep steps into the carriages. Then the train went through several long tunnels and emerged on a rocky plateau where a few sheep were grazing. It crept across this desolate terrain for some time before gradually descending into a valley and stopping at the town of Maleva.

'This is an important town,' said Dimitar. 'It is the centre of a district that produces much olive oil.'

The train sat in the station for about fifteen minutes. There were very few people about but Katy noticed one group of teenagers wearing red neckerchieves and carrying banners saying '*Popnikov, President!*'. They made a great deal of noise until a man of about thirty, who appeared to be their leader, silenced them and shepherded them on to the train.

'They are members of the People's Struggle Pioneers,' said Dimitar. 'It is the youth group of the People's Struggle Party based on the Soviet model. In Communist times it was compulsory for children to join it. Now it has very few members.'

'Where do you think they're going?'

'I'm afraid they may be going to Shkrapova. They have probably heard that you are visiting the village and they could be planning to have a demonstration against the monarchy. Do not worry. There is no danger. They are just children.'

'Quite big children,' said Katy with a wry smile.

The train started again and crossed a flat region of olive groves before climbing into the hills. Exactly three-and-a-half hours after leaving the capital, much to Katy's surprise, it pulled into the station at Shkrapova.

'You see,' said Dimitar, 'We are only half-an-hour late after all.'

A small brass band struck up the national anthem as they came out of the station and the mayor greeted Katy effusively and reeled off a great deal of information, most of which she couldn't understand. Dimitar translated.

'He says that we are now going to the village square where he will make his speech of welcome and you will reply. Then the children will give a display of folk dancing followed by a programme of traditional songs from the Shkrapova Male Voice Choir. The proceedings will end with a buffet lunch.'

The mayor beamed at Katy and she smiled her approval of the arrangements. They all set off down the main street to the square where a small crowd had gathered. They mounted the steps of the dais that had been set up and were escorted to some uncomfortable folding chairs. The Mayor was handed a microphone and launched into a long speech in which he repeatedly expressed the gratitude of the people of Shkrapova to Princess Katerina Borisovna for honouring them with her presence. Katy stifled a yawn. She'd heard this sort of stuff so often during the past few weeks. Soon she'd have to reply and she struggled to remember the few sentences of Maloslavian that she'd memorized. The stream of words flowed on - 'She brings with her hopes of a brighter future... Let us put the past behind us...Let us march forward together as one nation...' Then the Mayor stopped abruptly.

The crowd stared at Katy expectantly. She looked at them - old women in black, exhausted young women with pasty-faced children, youths in jeans and leather blousons chewing gum. She tried to speak but the words wouldn't come. Then, with a sudden burst of energy, she blurted out her short speech, thanking the people of Shkrapova for their welcome and promising that if she won the referendum she would work for the good of Maloslavia. There was some half-hearted applause and an old lady hobbled up to her, knelt down with difficulty, and kissed the hem of her skirt. She looked at Katy with tears rolling down her face and gabbled something excitedly. Dimitar translated: 'She says that she remembers the reign of your grandfather and that God has sent you to Maloslavia.' Katy was embarrassed but she smiled at the woman and helped her to her feet. At this moment the People's Struggle Pioneers appeared on the scene, waving their banners and shouting *'Doloy Manaheeyoo!*

Popnikov President!' Police had been stationed at strategic points and quickly dispersed the demonstrators without any display of violence, but the angry cries of 'Down with the monarchy!' had a depressing effect on the entertainment that had been planned; only a few people remained to watch it.

A group of children aged between ten and twelve ran into the square and performed a series of dances accompanied by an accordian. They stamped their feet and clapped their hands frequently and occasionally collided with one another when they forgot their next move. The girls wore embroidered blouses, stiffly pleated skirts and scarlet boots and the boys were in baggy linen shirts and trousers, the legs of which were bound with leather thongs. Their enthusiasm compensated for their mistakes and they were loudly applauded. The male voice choir which followed consisted of twelve young men who sang complicated polyphonic melodies with a high, curiously nasal tenor line accompanied by an unusually deep droning bass. Some of their songs were the cries of despair of a people who had suffered under Turkish occupation; others were lively dance tunes for feast days and festivals. They were definitely an acquired taste and Katy, who was beginning to feel hungry, longed for them to come to an end.

At last, at two o'clock, the performance finished and trestle tables were set up in the square. Dishes of various salads, hors-d'oeuvres and oriental pastries appeared, along with casks of beer and bottles of the local red wine. The people who had disappeared during the brief demonstration came back and started piling food on to paper plates. A few of the People's Struggle Pioneers also showed up again and mingled with the crowd, greedily eating anything that took their fancy.

Katy would have liked to go and help herself to the dishes that appealed to her but as a royal visitor her food was served to her on the dais. Dimitar and Yurek sat with their lunch trays balanced on their knees while Katy and the Mayor ate at a small folding table nearby. One of the dancers brought them glasses of wine and plates of tarama, aubergine caviar, ham and small pies filled with minced meat. After a few attempts at conversation, they ate in silence for the Mayor spoke very rapidly in Maloslavian and Katy had great difficulty in understanding him. She smiled and said '*Da*' and '*Nay*' from time to time, hoping it was the right response but in the end she gave up the struggle and concentrated on the food which was delicious, if not very filling. The dessert consisted of Turkish pastries and was followed by coffee, after which it was time to go back to the station for the return journey to Svyatograd.

The train was much slower than the one they had taken in the morning. It kept stopping in the middle of the countryside, sometimes for as much as fifteen minutes, but according to Dimitar this was quite normal. Katy tried to read, but she couldn't concentrate and her mind kept wandering back to the events of the day. The People's Struggle Pioneers had made her feel uneasy. They hadn't actually been violent but she felt the potential was there. She could imagine them smashing shop windows and hurling stones like the rioters she'd seen in Svyatograd and at the furniture factory. It was odd too that they'd managed to worm their way into the crowd and stuff themselves with food after the demonstration had been disbanded by the police. Why had nobody done anything to stop them?

The train ground to a halt again and she looked out of the window. She saw that they were back on the rocky plateau and it was beginning to get dark. She tried to pass the time by thinking about the Mahler concert she had gone to with Vladimir, hearing in her mind the great finale of the Resurrection Symphony and then suddenly she was seized by griping abdominal pains. She clenched her hands and leaned forward, writhing in agony.

'What's the matter?' asked Dimitar.

'I don't know. I don't feel very well.'

A few minutes later, as the train began to move again, she managed to stagger to the toilet at the end of the coach and was violently sick. She returned to the compartment and sank back in her seat feeling hot and shivering. She closed her eyes and clutched her stomach but the pain gave her no respite.

She felt sick again and Yurek fetched her a bucket which had been left in the toilet. The incessant vomiting exhausted her and she lay back moaning.

'She has a high fever,' said Dimitar, putting his hand on her forehead. 'We must get her to hospital.'

'Are we nearly there?' she whispered.

'It will be another hour at least. Try to sleep. I will phone for an ambulance to meet us at the station.'

It seemed as though the journey would never end but eventually Katy sank into a feverish doze. She drifted in and out of consciousness and was surprised to find herself in a teashop eating a cake covered in pink sugar icing. A cushion had been placed on her chair so that she could reach the table but her feet didn't touch the floor. A man sat opposite her, smiling. 'Would you like some orange juice?' he said and then his face became contorted and he fell forward on to the table, scattering the tea things in all directions.

She woke with a start in a cold sweat. Her heart thumped and she couldn't understand what was happening to her. Why was she lying on a stretcher? Why were they carrying her along the station platform? Was she ill? Then a wave of nausea reminded her.

'I've been poisoned,' she said in a faint voice before darkness engulfed her.

Chapter 9

Vladimir sat at the kitchen table drinking tea and trying to read *The Observer*. It was no good, he couldn't concentrate. He was thankful that it was Monday - his day off - and he could be alone with his thoughts. Since yesterday his mind had been in a turmoil. When the Sunday liturgy at St Nicolas had finished, Father Serge had told him that he had heard from the monastery on Mount Athos that they'd refused his application because of his disability. They suggested that he should approach an Orthodox monastery in England where living conditions would be easier.

Vladimir had half expected this decision but it was a blow nevertheless. Yet to his surprise it wasn't the refusal to let him go to Mount Athos that hurt most. Nor, he realized, did he want to try to enter an English monastery. It had gradually dawned on him that his desire to be a monk hadn't been a genuine vocation - it had sprung from loneliness and a feeling of rejection after Sofia left him. It had been a fantasy that, in his heart of hearts, he'd never really believed would become reality. He hadn't lost his faith, but for some time he had been thinking that he would find it very hard to renounce his simple pleasures - reading, cooking, listening to music, the cinema - and that perhaps it would be better to serve God in the world - 'seeing Him in other people' as Katy had once said. The hardest thing about the monastery's refusal was that it made him feel once again that he was different from other people. He'd always been careful to conceal the sense of inferiority that dogged him and when he began to find comfort in going to church he thought that at last he'd come to accept his disability with serenity. Now this new rejection brought memories of the past to the surface again with painful clarity.

He was two when he came to England with his parents. He was taken to a children's hospital in London and was pleased when he learned to walk, although he needed callipers and crutches. It was only when he went to primary school and saw the other children running about, fighting and playing boisterous games, that he realized there were things he would never be able to do. They stared at him with curiosity. 'What's the matter with you? Why do you wear those iron things?' they would ask and he would reply 'I had polio.' They would look at him, not understanding what polio was and then run away. Fortunately he was good at amusing himself. He loved reading, he was good at drawing and he had a toy theatre for which he spent hours designing scenery. At the age of eleven he had surgery on his legs and spent several months in bed in plaster casts. He hoped that after this he'd be able to discard his callipers, but he was told that he would still need to wear them. When he heard this, he decided he didn't believe in God and told his parents he wouldn't go to church any more. Because of his long stay in hospital he went to the grammar school a year late and there he began to feel really lonely. He would sit in the playground at break with his nose in a book, trying to show he didn't care that his classmates were chatting in little groups, ignoring him and probably making spiteful remarks about him. It was important to be good at sport and, while he could swim well, the fact that he couldn't play games automatically made him unpopular. He was clever and got good marks in most subjects which was another point against him, although the only time the other pupils took any notice of him was when they wanted his help with their homework. He gave it willingly but they still treated him as an outsider and in his desperation he discovered alcohol.

He hadn't enjoyed drinking; it had just been his way of expressing his loneliness, anger and frustration. Nearly every morning he woke with a splitting headache, but he still continued. It was strange that his parents never guessed what was going on. They trusted him and when they saw him, red-eyed at breakfast , they simply thought that he'd stayed up too late studying. They had no idea how unhappy he was and he would never have dreamt of telling them because he knew they'd done everything in their power to help him all his life. He solved the problem of disposing of empty bottles and beer cans by putting them in his rucksack and dropping them in a dustbin on the way to school; there were no traces in his bedroom of his secret addiction.

About a year after he began drinking, Sofia arrived in his class. They were drawn to one another by their mutual loneliness and their friendship quickly developed into a passionate first love. She was shocked by the quantity of alcohol he consumed and begged him to give it up. He was ashamed of his behaviour and now that he had someone who cared about him and whom he wanted to please, he found it quite easy to stop. Life became less complicated and he was treated with more respect by his classmates because he had a good-looking girlfriend.

When they finished school, Sofia suggested they live together and it was partly because of her that he'd given up the idea of going to university. But in the end she'd left him for someone else and although the breakup had been painful, he felt it had been inevitable. After their first few months in the little studio he'd begun to think that she was with him more out of pity than love. And their tastes were very different; he liked classical music but she hated it and wanted to play techno which got on his nerves. She enjoyed dancing and clubbing and he'd felt guilty that he couldn't participate, in spite of the fact that even if he could have done, he'd have been like a fish out of water. But although they had little in common and marriage would have been a mistake, he had the feeling that it was his disability that had driven them apart - a feeling that still hurt him occasionally.

He tried to blot out these memories and forced himself to get up. He put two slices of bread in the new toaster which he'd only bought the week before. He'd always insisted that the correct way to make real toast was under the grill of a gas cooker but Katy had laughed at him and said this was probably true if you remembered to remove the toast in time. He nearly always forgot and ended up scraping the burnt, blackened slices before masking them with generous layers of butter and marmalade. She'd suggested he buy a toaster but he'd scorned the idea at the time. Now, as the toast popped up, browned to perfection, he knew she'd been right.

He smiled, remembering her lively face and the sprinkling of freckles on her nose. She was so natural and honest and she wasn't embarrassed by his disability; she simply accepted it as part of him. She could be very funny too. They'd shared a lot of things and he realized how much he missed her. He wondered what was happening to her. He'd heard nothing from her and if she won the referendum he'd probably never see her again. Of course, it was very likely that she'd lose and in that case he could hardly imagine that she'd want to stay in Maloslavia. Perhaps she would come back to London.

* * *

Vladimir was in better spirits when he boarded the 74 bus on Tuesday morning to go to work at the bookshop. Basically he was an optimist and although he had occasional fits of despondency, helped by his faith he recovered quickly. He always tried to think positively and on reflection he could see that it would have been a great mistake for him to go to Mount Athos. Father Serge had suggested to him on Sunday that he should apply to study for a degree in theology and had mentioned the Institute for Orthodox Christian Studies in Cambridge. At the time he'd felt so discouraged by the monastery's rejection that he'd said he wasn't interested, but now he realized it was a good idea. After all, he couldn't stay working in the bookshop for ever. He had excellent A Level results and he was wasting his time by not going into higher education. If he had a degree he could become a university lecturer with a decent salary. Then he'd be able to afford to learn to drive and buy a car which would increase his mobility. He began to feel enthusiastic at the thought of it and decided to ring Father Serge to ask for his advice on applying for the theology course.

The bus stopped near South Kensington station about three minutes' walk from the small street where *The Bookworm* was situated. The shop was painted dark green and was crammed from floor to ceiling with an eclectic range of literature although it specialized in history and biography. It also had a good stock of scientific works because it catered for students from the Imperial College of Science and Technology nearby. It had been opened about ten years before by Patrick Donovan, a novelist who was growing tired of his secluded life as a writer and had decided he wanted to own a bookshop. At first he managed it single-handed and enjoyed discussing literature with customers, but then he began writing again and found that he didn't have enough time to devote to it. He took on Vladimir as his assistant and when he found that he was capable of running the shop on his own, he handed over the management to him and only came in once or twice a month to check the accounts and the orders for new stock. The arrangement suited them both and Vladimir enjoyed the freedom it gave him to organize things in his own way. On Monday, which was his day off, and during his holidays, his place was taken by Steve Montague, a rather unsuccessful free-lance journalist who needed to do odd jobs to supplement his income and also worked in a pub for part of the week.

Vladimir unlocked the door, turned the 'Open/Shut' notice round to 'Open' and went to his desk at the back of the shop. As soon as he had taken off his anorak he phoned Father Serge and made an appointment to see him on Thursday. Then he made coffee and began to check a box of books that had been delivered the day before and to enter them in his data base. He was meticulous in keeping his records up to date and although the shop was small and bursting at the seams he always knew whether a book was in stock and where it could be found. If it was on one of the top shelves he had to ask the customer to climb a ladder to get it but there was never any problem over this. He liked chatting to the people who came in, especially the students from Imperial College, and sometimes, if he wasn't too busy, he would offer them coffee.

Business was fairly slack on this Tuesday morning. A girl studying art history wanted a particular book on the Sienese school of painting. It wasn't in stock and Vladimir said he would order it for her and and phone her when it arrived. As she was leaving an elderly man who was a regular customer entered and, after browsing for a while, bought a biography of Thomas Hardy which was displayed on the New Books table. At eleven Vladimir's mother phoned and he knew that she was ringing him at work because he hadn't made his usual call to her on Sunday.

'Vladimir, we've been worried about you. You didn't ring on Sunday and yesterday we tried to phone you at home but the number was always engaged. Are you all right?'

'Of course I'm all right! I'm very sorry. I was with some friends on Sunday. I got back too late to ring and yesterday I accidentally left the phone off the hook.' He hated telling her a lie, but he couldn't explain that he hadn't called because he'd been depressed at being refused permission to enter a monastery and that he'd deliberately unplugged the phone.

'I can't help worrying when you don't call. Are you looking after yourself properly and eating enough?'

He laughed. '*Yes*! You know I enjoy cooking.'

'We haven't seen you for a long time. Have lunch with us on Sunday. Catch the eleven thirty and we'll meet you at the station.'

'Thanks mum. That'll be great. I'll have to ring off now because a customer's come in. I'll see you on Sunday.'

The woman who'd entered the shop didn't in fact appear to need assistance and was looking at travel guides, but he didn't want to get involved in a long telephone conversation with his mother. It would inevitably lead to an interrogation on his non-existent love life and his dead-end job. On Sunday he'd tell her about his decision to study for a degree and he knew she'd be pleased. His refusal to go to university had upset her and she'd attributed it to Sofia's influence, although she'd been equally upset when Sofia left him. He realized that she worried about his living on his own, no matter how often he assured her that he was coping very well. He loved her and didn't want to cause her anxiety; he was only thankful that she'd never found out about his plan to go to Mount Athos.

The woman who had been browsing among the travel books eventually bought a Lonely Planet guide to India, two students came in and placed an order for some textbooks and then it was one o'clock and time for lunch. Vladimir shut the shop and decided to go to the pub over the road where Steve worked. He hadn't been there for some time; he usually went to a pizzeria or bought a sandwich, but today he felt like something more substantial.

Steve was serving at the bar. 'Hi, you're quite a stranger,' he said. 'I haven't seen you in here for ages.'

'I don't often eat much at lunch-time but today I'm feeling hungry,' said Vladimir looking at the menu. 'I'll have the steak and kidney pie and a half of lager.'

'Okay. Sit over there by the window and I'll be with you in a minute.'

Steve brought the beer and the cutlery and set the table. He disappeared into the kitchen and a few minutes later came back with the pie. He sat down opposite Vladimir.

'Because I'm in *The Bookworm* on Monday and you're there the rest of the week our paths never seem to cross. I hope you found everything in order when you came in this morning. Did you find the box of books that was delivered yesterday?'

'Yes. I've checked them and entered them in the data base.'

'Well, what have you been up to lately?'

'Nothing much,' said Vladimir not wanting to get drawn into a conversation with Steve who knew nothing about the monastery project. 'Just the usual routine.'

'You mustn't get into a rut. You should find yourself another girlfriend.'

'In my situation that's not very easy.' Vladimir wished Steve would stop prying.

'That's rubbish! You've got a lot to offer. You're very intelligent, kind and reasonably good-looking. And above all, you've got a sense of humour. Incidentally, who was that red-haired girl I saw you with in a café at Earls Court a few months ago?'

'You mean Katy. She's gone abroad.'

'What a pity. She looked nice. Do you think she'll come back?'

'I don't know,' said Vladimir and added, quickly changing the subject, 'My compliments to the chef. This pie is superb.'

Steve realized that Vladimir didn't want to continue the

conversation and he returned to the bar where several customers were waiting to be served.

The shop reopened at two. The afternoon was fairly busy until about half-an-hour before closing time. By then all the customers had left apart from Mrs Fortescue, a fussy little lady with blue-rinsed white hair whom Vladimir knew only too well. She was a regular visitor but, to his knowledge, had never bought anything. She would stay, often for an hour or more, leafing through the books and then ask him if he had a certain title, usually a paperback romance. When he said they didn't stock it but he could order it for her, she would leave the shop. Today she was accompanied by a friend and they had been wandering around aimlessly for some time, taking books off the shelves and putting them back in the wrong place, rearranging the volumes on the New Books table and generally making a nuisance of themselves. He was wondering whether he should tell them that he would soon be closing the shop when, from behind a bookcase, he overheard Mrs Fortescue say to her friend in a penetrating whisper,

'He's a very good-looking young man isn't he? What a pity he's a cripple!'

He knew the best reaction would be to laugh or even to feel sorry for her but he couldn't suppress the anger that surged up in him. He'd fought his disability as hard as he could and all he wanted was to get on with his life and be treated as a normal human being. Was that too much to ask? On the spur of the moment, he rose and went over to her. Glaring at her, he said 'As you don't intend to buy anything, perhaps you would be kind enough to leave now. I'm about to close the shop.'

Mrs Fortescue looked at him in amazement. She didn't appear to understand why he looked so fierce and probably thought him rude. She took her friend by the arm and they left without a word.

Vladimir smiled. He couldn't help feeling pleased that he'd told her to go. Of course it would be nice to think she'd understood why he was angry but there was little chance of that. 'Cripple' was a disparaging word and a convenient label that those of her sort stuck on one because they were embarrassed, seeing only the disability and not the whole person.

He took the bus home and opened the front door. Some letters were lying on the mat and he bent down and picked them up. There was an electricity bill, the usual wad of publicity and, to his surprise, a letter with a Maloslavian stamp. He sat down and eagerly tore it open. It was from Katy, telling him about her experiences in Svyatograd. As he read the last sentence, he understood that the time they'd spent together had meant as much to her as it had to him. In astonishment he stared at the quotation that ended the letter:

But if the while I think on thee, dear friend,
All losses are restored and sorrows end.

He wanted to shout for joy. For a moment he felt as if he'd been given the most wonderful present, but then doubts set in. What did she really mean? Should he reply and if so, what should he say? She said she'd written the letter hoping that it wouldn't arrive too late, but realizing that he might already be on Mount Athos. Would she have written such a letter if she'd known that he wasn't going to be a monk? Was it a kind of farewell? Reluctantly, he decided that it was better not to answer. If she became Queen and never came back, he couldn't see any point in replying. If she did return, he'd see her again and discover what she really meant. He was afraid of reading more into her letter than she'd intended. Nevertheless, he kept it in his pocket and looked at it frequently.

Chapter 10

When Katy regained consciousness, she was lying in bed attached by tubes to various pieces of equipment. A tall dark-haired young man in a white coat was smiling at her.

'Where am I?' she said.

'You are in Svyatograd Clinic No. 1. I am Dr Kozlov.'

'You speak English?'

'I have done postgraduate studies in London.'

'I've been poisoned, haven't I?'

'We do not know yet the cause of your illness. You had a very high fever and you were delirious but now your temperature has dropped. You must not worry. You are in good hands and you will make a quick recovery.'

'But aren't you going to do tests to find out why this happened?'

'Everything necessary is being be done. We are examining samples of your blood in the laboratory and we are also investigating how the food you ate in Shkrapova was prepared.'

'Some of the People's Struggle Pioneers were helping themselves to the buffet. Could they have sprinkled poison on the dishes that were served to me?'

Dr Kozlov frowned. 'That is ridiculous. Your illness is almost certainly due to food being prepared in unhygienic conditions. It has probably been caused by Salmonella or Campylobacter.'

'My father died mysteriously, probably from poisoning. The same thing may have happened to me,' said Katy.

'It is highly unlikely. Your father died in the Communist period.

Such a thing would be impossible today.'

'I hope you're right. How long will I have to stay in here?'

'Until we get the results of the tests in three or four days time. Now you must rest and build up your strength. You can have some lunch today - rice and boiled chicken.'

Katy looked round the room. 'I think I've been to this clinic before,' she said.

'That is correct, Your Royal Highness. You visited the young policeman who was stabbed. He has made a good recovery.'

Dr Kozlov bowed and went out.

Katy lay back on her pillows. Because she was so weak, her mind wandered from one thing to another and disturbing images of her father flashed in front of her eyes. She was haunted by thoughts of his death. Her mother had always been reluctant to talk about it but she knew that in London her father had worked in his spare time with a group of young Maloslavian dissidents who wanted to bring about the collapse of the Communist régime. They came to him with stories of torture, psychiatric wards and sordid prison cells and he financed and edited a news bulletin in which he published reports of these atrocities. One day, when he returned from the office and had settled down with a drink, he told her mother that he had lunched with two refugees who said they were monarchists and needed his help. As he poured himself another whisky he was seized with excruciating pains in his limbs. He tried to reassure her mother that it was nothing serious and when dinner was ready he managed to stagger to the table. They began to drink the soup she had prepared, watched by two year-old Katy in her high chair. Suddenly he fell forward, sending plates and glasses crashing to the floor. With difficulty her mother managed to lift him so that he was in a sitting position, slumped against the back of the chair. She phoned for an ambulance, but before it could reach them he had a convulsion: his arms and legs were contorted and jerked so violently that he fell to the floor, saliva dribbling from his mouth. He lay motionless and by the time the paramedics arrived he was dead. Although every possible test was carried out, the exact cause of death was never established. It was clear that he had been poisoned, but the substance used had not been encountered before by the forensic laboratory and they were unable to identify it as it left no trace in the body. Suspicion fell on the two 'monarchist' refugees with whom Katy's father had lunched and who were probably KGB agents. Needless to say, they had vanished and the police never caught them. In any case there was insufficient evidence to charge them.

For the first time since she arrived in Svyatograd Katy was really frightened. If the Communists had killed her father, they could do the same to her; the People's Struggle Party was bitterly opposed to the monarchy. It was odd that the Pioneers had come back and infiltrated themselves into the crowd at the buffet and they could have easily poisoned her plate of food. But if the laboratory tests proved this to be true, would she be told? They could fob her off, saying she had Salmonella and it was possible that this was indeed the cause. Whatever the results showed, she felt that she never wanted to risk eating away from the hotel again. When she went on visits they would have to provide her with packed meals which had been tested for safety.

Katy's speculations were cut short when a nursing assistant came in with her lunch. As Dr Kozlov had told her, there was chicken with boiled rice (which was completely devoid of seasoning), a bottle of mineral water and a yoghourt. She was nauseous from lack of food and knew that she had to eat something but it was a colossal effort to swallow the tasteless meal and it took her a long time. Afterwards she felt better and decided to try to read. Then she realized she hadn't any books. Fortunately, at this moment a nurse came in to say that she had a visitor.

Boyana rushed into the room, carrying a pile of clean underwear and some magazines. She put them on the table and approached the bed looking worried. Katy was glad to see a familiar face and stretched out her arms. Boyana came closer and Katy hugged her.

Tears ran down Boyana's cheeks. '*Vwee nyay oomerayet?*'

Katy laughed. 'No, I'm not dying!' she said in Maloslavian.

'*Slava Bog!*' 'Thank God,' said Boyana, smiling with relief and began arranging the laundry in the small bedroom cupboard. While she was doing this, Yurek entered.

127

'I sleep in room next door. You better now?' he said.

'I think so,' said Katy.

Boyana finished putting the clothes away and sat down beside Yurek. They looked at Katy, grinning. Neither of them knew what to say and although Katy realized they meant well, she wished they would leave her alone. She was about to tell them she wanted to sleep when Dimitar came in and they left.

'We were very anxious about you, Your Royal Highness,' he said, 'but fortunately you will soon be well again.'

'I can't help feeling worried. I'm afraid I may have been poisoned, like my father.'

'That is impossible. Your father was helping dissident groups who opposed the Communist régime and the KGB probably had orders to kill him. The situation today is completely different.'

'But the People's Struggle Pioneers *are* Communists. They don't want a monarchy and they could easily have sprinkled poison on the plate of food that was given to me.'

Dimitar became angry. 'You are talking nonsense, Your Royal Highness! As Dr Kozlov told you, everything is being done to discover the cause of your illness. When we have the results of the tests, you will be informed and it will prove to you that your attack was due to unhygienic food preparation. Please do not interfere in matters that do not concern you.'

'Please do not talk to me in that tone! It does concern me when my life may be at stake. And in future, whatever the test results show, I don't want to eat anything that hasn't been prepared in the hotel kitchen even if it means taking packed meals on visits. Please make sure that all my food is vetted before it's brought to me.'

Dimitar tried to pacify her. 'Of course, Your Royal Highness. It is a wise decision. Everything will be done according to your instructions.'

'Please see that it is. Now I'd be grateful if you could leave as I'm very tired and I need to sleep.'

Dimitar left and Katy lay down, exhausted.

* * *

Four days later she was feeling much stronger. She had regained her appetite and was able to get up and take a walk down the corridor. She was sitting on her balcony, enjoying the spring sunshine when Dr Kozlov entered smiling.

'Good morning, Your Royal Highness,' he said. ' I am glad to see you looking so much better. Your temperature and pulse are normal and you can go back to the hotel this afternoon. But you must not undertake any strenuous engagements outside Svyatograd for at least a week.'

'Do you have the results of the tests?' asked Katy.

'Yes, we have them. As I expected, your illness was caused by Salmonella-contaminated food. The little *pirojki,* or should I say pies, were made with minced meat which had undoubtedly been left lying about in the hot sun exposed to flies and other pests. People in the villages are careless about food hygiene.'

'But how did you manage to test these pies? Weren't they all eaten at the buffet lunch? There was a big crowd there grabbing everything they could lay their hands on.'

'Fortunately one or two pies remained and they were given to a member of our laboratory staff for testing.'

'But they could have become contaminated with Salmonella *after* the lunch if they weren't refrigerated. Were any of the other people who ate the pies taken ill?'

Dr Kozlov looked embarrassed. 'Er, not that we know of. You appear to be the only one who was stricken. But that proves nothing. You were unlucky enough to eat a contaminated pie but it does not follow that all the others were infected with Salmonella. It could be that only a small part of the meat was tainted.'

'It sounds very suspicious. Somebody could easily have poisoned the plate of food intended for me. What about the other items that were on my plate?'

'We could not test them because there were no samples of those dishes available. They had all been consumed.'

'Dr Kozlov, surely you can understand that I'm worried. You know what happened to my father. I could have died in the same way. I'm sorry, but I'm not convinced by your explanations.'

Dr Kozlov's voice was cold. 'Your Royal Highness, I am afraid there is no other explanation that I can give you, so you will have to accept it. Your blood tests showed that you were infected with Salmonella but I am happy to say that your latest test shows that you are now free from this infection. You should be thankful for this.'

'I *am* thankful but I don't want it to happen again.'

'Rest assured it will not happen again. Everything you eat from now on will be carefully monitored by an expert. But I would like to point out that this is not because we are afraid you could be poisoned; it is simply because food hygiene in this country is poor.'

Katy found it hard to believe what Dr Kozlov had told her, but there wasn't much she could do about it. At least she was making a good recovery and they would check all her meals in future.

'Thank you for all the care and attention you've given me during my illness,' she said in a conciliatory tone, 'I'm very grateful for the good treatment I've received.'

Dr Kozlov bowed. 'It was an honour for me, Your Royal Highness, but if I may be permitted, I would like to make a suggestion.'

'What's that?'

'I would advise you to trust those who are responsible for your safety and not to ask so many questions. Your well-being is our prime concern.'

'I hope so, Dr Kozlov,' said Katy with a wry smile.

* * *

For the next few days Katy rested at the hotel and made no official visits. By the end of the week she had fully recovered and Dimitar told her they would have to intensify their referendum campaign as time was running out. She must give a press conference, there were some important towns she still had to visit and she would also appear at the military parade on Heroes' Day which was a national holiday at the end of May.

The press conference took place in Svyatograd's town hall and was attended by foreign and local journalists. Dimitar briefed Katy beforehand and translated the questions and her replies. She was asked how she thought it would benefit the country if she were to become Queen and she said that she would listen to the people and work to improve their living conditions. She would also live as simply as possible and wouldn't occupy the Royal Palace which she planned to convert into a hospital or a school. She felt the journalists were slightly hostile towards her, especially those from the foreign press. They tried to catch her out with awkward questions but Dimitar succeeded in fencing them off. The following day there were photos of Katy in all the national papers with reports on the conference. The Maloslavian Front-controlled *Our Country* gave a glowing account but *Our Fight,* the organ of the People's Struggle Party had a banner headline saying 'Fight the royalist cancer NOW!' with an arrow pointing at Katy's photo. She saw the paper the following morning when she was having her breakfast.

'I might as well go home. They really hate me,' she thought and got up without drinking her coffee or finishing her croissant.

In spite of the hostile press, Katy was obliged to continue her visits to various parts of the country. Her first trip after her illness was to the town of Bogonda in the north of the country and this time they travelled by road in the Volga and took a packed lunch which had been carefully inspected by a food technician. It was only a hundred kilometres to Bogonda but the road was in a dreadful state; the surface was full of potholes and the car rocked up and down as if it were on a rough sea. The landscape was depressing - an endless grassy plain scattered with piles of rubbish and the rusty skeletons of abandoned cars, although there were occasional small patches of cultivated land and a few goats and sheep. Katy caught sight of a cow tethered in the front garden of a ramshackle cottage.

Eventually they reached a range of mountains and the narrow unprotected road climbed in a series of terrifying hairpin bends with sheer drops to the valley below. Bogonda clung to the side of a steep crag and had the usual collection of half-finished new buildings and decrepit old shacks. The Mayor made the customary speech of welcome and Katy replied. Then she visited a primary school and a handicraft centre where girls were learning to weave kilims. She also met the oldest lady in the town who was ninety-five. Her deeply tanned, wrinkled skin was peppered with warts and she had a hawk-like nose. Her black eyes blazed with fury when she spoke about her miserable pension and how her meagre savings had evaporated in the transformation to capitalism. Katy promised to see what could be done for her.

She travelled to some other towns nearer Svyatograd, but she really wanted to visit St Paraskeva's convent and orphanage which had been the country estate of the Fedorovitch family until it was seized by the Communists. When Count Stefan had told her at the reception in Hampstead how his father, Count Yaroslav, was trying to reclaim it from the Government, he had sounded so scornful and indifferent to the needs of the orphans that she was determined to investigate further. The Count's only concern had been that his family could no longer go hunting on the estate and it had appeared more important to him than a bunch of under-nourished children.

She asked Dimitar to organize a trip to the orphanage but he was evasive.

'I do not think that will be possible. The place is very isolated.'

'But it's only 30 kilometres from Svyatograd and on the map the road to it looks very good. We've been to far more remote places than that!'

'The nuns who run the orphanage do not welcome visitors.'

'That's nonsense! The priest at my church in London told me they were desperate for help. They're lacking the most basic medical equipment and they don't have enough money to give the children a healthy diet.'

'Although the nuns from the convent run it, the orphanage belongs to the State and the Government provides everything that is necessary.'

'Well, it doesn't sound as though it's doing a very good job does it? I want to see if I can help.'

'There is also another problem. You may not know that Count Yaroslav Fedorovitch is in negotiation with the Government for the return of the orphanage to his family. It was their hunting lodge before the Communists took over.'

'And where will the orphans go if this happens?' asked Katy.

'We do not know. There is no suitable accommodation for them at present. It is a very difficult problem. That is why it is not a good idea for you to go to the orphanage for the time being. It could make things worse.'

'You mean I could expose a situation which you're trying to hush up! Aren't the lives of some unfortunate children more important than a few aristocrats hunting bears? Please try to organize a visit.'

Dimitar sighed wearily. 'Very well, Your Royal Highness. I will see what can be done. I will telephone the nuns and arrange for us to go to St Paraskeva's privately. The Ministry of Health and Social Services is responsible for the orphanage, but I will not mention our trip to them because they would be very annoyed. I hope there will be no unfortunate repercussions from your decision.'

'I'll take full responsibility,' said Katy firmly.

* * *

Two days later Katy, Dimitar and Yurek drove to the orphanage. The road was surprisingly good until they branched off on to a dirt track through a forest for the last five kilometres. St Paraskeva's Convent was situated in a clearing on a steep hill and had only been built after the collapse of the Communist régime, but the orphanage itself was housed next to it in the Fedorovitch family's nineteenth century hunting lodge, a yellow stone mansion that resembled those in Austria and Hungary. It was badly in need of repair; the walls were cracked in many places and some of the windows had been broken and were boarded up. In front of it a formal garden in the French style sloped down the hill, but it was overgrown with weeds and long, untended grass.

They parked the car in front of the convent building and a pale, slender young nun, wearing steel-rimmed spectacles, ran out and greeted them in excellent English.

'We are so happy that you have come to see us, Your Royal Highness,' she said. 'I am Sister Athanasia. I studied English at university and so I have been designated by the other sisters to show you round the orphanage.'

They went into the hunting lodge building and entered a wood-panelled Gothic-style hall. Stags' heads and other trophies still hung on the walls and the atmosphere was oppressive. There was no furniture apart from cheap trestle tables and folding chairs.

'This is the refectory,' said Sister Athanasia. 'It is not very practical and it is a long way from the kitchen but there is nowhere else that is suitable. Come and meet the children.' She led them down a corridor to a room where about twenty small boys and girls were sitting on the floor engrossed in a cartoon film on an ancient television set. Several of them turned and looked at Katy and she could see that they were very thin and their eyes looked enormous in their pinched faces.

'These children are small for their age.' said the nun. 'They are anaemic and they are not growing properly because we cannot afford to give them the kind of food they need. They would make rapid progress if they had a better diet.'

'But couldn't you grow vegetables and keep hens?' suggested Katy.

'We try. The older children work in the garden but it is difficult for them. The soil is poor and stony and digging is hard. There is only one man from the village who helps them but what they grow and the eggs the hens produce are not enough to feed everyone in the orphanage.

'Don't you buy food in the market?'

'Yes, but fresh fruit and vegetables are expensive. The Ministry of Health does not give us enough money for anything but the cheapest food - pasta, rice and potatoes. We can only buy meat occasionally and we cannot even afford the equipment and medicines we need to treat the disabled children properly.'

'Are many of the children here disabled?'

'Twenty of them have a physical handicap - in most cases it is cerebral palsy. Some of them are not even orphans: their parents abandoned them because they were ashamed of them. In other cases they had to be removed from families where the father drank and beat or sexually abused them. We do the best we can to help them but they need drugs and walking aids that are only available abroad.'

'Have you asked the Ministry of Health to increase the funding of the orphanage?'

'We have tried but they have done nothing,' said Sister Athanasia.

She led them through a labyrinth of stone passages to the other side of the building. They entered a large room which smelled musty. There were damp patches on the dingy beige walls and peeling paint indicated a leaking roof. On one side of the room half-a-dozen children lay flat on their backs on iron beds, staring at the ceiling.

'These children all have cerebral palsy. They cannot walk but they might be able to if they had the right treatment. We do not have enough wheelchairs for everyone so they have to take turns in using them. One week they stay in bed all day and the following week they sit in a wheelchair.'

'That must be very bad for them.'

'Of course it is. We should be helping them to get out of the wheelchairs and learn to use crutches.'

Katy walked down the row of beds and sat on one of them which was occupied by a girl of about seven. The child clutched her hand and struggled to ask for something.

'She wants you to help her sit up,' said Sister Athanasia.

Fighting back tears, Katy lifted the little girl and propped her against a pile of pillows. 'What's your name?' she asked her in Maloslavian. The child's face twitched in a violent spasm as she tried to force out the word 'Maria.'

Sister Athanasia sighed. 'Maria has cerebral palsy. She has difficulty in speaking and her legs are affected but she is very intelligent. When it is her turn to be in a wheelchair she likes to watch television and she would love to learn to read.'

'So she's not getting any education?'

'It is not possible at the moment. The children who have no disabilities walk to the village school and those who have milder handicaps are taken there by bus. Unfortunately the teachers cannot deal with the more serious cases.'

'But can't one of the sisters teach them here?'

'There are only five sisters to run an orphanage of seventy children with help from some unqualified village girls who work in the kitchen, do the cleaning and some elementary nursing duties. We do not have time for any teaching but we have asked our mother convent in Svyatograd to send us another sister who could hold classes in reading and writing.'

'Don't the orphans ever see a doctor?'

'The local doctor comes here every three months and examines them but there is little he can do without the right equipment and medicines. One child has epilepsy but we do not have the correct drugs to control his fits.'

They moved to the other side of the room where six small boys sat round a table painting and a little girl aged about five was crawling along the floor.

'Anna was born with club feet,' said Sister Athanasia. 'The condition could have easily been corrected when she was a baby but her parents did nothing to help her and then they began kicking and beating her. Finally they left her here. She is still very frightened after what she has suffered and she refuses to try to walk with crutches. She feels happier crawling.'

Katy knelt down and took the little girl in her arms The child smiled and Katy saw that she was pretty with large blue eyes and dimples. Two of the boys, who were in wheelchairs, left their painting and propelled themselves across the room to join them.

'*Otkoodah tee*?' they asked eager to know where Katy came from.

'*Ot Anglee*,' she replied and they told her that they went to school and knew where England was because they had seen it on a map.

The other four boys came over and Katy found herself surrounded by a group of excited children all talking at once. They handed her their paintings and she wanted to cry when she looked at the pictures which depicted their limited world and the cruelty to which they'd been subjected. They showed children in wheelchairs or lying in bed and in one of them a girl was being beaten by a fierce looking man. But there were also pictures of cottages surrounded by flowers and trees under a blue sky.

'Don't the children in those beds ever go outside?' Katy asked.

'When it is their turn to be in the wheelchairs they are taken into the garden. We try to see they all get as much fresh air as possible,' said Sister Athanasia.

'I think it's a pity to isolate disabled children like this. Wouldn't it be better to let them mix with the others so that they could learn to live together and help one another?'

The nun looked embarrassed. 'You are right. I have been suggesting this for a long time but two of the older sisters are against it. I will tell them what you have said and we will see what can be done.'

It was time to leave as Sister Athanasia said she had to go to vespers in the convent chapel. Some of the children shouted 'Goodbye!' in English and Katy waved to them.

'You have been a great success with them,' said the nun as they walked back to the entrance. 'It is good for them to have someone to talk to. We do not have much time to do that.'

'I know how difficult things must be for you and I want to help,' said Katy. 'If I become Queen I'll do everything I can to improve conditions in the orphanage and if I don't win the referendum and return to London, I'll try to organize a campaign to raise money for medicines, medical equipment and whatever else you need.'

Sister Athanasia smiled. 'Thank you, Your Royal Highness. That would be wonderful. But there is another problem.'

'What's that?'

'Perhaps you know that Count Yaroslav Fedorovitch is negotiating with the Government for the return of this building to him. If that happens I do not know where we will go. The Ministry of Health did mention a former Communist Party workers' holiday camp in the north of the country but it is quite unsuitable. It has not been used for many years and it consists of a number of chalets and cottages which are damp and cold. This hunting lodge could easily be repaired if we had enough money but the holiday camp would need to be completely rebuilt.'

'I'll do my best to prevent this happening,' said Katy. 'I'll ask to see the Prime Minister and perhaps I can talk to the Count. I once met his son in London.'

' Count Yaroslav is a hard man and it will be difficult. He came here recently to look at the building and he was very rude. He behaved as though we did not exist and he was only interested in the possibilities for hunting when he recovered the estate.'

'Don't worry,' said Katy. ' I'll think of a way to stop the Count.'

* * *

'You are wasting your time,' said Dimitar when Katy told him she wanted him to arrange a meeting with the Prime Minister. 'If Count Yaroslav wishes to reclaim his hunting lodge the Government cannot stop him. He is a valued friend of our country with business interests here. His investments in our furniture factories are of great importance to us.'

'So returning the hunting lodge to him is his reward for trying to shore up the crumbling economy?'

'It is only right that his property, which was seized by the Communists, should be restored to him.'

'Yes, if the children can be housed in another suitable building. Unfortunately it seems they can't. The Government has done absolutely nothing to find satisfactory accommodation. A damp, decrepit holiday camp won't do.'

Dimitar looked sheepish. 'Very well,' he said, 'I will try to fix an appointment with Ivan Petrovitch.'

Katy was afraid he would find some excuse to avoid taking the matter further but the following day he told her he had managed to arrange a meeting with the Prime Minister for the following Tuesday afternoon. It so happened that Count Yaroslav would be in Svyatograd on that day and would also be present.

It was only the middle of May, but the weather in Svyatograd was unusually hot. By noon on Tuesday the temperature had risen to 40°C. Katy felt weak and faint when she entered the Prime Minister's office in a nineteenth century building without air conditioning on the Boulevard Victoria.

Ivan Petrovitch greeted her, smiling nervously, and introduced Count Yaroslav who bowed and gave her a cold smile. He reminded

Katy disagreeably of his son, Count Stefan, for he too was tall, with a slobbery mouth and protuberant eyes behind thick glasses but his few remaining tufts of hair were white and he stooped slightly.

Ivan Petrovitch asked a secretary to bring tea and turning to the Count said 'Her Royal Highness has visited St Paraskeva's Orphanage and was very disturbed by the conditions there.'

'The conditions there are not my responsibility,' said the Count. 'I do not run the orphanage and if things are as bad as you say, then it would surely be better to move the children elsewhere and return my property to me.'

'But as I explained to you before, there is no suitable alternative accommodation for the orphanage,' said Ivan Petrovitch. 'The children would have to be housed in a damp, disused workers' rest home.'

'It would be shameful to do that,' interrupted Katy. 'If Maloslavia were part of the European Union it would be illegal!'

'Your Royal Highness believes in plain speaking,' said the Count with a cynical smile. 'I don't think we should get emotional about this.'

' But surely you, as a Maloslavian, care about what happens to these children? You would probably only use the lodge occasionally whereas they live there all the time. Couldn't you wait, say another five years, during which time suitable new accommodation could be found?'

'That is a possibility,' said Ivan Petrovitch. 'Would you be prepared to consider such a solution?'

The secretary arrived with the tea and offered a glass to the Count who refused it with a brush of the hand, saying 'I have waited long enough. It was not possible to reclaim the lodge during the Communist period but now there is absolutely no legitimate reason why I cannot have what is mine. It is the fault of the Government that suitable provision has not been made for the orphanage and I don't see why I should be deprived of my inheritance because of a bunch of children who had no right to be there in the first place!'

Katy stood up, all semblance of royal dignity forgotten.

'I never suggested you should renounce your inheritance - simply that you might wait until the orphanage could be moved to a suitable place. I mean to let the world know what the conditions there are like and to try to raise money to give the children medical aid and better food but what's the point if you throw them out. This is the only worthwhile thing I've done since I came to this country. Maloslavia doesn't need a monarchy and if you insist on reclaiming your property I won't take part in the referendum and I'll go straight back to London.'

'Please, Your Royal Highness...' stammered Ivan Petrovitch.

But without waiting to hear any more, Katy stormed out of the room.

As they drove back to the hotel Dimitar said 'That was a most regrettable outburst, Your Royal Highness. You have offended the Count and he could terminate his business interests here.'

'I'm sorry, but I had to say something. All that man cares about is getting back his lodge so that he can kill a few unfortunate bears. I only asked that he should wait a few years.'

Dimitar looked at her as if she was a naughty child. 'You delivered an ultimatum. You threatened to return to London. That was childish. You have a lot to learn, Your Royal Highness.'

* * *

On Wednesday the temperature again reached 40°C and Katy heard on the news that it was the hottest May since 1900. Water was becoming scarce and was cut off for several hours without warning and to make matters worse there was an unannounced general strike which completely paralysed the country for twenty-four hours. People couldn't get to work but were thankful to stay at home. Katy spent the morning sitting on the balcony, dripping with perspiration. She was in disgrace and Dimitar did not come to see her. She knew her behaviour hadn't been that of a prospective queen - royalty in the modern world weren't allowed to speak their mind and had to smile sweetly and keep quiet. She wondered what would happen now. Would they cancel the referendum and send her back to England? Well, she didn't care if they did.

Shortly before lunch the phone rang. Katy picked it up and she groaned inwardly when she recognized the unctuous tones of Count Stefan.

'Your Royal Highness, what an unexpected pleasure,' he said.

'I didn't know you were in Svyatograd,' she replied in an expressionless voice.

'I decided to accompany my father. I'd never been to Maloslavia and I felt it was time to have a look at the old country and visit our estate. I've only just arrived in Svyatograd. I hired a car and I've been travelling around. My God, what a dump!'

'But the countryside is beautiful.' said Katy.

'If you say so, but I don't envy you. You must be rather bored with it all. Anyway, Countess Elena suggested that it would make a nice change for you if I paid you a visit.'

Katy felt trapped. She found Count Stefan repulsive and she didn't want to see him but because of the delicate situation with his father it was difficult to refuse. She decided that the safest solution was to invite him for tea. If he came to dinner he could easily become amorous and she didn't want to have to fight him off. She said 'Would you like to come this afternoon around four? We can have tea.'

He sounded disappointed. 'Tea! How very British!'

'Actually it will be more Austrian than British,' said Katy. 'The chef trained in Vienna and he makes delicious Viennese pastries.'

'I *adore* Sachertorte with whipped cream! I shall look forward to it and, needless to say, I look forward very much to seeing *you* again! *A tout à l'heure.*'

'Goodbye,' said Katy and flopped on the bed exhausted. 'The heatwave was bad enough without having to cope with Count Stefan. She wondered whether he'd heard of her outburst to his father the day before and decided that he probably didn't know about it. After all, it seemed that he'd only just arrived in Svyatograd.

At four o'clock precisely Boyana announced Count Stefan. He entered, sweeping off his Panama hat, and bowing with mock gallantry. He kissed Katy's hand and she instinctively recoiled at the touch of his lips. He paid no attention to her reaction and said, smiling 'I am delighted to see you again in your new surroundings.'

'Shall we go outside?' said Katy. 'The view of Liberation Square is very pleasant.'

They went on to the balcony but although it was protected from the sun by an awning, the afternoon heat was suffocating.

'Do sit down,' said Katy, uncomfortably aware of the way his eyes were fixed on the opening of her blouse.

They sat facing one another on uncomfortable wrought iron chairs. Count Stefan had put on weight and she thought he looked even more unattractive in casual attire than he had in evening dress. His stomach bulged slightly over the top of his Armani jeans and his striped open necked shirt revealed a glimpse of a chest covered in black fuzz.

Katy tried to make conversation, carefully avoiding the subject of the orphanage. She told him about the visits she'd made since her arrival in Maloslavia and asked him about his journey round the country.'

'The worst place I stayed in was the hotel in Shkrapova.' he said.

'I went to Shkrapova,' said Katy.

'You obviously didn't stay in the Friendship Hotel. God, it was awful - filthy bathroom, loo that didn't flush and flies and mosquitoes everywhere.'

'Conditions are quite primitive outside the capital,' said Katy, thankful to see the waiter arriving with the tea and a Sachertorte. She sliced the cake and handed a plate to Count Stefan.

'Do help yourself,' she said pouring the tea and handing him a cup.

Count Stefan took a large portion of the Sachertorte and covered it with whipped cream. He devoured it with obvious appreciation.

'This is really excellent,' he said. He took another slice, scooping up the rapidly melting chocolate icing with a spoon. ' I would never have expected to find a Sachertorte of such quality in this dump even if the chef was trained in Vienna.'

'It *is* a five star hotel, but apart from cakes the food isn't very good,' said Katy.

'Well, I suppose you can always live on cake like Marie Antoinette.'

'Marie Antoinette did *not* live on cake. She is *supposed* to have said "Let them eat cake" when she was told the people had no bread. But actually it's a legend,' said Katy. Count Stefan was already starting to get on her nerves.

'You've always got to have the last word haven't you? But of course, your piquancy is part of your charm,' he said. moving his chair until it was close to hers.

She ignored this remark but undeterred he put his arm round her and looked at her with a smile that was almost a leer. Beads of perspiration trickled down his face.

'You're very alluring you know,' he whispered. 'I've often thought about you since we met at that New Year's ball. I've been waiting for a chance to get to know you better.'

'But I don't think this is the right time,' said Katy, wondering how to extricate herself.

'Oh, but it is! It must be terribly boring for you in this ghastly place. Let's relax and have a bit of fun together.'

'I don't think so,' said Katy. She tried to pull away but before she knew what was happening, he leaned forward and slipped a sweaty hand inside her blouse, groping for her breasts. She pushed him away with all her strength. 'Get *off*!' she shouted and slapped his face hard.

'You disgust me,' she said.

Count Stefan rubbed his cheek, deeply offended. 'You're a proper little spitfire, aren't you?' he said. 'I came here because I thought you needed cheering up. Your behaviour isn't exactly that of a future queen.'

'Well, you haven't shown much respect for a future queen,' retorted Katy.

'You're making a big mistake,' said Count Stefan. 'If you were nice to me I could persuade my father to allow your precious orphan brats to remain on our estate. You'll be sorry for this.'

'Get out!' said Katy and he left, slamming the door.

She went back into the sitting room and sank down on the sofa. What would happen now? The situation over the orphanage wasn't very promising and she wondered whether her rejection of Count Stefan would make any difference either way. She doubted that he'd tell his father about the afternoon's events because in fact they reflected badly on him. Moreover, Count Yaroslav was probably well aware of his son's reputation with women and possibly disapproved of it. There was nothing she could do except keep quiet and hope for the best.

The heatwave continued until Sunday. That night there was a violent storm and Monday morning was pleasantly cool. Katy was eating her breakfast when Boyana suddenly appeared with Ivan Petrovitch.

'I have good news, Your Royal Highness,' he said smiling.

'That will be a pleasant change.'

'On reflection Count Yaroslav has decided to postpone reclaiming his property for a period of up to five years. I persuaded him to visit the orphanage again with me and finally convinced him that the children needed a stable environment. They will remain where they are for the time being and I am instructing the Ministry of Health and Social Services to abandon the idea of moving them to the camp. I have told the Minister to increase his efforts to find suitable alternative accommodation for them and even to consider the possibility of building a new orphanage.'

So presumably Count Stefan had said nothing about her rejection of him!

'I'm very pleased about this news, Prime Minister,' said Katy, trying to conceal her feeling of triumph.

'Your influence in such matters is of the utmost importance, Your Royal Highness,' said Ivan Petrovitch. 'You may well become the conscience of the nation, alerting us to areas of need.'

Katy laughed. 'Let's not exaggerate. But if something needs doing I can't help saying so and trying to get it done. As far as I can see it's the only useful role I can play as Queen.'

'Let us hope that the people will allow you to play it.'

Chapter 11

Katy was dreading the ceremonies on the thirty-first of May, Heroes' Day, which was a national holiday. It commemorated the Maloslavian rising against the Turks in 1848 when several hundred people in Svyatograd had been brutally massacred. Although independence hadn't come until 1880, the rising had heralded a decline in Turkish control over the country and a number of restrictions had been lifted.

Since the collapse of Communism, the day always began with a service in the Cathedral of the Redeemer. This was followed by a military parade down the Avenue of Heroes to Liberation Square, where in previous years President Grobov had taken the salute from the balcony of the Royal Palace. Latterly he had been in a wheelchair and although he didn't understand what was happening he would wave feebly to the crowds. This year it was proposed that Katy should take the salute with Nicola Popnikov but the idea didn't appeal to her.

'Popnikov is the acting president and he's opposed to the monarchy. Wouldn't it be better for him to appear on the balcony alone?' she said to Ivan Petrovitch.

'No, Your Royal Highness. It will be good for the public to see you both on the balcony and it could have an influence on the choice they make in the referendum.'

'I've never met Popnikov. He'll probably be hostile to me.'

'You will stand one at each end of the balcony and if you do not wish to speak to him it will not be necessary, apart from greeting him when you arrive and saying goodbye when you leave.'

It had been decided that Katy would not attend the service in the cathedral but would go straight to the palace to await the arrival of the parade. On the morning of Heroes' Day she and Dimitar were driven across the square and taken to the reception room where a few weeks earlier they had met President Grobov. Popnikov was already there, surrounded by half-a-dozen bodyguards, talking angrily to a secretary. He ignored Katy's arrival and continued his conversation, so she sat near the open doors leading on to the balcony and looked down at the square.

'You must greet Nicola Popnikov, Your Royal Highness,' whispered Dimitar.

'Well, I'd be happy to do so, but he seems intent on ignoring me.'

'Come with me,' said Dimitar.

They went over to the group surrounding Popnikov. He stopped speaking and glared at them.

'Mr Acting-President,' said Dimitar in Maloslavian, 'May I have the honour to present you to the Princess Katerina Bogdanova, heir to the throne of Maloslavia.'

'*Shto?*' cried Popnikov going red in the face. '*Ya nyay "Acteeng". Ya President!*' He snatched at Katy's hand and shook it briefly, then turned his back on her and went on talking as though she didn't exist.

'We had better go back and sit near the balcony doors,' said Dimitar. 'He is just a vulgar peasant. He has no breeding and no manners. He is angry because I addressed him as "acting president" but it is the truth whether he likes it or not.'

They sat waiting for the parade to arrive for what seemed a very long time while in the background Popnikov talked endlessly in a loud voice interspersed with raucous laughter. Near him, on an eighteenth century cherry wood table, was a generous supply of beer and vodka and he frequently helped himself to it, drinking straight from the bottle.

'He's following in President Grobov's footsteps,' whispered Katy to Dimitar as Popnikov became more and more drunk, repeatedly shouting '*Ya President!*' Finally, as military music heralded the approach of the parade down the Avenue of Heroes, he vomited explosively on the immaculately polished Hungarian point parquet and slumped back in a chair. A maid was summoned with a bucket and mop. She hurriedly cleaned the floor and disappeared.

The procession was drawing ever nearer but Popnikov lay in a stupor, groaning. Prompted by Dimitar, Katy went out on to the balcony alone just as the band appeared playing the Radetsky March. They were followed by the members of the National Guard in their shoddy hussar-style uniforms, goose-stepping across the square. As one man, they turned their heads towards her and saluted and she returned their greeting with a slight wave of the hand. Some troops in camouflage battle dress came next and then a handful of girls and boys in the uniform of the Maloslavian Orthodox Scout Brigade who sang the patriotic song *Blood of our Fathers*. A couple of antiquated tanks and a tractor trundled into the square behind them and after them came a group of athletes in white trousers and tee shirts. Another small military band brought up the rear playing the triumphal march from *Aida* off-key.

The parade was a small-scale affair and there was plenty of room in Liberation Square for all the participants who now lined up in ranks facing the Palace balcony. They were watched by crowds of onlookers jostling in front of the Hotel Franz Josef and the Svyatograd Hilton. They wore paper hats and waved flags in the Maloslavian colours and had already succeeded in littering the pavement with empty ice cream cartons, chip bags and Coca Cola bottles. A cordon of police struggled to maintain order but found it difficult to control the people who kept pushing in their attempts to get a better view. Black clouds were gathering and there was a distant rumble of thunder. Katy's thin silk dress clung to her damp body and she felt sick in the oppressive midday heat. She wondered how much longer she would have to stand watching this pathetic little circus. If they couldn't put on a decent show, then they shouldn't have a parade at all. It simply made them look ridiculous in the eyes of the world, if indeed any foreign journalists took the trouble to report on the event.

The two military bands struck up the national anthem, *O Blessed Maloslavia,* and everyone in the square began to sing. Just as they reached the line *We'll fight and kill our foes*, a shot rang out and a bullet whizzed past Katy into the room beyond, shattering a bottle of vodka on the cherry wood table and scattering fragments of glass on Popnikov's recumbent body. Before she could take in what had happened, two bodyguards seized her, dragged her inside and seated her in a chair. One of them handed her a glass of water but her hands were trembling so violently that she nearly dropped it and he took it and held it to her lips. Her mouth was parched and she drank until her thirst was quenched. Her heart thumped and although her palms were clammy with sweat she felt cold.

'Please, get me out of here,' she whispered. 'I want to go back to the hotel.'

'We cannot leave yet,' said Dimitar. 'It would be too dangerous. The square has to be cleared first. You can rest here for a while. You must lie down and we will fetch a doctor.'

The two bodyguards helped Katy to her feet and, holding her by the arms, took her to the adjoining room which was dominated by President Grobov's massive bed. She was lifted on to it and laid on the gold brocade counterpane. It suddenly flashed through her mind that this was the copy of Marie-Antoinette's bed at Versailles and then revulsion swept over her as she realized it was also the bed on which the drink-sodden, senile President had breathed his last. After a few minutes, a grey-haired, bearded doctor arrived who had been Grobov's personal physician. He took her blood pressure, felt her pulse and pronounced himself satisfied.

'You have had a terrible shock, Your Royal Highness,' he said 'but no harm has been done. When the crowds have dispersed you can return to the hotel and rest quietly for the rest of the day.'

'But will it be safe to cross the square?' asked Katy.

Dimitar, who had just received a call on his mobile phone, reassured her.

'They have arrested the boy who fired the shot. He was wearing Scout's uniform but he was clearly a member of the People's Struggle Pioneers who had infiltrated the Scout movement. He has been taken for questioning. We can leave now.'

Yurek took Katy's arm and they went downstairs to the car. The square was deserted but litter was blowing about in the hot wind that had arisen and the smell of tear gas lingered in the air. As they entered the Hotel Franz Josef, the storm broke and the rain came down in torrents. Katy went to her room and lay on the bed looking at the sheets of water cascading down the window from a blocked gutter. Boyana came in with lunch on a tray looking terrified. She had seen the assassination attempt from the balcony where she had been watching the parade. She put the food on a small table and sat beside Katy without speaking.

Katy knew Boyana wanted to comfort her but she needed to be alone. She patted her on the arm and told her that there was nothing that she needed for the time being. She forced herself to swallow some cold chicken and salad and lay down again wondering how she was going to get through the remaining three weeks until the referendum. And after the referendum, what then? How would she cope if she won? But before she could answer this question she fell into a doze.

* * *

Janko lay on a straw mattress on the stone floor sobbing with pain. He wanted to sleep, but his battered body wouldn't let him. When he'd refused to say who had ordered him to shoot the Princess, the police had beaten him on his back, his arms and legs and then they'd kicked him in the stomach and punched him in the face. His left eye was swollen and had closed up but with his right eye he could see the small barred window high up in the wall facing him. It provided the only light and he realized that the cell was bare and so tiny that he could touch the walls on each side of him.

Why had he been such a fool? When the Pioneers first asked him to carry out this crazy operation, he'd refused. They'd laughed at him and called him a coward and a *krevetka* - a word he hated which meant 'shrimp'. He hated being so much smaller than the rest of them - he was just over five foot - and being the butt of their jokes. He'd tried hard to be like them but he was always the outsider. When their taunts proved unsuccessful, they used persuasion. They told him that if he killed the Princess he would be acclaimed as a hero in the glorious new Communist state that Popnikov would establish. He didn't really believe this but he wanted so much to prove that he was capable of a daring act that he'd finally agreed to their plans.

His parents hadn't wanted him to join the Pioneers. They'd suggested he become a member of the Orthodox Scout Brigade instead but he'd upset them by saying the Scouts were pious wimps and anyway he didn't believe in God any more. His mother, who was very religious and had made sure he was baptized as a baby, had cried and pleaded with him but he took no notice. He liked the Pioneers' uniform with its red neckerchief and the way they marched, goose-stepping and singing patriotic songs. He attended a few meetings and was impressed with their fiery speeches about fighting for a better future. When he was fourteen he signed up as a member and took the oath to work for the Socialist cause and to serve the Motherland whatever the cost. At first he enjoyed being a Pioneer, but when he went to the summer training camp he began to feel uneasy. He didn't like the classes where they were instructed in the use of various weapons, including Kalashnikovs, and taught different techniques for starting a riot and inciting people to violence. When he timidly ventured to say that he thought it might be better to achieve their goals by peaceful means, they jeered at him. He became a figure of fun. 'Hey, *krevetka!*' they'd shout when they saw him and he'd laugh and pretend he didn't mind.

One day, Stenko, the captain of the troup, told him they'd got a job for him. He was to put away his uniform, pretend he wasn't a Pioneer and go to the Orthodox Scout Brigade to ask if he could join them. In spite of Popnikov's insistence, the Pioneers would not be allowed to attend the Heroes' Day parade, but the scout brigade would be there. Janko was to become a scout, take part in all their activities and attend Orthodox services. Nobody would doubt his sincerity. Then, on Heroes' Day, when the Brigade was lined up in front of the Palace, he would pull out a small Ruger revolver concealed in a holster under his shirt, and fire at the Princess.

After he'd agreed to carry out the assassination, he began in a strange way to enjoy the preparations for it. Infiltrating the scout brigade gave him a kind of thrill. He felt that he was a spy, a secret agent, and it gave him a sense of importance. But at the same time he was happy with the scouts and had to admit that they were a nice, friendly group even though their values were diametrically opposed to those of the Pioneers. When Heroes' Day arrived, he had mixed feelings about the task he had to perform but he told himself firmly that it was for the good of the country and that he was going to show everyone how courageous he could be. As he stood in Liberation Square and the people began singing *O Blessed Maloslavia*, a wave of patriotism surged over him and all his doubts vanished. He wanted to serve the Motherland! In a state of euphoria he drew the revolver from under his shirt and fired. It was so easy! Why had he been afraid? He was a hero! But then, seconds later, he was dragged away and bundled into a police van.

Janko tried to find a more comfortable position on the lumpy mattress but every movement was torture. His head ached and his eye throbbed unbearably. He understood now that the Pioneers had picked on him to do their dirty work because they despised him and thought him weak. He also realized that the police who had beaten him so savagely were probably those who'd carried out similar acts under the Communists and had never been removed from their posts. To think that he'd messed up his life fighting to restore their rotten regime!

A guard appeared and left a bowl and a tin mug by the mattress. Then the heavy steel door was slammed shut again. Janko managed to raise himself slightly and drank some water from the mug. He took the bowl which contained a kind of glutinous gruel. It was nauseating but he forced it down. It was important to keep up his strength and he was going to swallow whatever lousy food they gave him. And next time they questioned him he'd tell them the truth. He'd give them the names of the boys who'd persuaded him to shoot the Princess. Why should they get away with it? If he was going down he'd bring them down too!

* * *

When Katy woke it was already getting dark. She got up and switched on the television news. The heavy rain had brought severe flooding and they spoke of a national disaster. Rivers had burst their banks, villages were cut off and crops ruined. In Svyatograd, Liberation Square was under several inches of water. It was only after extensive coverage of the floods that they showed film of the assassination attempt. Katy saw herself on the palace balcony taking the salute and then the bullet whizzing past her. There were pictures of an angry young boy shouting 'Royalist scum!' as he was dragged away by the police. He was apparently called Janko Drobovitch, he was only sixteen and he was being interrogated. She watched, horrified to think that someone so young should have tried to kill her in cold blood but before the bulletin ended Boyana came in and told her that the Prime Minister was waiting to see her. She dressed quickly and went into the sitting room.

'Your Royal Highness, I am profoundly shocked by what has happened and I deeply regret that you were exposed to such a terrible ordeal,' said Ivan Petrovitch. 'I trust that your health has not been greatly affected by this unfortunate incident?'

'Fortunately not, but I've had a lucky escape. To think that a boy of sixteen should want to kill me. And it's not the first time there's been an attempt on my life. Don't forget people tried to poison me when I visited Shkrapova.'

'That has never been proved. Your illness was caused by Salmonella.'

'That's what they say but I don't believe it. How can I believe it when I know how my father died? Callously poisoned by Communist thugs! It's pretty clear to me that the people don't want a Queen and I don't think they need one.'

'But, Your Royal Highness...'

'Please,' said Katy, interrupting him. 'Let's not argue about it. The point is that although I've tried to serve Maloslavia to the best of my ability, I've been very unhappy here and now it looks as though I'm in danger of losing my life. I would like to go back to England as soon as possible.'

'To return would be to lose all credibility and you will be needed here to comfort the people who have been stricken by these terrible floods. You must not give in to a few terrorists - they are a minority.'

'Perhaps, but the latest opinion polls show that sixty-five percent of the population are against the restoration of the monarchy.'

'You must not take any notice of opinion polls, Your Royal Highness. People do not decide how they will vote until the last minute. I beg you to stay until the referendum. I give you my word that police protection will be increased. You cannot leave now. You have done a great deal of good in helping the poor and the sick.'

'I've done what I could, but it's not much,' said Katy. 'Your government should take responsibility for these people but it's too corrupt and inefficient to care. I'll stay until the referendum but if I lose, which seems almost certain, I don't think the people will want me to remain here. Can I have your word that if the majority vote "No" you will arrange for my immediate return to London?'

'Very well, Your Royal Highness,' said Ivan Petrovitch reluctantly, 'I give you my word.'

* * *

The three weeks leading up to the referendum seemed never-ending. Nikola Popnikov was touring the country giving fiery speeches against the monarchy and making wild promises of lavish financial aid to the flood victims. The newspapers printed photos of him surrounded by cheering crowds waving the Maloslavian flag. Because of the volatile situation after the attempt on her life, Katy was confined to her rooms at the hotel for much of the time and felt more like a prisoner than ever. She had by now read all the books she'd brought with her and spent her days studying Maloslavian grammar and watching television. From Dimitar she learned that Janko Drobovitch at his second interrogation had given the names of the boys who had ordered him to kill her and they had been arrested. There were four of them and they were all aged eighteen and, unlike Janko, too old to be tried in a juvenile court.

When Katy heard from Dimitar that Janko had been virtually forced into the assassination attempt and was sorry for what he'd done, she was curious and asked if she could talk to him. Dimitar told her firmly that this was out of the question.

'Nobody is allowed to see him at present. He is not very well. After his second interrogation he was moved to a better cell and a doctor has examined him. He is receiving treatment for his ... er, he is being treated.'

'What do you mean - for his? For his what? For his injuries? Were you going to say that he was beaten up?'

'He refused to give any names during his first interrogation and the police were, shall we say, a little harsh.'

'I suppose he was beaten to a pulp? Whatever he's done, he's only a kid for God's sake!'

'Now that he has given the police the information they require he is being well treated and he will be tried in a juvenile court because he is only sixteen. After he is sentenced, you will be allowed to see him if you are still here.'

Katy was silent. It was obvious to her that the police were using the same methods as they had done under the Communists and she realized that she couldn't visit Janko because they didn't want her to see his injuries.

The bad weather continued for nearly a week with torrential rain and thousands of people in areas bordering the river Drin saw their fragile wooden cottages swept away in the flood waters. When conditions finally improved, Dimitar told Katy she was to tour the regions hit by the disaster but that security would be much stricter than before: in addition to her usual bodyguard there would be an escort of police on motor bikes accompanying her car.

The journey was difficult. The waters had subsided leaving a sea of mud behind them. Fields had been transformed into swamps and the potholed roads were slippery and dangerous. The villages bordering the river had suffered severe damage and many of the old Turkish-style houses and shacks had collapsed completely. In the village of Bozena there was a strong smell of sewage everywhere and people were told that on no account must they drink any water. Katy was surrounded by angry crowds complaining that supplies of mineral water had run out. How could they cook? What were they supposed to drink? Many of the men had solved this problem by looting the village shop and swallowing large quantities of alcohol. They staggered around the streets shouting while their wives tried to clean up what remained of their houses as best they could.

One young woman caught Katy by the arm and begged her to visit her home. Katy followed her to a one-storey concrete hut. A rickety table, a few chairs, an oil lamp and some boxes of crockery, saucepans and blankets were piled up outside and three small children - two boys and a girl - were sitting on the muddy ground by the door. She went into the hut which consisted of one room with two small windows. Pools of water still lay on the floor and the walls, which glistened with moisture, had already developed patches of an evil-smelling green fungus.

'Smotree!' (Look!) cried the woman angrily, dragging a sodden mattress towards Katy. *'Kak moshna spat?'* (How can we sleep?) And she threw the mattress on the ground and flung herself down on it, sobbing.

'What is being done to help her?' asked Katy turning to a young man who had followed her into the hut and who appeared to be the only relief worker in the village.

'At present she, and all those whose homes are damaged, are sleeping in the church hall but the conditions are not good.'

'Why aren't there more relief workers here? Isn't the Government doing anything?' said Katy. It occurred to her that in practically every situation in which she'd found herself she'd had to ask the same question.

'Of course appropriate measures are being taken but we are dealing with a major disaster. It takes time.'

'Surely it's possible to deliver supplies of mineral water? If these people don't get drinking water there must be a risk of epidemics.'

'We have contacted the Ministry of Health and told them the matter is urgent.'

It was pointless to continue the conversation. The young woman was still sitting on the floor crying and Katy knelt down beside her. There was nothing she could say and she simply took her in her arms and held her for a moment.

The relief worker took Katy to the church hall which was situated on a hill above the river and had not been affected by the floods. The homeless villagers were lodging there and the floor was strewn with mattresses on which mothers were sitting feeding babies or trying to calm boisterous toddlers. Several very old women occupied the few chairs, staring blankly as if they could not understand what had happened to them. Others were queuing for bowls of soup that were being served from a large urn at the end of the room. Although living conditions were rudimentary, great efforts had been made with the limited resources available.

After visiting four more villages, Katy drove back to Svyatograd, overwhelmed by what she had seen. Dimitar, however, seemed more concerned about the referendum campaign.

'On Sunday you will appear on television again and we must also hold another press conference. Next week you will visit more places in the Svyatograd area because this is where you will probably pick up the most votes.'

She nodded meekly. Official visits, speeches full of platitudes, conferences - it was all becoming a dreary routine and she went through it like a robot, counting the days until, hopefully, she would be able to return to England. She wasn't nervous any more - she simply did what she was told as though she was on automatic pilot. She was numbed by it all and it was only when she was face to face with genuine human suffering that she came alive again and longed to help.

* * *

The viewing figures for Katy's television broadcast were poor, but Popnikov, speaking the following night attracted a huge audience, probably because he promised unrealistically large sums of money to the flood victims; Katy could only offer sympathy and vague promises of financial aid and had a fierce argument about her speech with Dimitar who had written it.

'Shouldn't we be more specific about the help we are going to give to the homeless?'

'It is not for the prospective monarch to enter into the financial details. That is the responsibility of the Government and in due course the Prime Minister will announce the arrangements that have been made. Your role is to be compassionate and understanding.'

'Being compassionate and understanding won't build those people new homes. They need help *quickly*.'

'Do not worry, Your Royal Highness. The matter is being dealt with at the highest level.'

It was unfortunate that Popnikov's broadcast took place the night after Katy's rather feeble speech. Not only did he make extravagant promises to the flood victims but he also laid heavy emphasis on the Fascist, pro-Nazi attitude of Katy's grandfather during the Second World War, pointing out that he had done nothing to stop Jews being herded off to concentration camps. Moreover, her father had only reigned five years and had been a weak, inexperienced young man who would undoubtedly also have developed Fascist tendencies if he had not been forced to abdicate. What guarantee was there, he asked, that his daughter, who had been born and bred in a decadent capitalist country and had not set foot in Maloslavia until four months ago, would not turn out the same way? 'Protect democracy!' cried Popnikov. 'Say no to the royalist cancer!'

The figures in the public opinion polls after these two broadcasts were even more discouraging than the previous ones. Katy's share of the vote had dropped to twenty-five per cent and she began to think about starting to pack her bags. She felt it was pointless to hold a press conference attended by the international press and that she would be a laughing stock, but Dimitar was insistent.

'It is important to have world opinion on our side,' he said firmly.

'But it won't be. Those journalists will tear me to pieces.'

'I will not let that happen. I will be there to field off awkward questions.'

Katy was proved right. The press conference, which took place in the town hall, was a nightmare. It was humiliating to be interrogated mercilessly by journalists from papers such as *Le Monde*, *The Times*, *El Pais* and *Die Welt*. They thoroughly enjoyed themselves and played with her like a cat with a mouse, relentlessly throwing questions at her which she couldn't answer on Maloslavia's foreign policy, its human rights record and its weak economy. Dimitar tried to take the pressure off her, giving his usual evasive replies, but the journalists were having a good time exposing the corrupt little country to ridicule.

The final question came from the correspondent of the French Communist *L'Humanité*:

'Does *Her Royal Highness*,' (he pronounced these words with heavy irony), 'really think that a monarch can play any useful role in a poor country like Maloslavia where a considerable proportion of the population live below subsistence level?'

Anger suddenly gave Katy confidence. She could answer this question with sincerity.

'I believe there is a role for a constitutional monarchy in this country because a monarch guarantees continuity and should be above politics. A monarch's role should be to listen to the people, sympathize with their hardships and difficulties and alert the government to areas where help is needed. I have tried my best to fulfil this role and I have been moved by the poverty and suffering of many members of the population. I wanted to help them in a practical way but it has been difficult to do this without the cooperation of an administration which is free from corruption and inertia.'

She was surprised at her eloquence. She didn't know where the words had come from but she'd spoken from the heart and for the first time during the conference there was a burst of applause. She realized that Dimitar and Ivan Petrovitch would probably be furious with her for her criticism of the government but what did it matter now? She was going to lose the referendum and it was worth saying what she felt.

* * *

The Maloslavian papers' coverage of the press conference was poor but the international press carried a number of features on the political situation in the country, most of them expressing doubts on the advisability of restoring the monarchy. *The Times* had a lengthy article with a photo of Katy under the headline *Princess Katerina - an Unfortunate Pawn in a New Balkan Chess Game*? When she saw this, Katy realized with a sinking heart that her face would now become familiar to the British public and that if she went back, people would recognize her. She would have to alter her appearance in some way because she intended to transform herself back into plain Katy Brennan. Never again would she be Princess Katerina. That chapter of her life would be over.

The Sunday of the referendum arrived at last and Svyatograd was strangely quiet. Armed police were everywhere, anticipating trouble, but there were few people on the streets. Many had undoubtedly taken advantage of the fine June weather to go to the country and polling stations were half empty. Katy spent most of the day on her balcony. She tried to read but she couldn't concentrate and became increasingly nervous as the the long, hot afternoon wore on. She was almost certain she'd lose the referendum and prayed that she would, but the uncertainty was hard to bear. The voting would end at eight o'clock and the results would be announced at ten. How was she going to get through the hours until then?

At six she went indoors, had a shower and ate a light supper. Then she watched *Brief Encounter* on television, which for once was shown in English with Maloslavian subtitles. The film seemed dated but she enjoyed it nevertheless and for a short time it took her mind off the referendum. When it ended there was still another hour to go until the results were announced and it was taken up by a quiz show. She turned the television sound off and tried to read again, nervously looking at the screen from time to time. Then at last it was ten o'clock. Her heart thumped as she turned up the sound. An announcer appeared pointing to a chart. She breathed a sigh of relief. Eighty per cent had voted 'No'! A group of men seated round a table began to analyse the results, stressing that there had been a very low turnout; only fifty per cent of the population had taken the trouble to vote. She didn't care. She was going home! She switched the television off and at that moment Ivan Petrovitch walked into the room.

'Your Royal Highness, this is a sad day for Maloslavia,' he said.

'I'm not sure that it is. It's simply proved that the people don't want the return of the monarchy and that having a queen won't solve Maloslavia's problems. The Government must do that.'

'Then you are determined to return to England? You might be able still to do some valuable work here?'

'I've made up my mind. It would be extremely difficult, and probably dangerous, for me to stay here in the present circumstances. I've done what you asked of me but now it's over. I can be of far more use in England trying to alert the public to the problems of your orphanages and to raise money for them.'

'Perhaps you are right,' said Ivan Petrovitch reluctantly. 'And now I suppose you wish me to arrange for your return to London?'

'I would like to go back immediately. Would it be possible to book a flight for me for tomorrow?'

'I will give instructions for the arrangements to be made, but before you leave you will have to sign a document renouncing the throne for yourself and your heirs. Are you prepared to do this?'

'With pleasure,' said Katy smiling.

Chapter 12

Ivan Petrovitch watched Katy sign the lengthy deed of abdication after only a perfunctory glance.

'You must read the document carefully, Your Royal Highness,' he said. 'You are renouncing your right to the throne for yourself and your heirs and I am afraid you may live to regret it.'

'I don't think so,' said Katy. 'A monarchy won't solve Maloslavia's problems - only a government free of corruption can do that. But I'm grateful for the time I've spent in this country.'

Ivan Petrovitch bowed and kissed Katy's hand. 'Thank you for all you have done for us. I wish you every success in the future,' he said.

Dimitar added his good wishes and told her that Elena Slobovna was unable to come to say goodbye because a brain tumour had been diagnosed and she was seriously ill.

'I'm so sorry,' said Katy. 'Please tell her I'm thinking of her.'

Ivan Petrovitch and Dimitar bowed and departed, leaving her to finish her packing. She was closing her suitcases when Boyana rushed into the room in tears.

'I don't want you go,' she sobbed. 'They send me back to kitchen!'

'No they won't,' said Katy. 'I've told the Manager how well you've worked for me and recommended that they give you a better job.'

She handed Boyana several trouser suits, skirts and sweaters. 'These are for you.'

Boyana's eyes shone at the sight of the expensive designer clothes. She hugged Katy, laughing and crying at the same time.

'*Spasob*! Thank you! God bless!' she cried and was picking up

Katy's heavy cases when Yurek appeared and took them from her.

'Time to go,' he said.

Katy kissed Boyana and went with him down to the car that was waiting outside the hotel. She was wearing jeans and a tee shirt and wore dark glasses. As she had hoped nobody recognized her when she arrived at the airport and walked across the tarmac towards the Ilyushin that would take her to Vienna. Yurek looked at her sadly.

'What will you do now?' she asked.

'With you it was good but I don't want to be bodyguard again. I go back to farm,' he said, shaking her hand with a firm grip.

'Goodbye, good luck and thank you for everything,' she said and went up the steps into the plane.

* * *

Never had Katy been so pleased to see Disraeli Road. When she left the trees had been bare; now they were in full leaf but otherwise everything looked the same. She ran up the steps of No. 32 and unlocked the door of her flat, thankful that her tenant had left a few weeks earlier. Her four months in Maloslavia had seemed an eternity, yet now that she was back everything suddenly came into perspective and she felt as though she'd never been away. She sat on the sofa, happy to be home, and began to make plans. Her priority was the campaign to help the orphanage. Father Serge could advise her on how to proceed and if by any chance Vladimir was still in London she was sure he would help her. Although he hadn't replied to her letter she decided she would phone him in a few days time. But she also had to find a job that she really liked and that suited her talents. On top of all this, her flat was badly in need of redecorating and she wanted to find time to study drawing and painting again.

She woke the next morning full of energy and during the week that followed she cleared out the flat, bought decorating materials in Homebase and repainted the sitting room in a pale apricot shade. Then she went to the Putney School of Art and enrolled for the autumn term. She also visited two employment agencies and scanned job advertisements. To her surprise, she found something that appealed to her quite quickly. A monthly magazine for amateur artists was looking for a features writer and she applied. She was afraid that she hadn't the right qualifications as she had never written for a magazine before, but her experience with *The English Countrywoman* and her work as an amateur painter stood her in good stead and after two interviews she was told they were going to employ her. The job sounded interesting and she would only be working four days a week which would give her time to paint. The pay wasn't particularly good, but as she owned her flat and had no mortgage she could just about manage. Anyway, it was more important to be free to do what she enjoyed than to slave away for long hours in return for a high salary.

One evening she heard on the news that the Maloslavian government had collapsed and Ivan Petrovitch had resigned. The new prime minister was trying with little success to stitch together another coalition but Katy didn't pay much attention. As far as she was concerned, apart from helping the orphanage, her Maloslavian interlude was over and she was thankful that her return to London had passed almost unnoticed in the media. There had been no mention of her on television or the radio and *The Times* was the only paper to print a short paragraph saying that after losing a referendum to restore the monarchy, Princess Katerina had renounced her rights to the throne and returned to Britain. There were no photographs of her in the paper and she was relieved that nobody recognized her when she walked around Putney, deliberately scruffy in old jeans.

A couple of weeks went by and she still hadn't contacted Vladimir. Telling herself that he was probably already on Mount Athos, she finally plucked up courage and phoned. To her surprise he answered and sounded pleased to hear her voice.

'Katy! I was hoping you'd return. It's good to hear from you.'

'You too! I was afraid you'd be in the monastery or else away on holiday.'

'I've already had my holiday. I rented a cottage in Cornwall for a week with Kiril and Marina. Let's meet tomorrow afternoon in the usual café. I've got a lot to tell you.'

Before setting out the following day, Katy paid more attention than usual to her hair and makeup and put on her favourite green suède jacket. She told herself she was silly to worry about her appearance as Vladimir, the future monk, wouldn't even notice what she was wearing. She wished she hadn't sent him the letter with the quotation from Shakespeare but at the time she'd been homesick and it had seemed a good idea. He'd probably been embarrassed by it and she wondered what she would say to him.

When she arrived at the café he was already at a table by the window and on seeing him she was immediately reassured.

'Hullo Katy,' he said with a smile that lit up his whole face.

She sat down beside him and he put his arms round her in a bear-like hug. She looked at him in surprise.

'What have you done with your beard?'

'I shaved it off! It made me look too much like a monk!' he said with a grin.

'But I thought you *wanted* to be a monk!'

He laughed at her bewildered expression. 'Well, it's not going to happen.'

'I'm pleased to hear it! I never felt it was right for you.'

He explained how the monks had rejected him because of his disability.

'It was a great blow at the time. Then I began to see I'd been pursuing a vocation that didn't really exist: it was all in my head and if I hadn't read all those books on monasticism it would never have happened. Anyway, Father Serge suggested that I do a course at the Institute for Orthodox Christian Studies in Cambridge and when I thought it over I realized it was a good idea. I applied too late for this year but I'm going next year in October and I'll live there until I get my degree. I won't become a priest but I can be a lecturer on Orthodoxy.'

'It sounds just the right thing for you,' said Katy, who was surprised by the change in him.

'Now I want to hear all about Maloslavia,' Vladimir continued, pouring out the tea. 'I read that you'd lost the referendum.'

Katy related her experiences in Svyatograd - the corruption, the poverty, the riots and the referendum. He was horrified to learn about her mysterious illness and the assassination attempt.

'I knew things would be difficult but I'd no idea you'd be in such danger. I don't believe a word of their story about Salmonella - it must have been poison and you were lucky to survive. What about the boy who tried to shoot you?'

'He was apparently forced into it by members of the People's Struggle Pioneers. He's in prison awaiting trial and they say he's sorry for what he's done. He's only sixteen and I gather he was badly beaten up by the police when they interrogated him.'

'What a barbaric country! I read they want to join the EU but they've got to clean up their act a lot before that happens!'

'There's something else I want to talk about,' said Katy and she told him about the orphanage - the dilapidated building, the poor food and the disabled children who were bedridden because of the shortage of wheelchairs. 'There aren't enough trained staff either, although the nuns are devoted to the children and do the best they can. I promised them that even if I didn't become Queen, I'd do everything I could to assist them and I mean to keep my promise. Will you help me?'

'It's a splendid idea,' said Vladimir. 'Of course I'll help. Why don't you come to supper on Thursday and we'll work out a plan of campaign.'

Katy went home happy. It had been good to see Vladimir again and to know he wasn't going to enter a monastery after all. Suddenly it occurred to her that never in her life had she felt so much at ease with anyone.

* * *

A powerful aroma of cooking greeted Katy when she arrived at Vladimir's flat on Thursday evening.

'Something smells good,' she said, handing him a bottle of *Moulin à Vent*.

'It's a Ukrainian recipe - a kind of lamb stew with prunes. Let's have a Kir.'

Over the apéritif, Katy told Vladimir about her new job. 'I'm starting on Monday and I'm looking forward to it. It'll be a welcome change to be working on something creative instead of that ghastly *English Countrywoman*.'

'It's much more suitable.'

'How's the bookshop?'

'Okay. I like the work but I'll only be there until October next year when I start my studies.'

He went into the kitchen. 'Can I help?' called Katy.

'Not really, but I'll show you how to cook buckwheat to go with the stew.'

Vladimir browned the grains of buckwheat in butter in a saucepan. Then he added water and salt and stirred the grains with a wooden spoon.

'Watching you actually makes me want to learn to cook well!' said Katy.

Vladimir smiled. 'I can teach you! It's easier than Maloslavian!'

They opened the bottle of wine and sat down to eat, chatting about this and that, one subject leading to another, and Katy thought to herself, 'I never get bored talking to him and he makes me feel so happy.'

'I've cooked a Russian cheesecake for the dessert,' said Vladimir when they had finished eating the stew. You'll like it.'

They both had two helpings, after which Katy insisted on doing the washing up while Vladimir made coffee. As they were drinking it, sitting on the sofa, he said, looking down at his cup,

'I'm sorry I didn't answer your letter. It arrived when I was feeling depressed - just after I'd heard my application to join the monastery had been rejected. But it meant a lot to me. That was a beautiful quotation from the Shakespeare sonnet. Is that what you really think?'

'You know it is,' she said. Their eyes met and for a moment they were silent. Then he looked away and hurriedly began talking about the orphanage.

'We must think about your plans for St Paraskeva's. I've been making some enquiries. If we tried to set up a fully registered charity it would take a long time and we want to get help to the children as soon as possible. Why don't we ask Father Serge on Sunday if we can hold a fund raising meeting in the church hall, followed by a buffet supper?'

'That's a great idea,' said Katy. 'I'll organize the food and talk about what I saw at the orphanage. And you must speak too.'

'But I've got nothing to say!'

'Yes, you have! You can speak about how you caught polio in Maloslavia because there was no proper vaccination scheme and how you'd never have learnt to walk if you'd stayed there.'

'Well, I'm not very keen on the idea but I'll do it. And after the meeting we can organize other things too - a bring-and-buy sale, concerts by the church choir. I'm sure people will come.'

'We must contact the press, the BBC and medical charities working in Eastern Europe to see what support and publicity we can get.'

'I'm not sure about that,' said Vladimir. 'You say you want to be plain Katy Brennan again. But if we start involving the national press and the media, it's bound to get out that you're Princess Katerina who lost the referendum and we'll be hounded by reporters and photographers. Would you like that?'

'No! I'd hate it. But what can we do?'

'I don't think we need to do things on such a big scale at the beginning. Between now and Christmas we can probably raise enough money for the wheelchairs and medecines by holding fund raising events at St Nicholas. It doesn't matter too much if the parishioners know you're a princess. They'll be sensible about it and if the local press get hold of it that'll probably be all right too. Let's keep it low key and see how it goes.'

'You're right,' said Katy. 'I want to forget all this Royal Highness stuff.'

'A doctor ought to go to Svyatograd to examine the children and draw up lists of the most urgent things,' said Vladimir. 'Dr Stenkovic who goes to St Nicolas was brought up in Maloslavia. Perhaps he'd agree to take two weeks off to visit the orphanage at his own expense. He knows how bad the conditions are there and he might be pleased to help. He could let us know what the priorities are and when we've collected enough money, we could hire a van and drive to Maloslavia with the equipment. Marina and Kiril could come with us.'

'That would be the cheapest way of doing it.'

'Kiril drives. You could share the driving between the two of you and I'd be navigator and interpreter. It would be fun. Do you think you could drive a van?'

'I can drive a car, but I've never driven a van! I might need some lessons and perhaps I'd have to pass another test. I'll look into it.'

It was nearly midnight. 'I must go or I'll miss the last train,' she said, glancing at her watch.

Vladimir helped her into her jacket and followed her to the door.

'Thank you for the delicious meal,' she said and was wondering how to say goodbye when he settled the matter and kissed her lightly on the lips. She smiled and gently touched his cheek, then quickly turned and hurried to the Underground.

* * *

The following Sunday morning Katy went to St Nicolas for the first time since she returned to London. She was pleased to be back, standing beside Vladimir, listening to the choir's magnificent singing. As she had been to confession the day before and fasted from midnight, she received communion with him and said a prayer of thanks that she had come back safely from Maloslavia. After the service they asked if they could talk to Father Serge and he invited them both to have lunch.

'Marfa Andreevna has cooked stuffed cabbage today. We would be delighted if you joined us. We want to hear all about your experiences in Svyatograd, Katerina.'

The meal took a long time. The stuffed cabbage was extremely filling and was followed by a cheesecake similar to the one that Vladimir had made. Katy found it difficult to eat because Father Serge kept asking her questions about Maloslavia. He was shocked to learn of the conditions in the orphanage.

'I had no idea the situation was so bad.' he said.

'That's one of the reasons I wanted to see you,' said Katy and she told him about her plans to help St Paraskeva's.

'Vladimir is going to work with me and we wondered if you'd let us use the church hall for a meeting to launch the project and afterwards for fund-raising events - perhaps a concert by the choir, a bring and buy sale and coffee mornings.'

'And we also thought you might be able to persuade Dr Stenkovic to go to Maloslavia to examine the children and see what are the most urgent needs,' interrupted Vladimir.

'This is a splendid idea!' said Father Serge. 'I shall be happy to assist you in any way I can and I am sure the members of our congregation will support you. When were you thinking of holding the opening meeting?'

'A lot of people will be away in July and August,' said Katy. 'What about September?'

'Would the first Saturday in September suit you?'

'That would be ideal,' said Katy. 'We'll start making plans right away.' She was excited. Her project was going ahead, Vladimir was going to help her and together they'd make a success of it.

Father Serge smiled. 'So Katerina, your attempt to become Queen will not have been in vain. With God's help, some good may come out of it after all!'

Chapter 13

Katy and Vladimir were eating a supper of sweet and sour pork and for the first time since they became friends, she found it difficult to know how to behave with him. They'd got into the habit of meeting at his flat one or two evenings a week or at weekends to work on the orphanage project and afterwards they usually ate a pizza or a Chinese take-away. While they discussed plans, they argued, laughed and joked as easily as in the past but when they stopped working, neither of them seemed to know what to say. Katy tried to talk about subjects that had interested them before, but her voice sounded unnatural and Vladimir's replies were curt and dismissive making her feel stupid. On several occasions she'd glanced up from the computer keyboard and caught him looking at her intently but when she met his gaze he turned away.

'I've been looking at my photos of the orphanage,' she said. 'I thought we could use some of them for our campaign posters.'

'Sounds a good idea. I'll look at them later,' Vladimir smiled at her and then quickly looked down at his plate.

There was a long pause. Then Katy said, 'I don't think I can do all the catering for the buffet supper after the meeting. I thought I'd make an appeal at the church for people to contribute food.'

'You shouldn't have much trouble in finding helpers. There are some very good cooks at St Nicolas,' said Vladimir, helping himself to more rice.

They were silent again and Katy tried desperately to think of something to talk about. At last she said,

'How's the bookshop?'

'Okay. Business is rather slack though and it's just as well I'll be leaving in September next year. I wonder whether Patrick will bother to replace me and I'm afraid he may have to close down. Small bookshops can't compete with big chains that can afford to make special offers - three paperbacks for the price of two.'

'But your job's safe until you go to Cambridge?'

'Oh yes. Patrick knows I'm leaving and he won't close the shop before then unless things get really bad. At the moment we manage to tick over thanks to the students from Imperial College ordering their textbooks from us.'

They finished their meal and she helped him wash up. Neither of them spoke until he said suddenly,

'*Cyrano de Bergerac* with Gérard Dépardieu is on near here at a small cinema that shows foreign films. Why don't we go and see it on Saturday evening?'

It was the first time he'd suggested an outing since her return to London.

'I'd like that very much. I read it when I was an *au pair* in Paris. The last act always makes me cry.'

Vladimir laughed. 'Well, we'd better take a supply of Kleenex!'

* * *

On Saturday they met outside Earls Court Underground. Katy wondered what sort of mood Vladimir would be in but he seemed very relaxed.

'There's a sushi bar near the cinema,' he said. 'We've got time for a quick meal there before the film.'

It was starting to rain but Katy had an umbrella which she held over them both as they walked down the street.

'Thanks! That's sweet of you,' he said, smiling at her.

The sushi bar was small and brightly lit with a large television on the wall showing Japanese publicity clips. Customers sat on stools in front of a carousel and helped themselves to the dishes as they passed in front of them. Katy and Vladimir liked the prawn sushi best.

'Isn't this fun? I've often walked past this place and I've always wanted to try it,' said Vladimir. 'Now tell me about your job.'

'It's hectic but I'm enjoying it. I interview promising young painters and I have to attend exhibitions and prepare articles on them. I've never written much before so I'm pleased to find I can actually do it and that my boss seems satisfied.'

'That's great. You deserve it after all you went through in Maloslavia.'

They both had six plates of sushi washed down with green tea, and then it was time to go. Vladimir asked for the bill. 'This is on me,' he said firmly as he took out his wallet and Katy realized that he'd be offended if she suggested paying her share.

The tiny art house cinema was next door to the sushi bar but they arrived with only five minutes to spare and there were very few places left . They found two at the far end of a row but to reach them they had to squeeze past the people in the other seats which was difficult for Vladimir. They sat down and stowed his crutches away just as *Cyrano de Bergerac* began.

The film exceeded Katy's expectations and she was caught up in the atmosphere of seventeenth century France - the gorgeous clothes, the Parisian theatre full of noisy, ill-mannered spectators and the savage battle scenes. She found Dépardieu very moving in the tragic final scene under the falling autumn leaves in the convent courtyard. When Roxane cried out *Vous m'aimiez!* and the dying Cyrano whispered *Non, non, mon cher amour, je ne vous aimais pas!* tears rolled down her cheeks. Vladimir glanced at her and took her hand which made her feel ridiculously happy for it was the first time he'd done such a thing.

As they came out of the cinema, she said 'If only Cyrano had told Roxane he loved her. He had such wit and courage and he was a wonderful poet. She wouldn't have cared about his big nose.'

She hoped Vladimir would understand what she was trying to tell him but he only said,

'Yes, but then there wouldn't have been a play would there? You're such a romantic! Life isn't like that.'

'It could be!' she murmured, feeling crushed by his attitude.

They went down the street in an uncomfortable silence. It was raining heavily now and Katy held the umbrella over them both. Vladimir seemed tired and walked more slowly than usual, taking care not to slip on the wet pavement. When they reached the Underground, he turned towards her.

'I shan't be at church tomorrow. I've got to go to Redhill and have lunch with my parents.' He gave her a quick peck on the cheek. 'Goodnight,' he said brusquely and with a sudden burst of energy he moved away, swinging himself along rapidly on his crutches.

The kiss on the cheek was like a slap in the face for Katy. Lately Vladimir had been kissing her on the lips when they said goodbye and she couldn't understand his change of attitude. She knew that she was in love with him and she had the impression that he felt the same way but because of his disability was afraid, like Cyrano, to show his feelings . By talking about Roxane's attitude to Cyrano's ugly nose, she'd hoped he'd see that his handicap wasn't a problem for her but he hadn't understood and had been cynical.

In the middle of the night she woke up and for a long time she lay thinking about him. Their friendship had been uncomplicated before she went away. Sex hadn't come into it and they'd both known it wasn't on the cards - he intended to become a monk and she was about to go to Maloslavia. She'd been attracted to him but she was content to have a platonic relationship after her unhappy love affair with Richard and there'd been a barrier round their friendship that couldn't be crossed. Now it no longer existed. They couldn't go back to where they were before she went away but they didn't seem to know how to go forward. She wanted to tell him that his disability made no difference to the way she felt, that she loved everything about him - his courage, his humour, his kindness and his intelligence - but she was afraid of misinterpreting his attitude and destroying their friendship by a clumsy move. 'I'll find the right moment to say something,' she thought and fell asleep again.

* * *

Vladimir returned to his flat, unlocked the door and sat down in the kitchen, resting his elbows on the table. He'd understood very well what Katy had been trying to tell him when she'd said Roxane wouldn't have cared about Cyrano's big nose and he'd wanted to put his arms round her and kiss her on the lips. Instead he'd been cynical and called her a romantic. Why? Even when he first met her, although he thought he was called to be a monk, he'd been bowled over by her quirky charm. He'd struggled to suppress his feelings and told himself he was being foolish - that she was going away and probably wouldn't return. Then, after his application to the monastery was refused he'd been overjoyed to receive her letter and he'd hoped she'd come back. Well, now she was back and he was in love with her. He sometimes thought she had feelings for him too but was she just being kind? He longed to make love to her but how would she react when she saw his wasted legs? Every time he decided to tell her how he felt, the thought of his callipers and crutches stopped him. How could he hope a girl like Katy would want him?

He got out of bed the next day in a black mood. He didn't want to have lunch with his parents because there would almost certainly be an interrogation by his mother. She was glad that he was at last going to embark on a course of study in Cambridge but she still kept nagging him to find a girlfriend and 'settle down' as she put it. He hadn't told her about Katy for he knew that she would immediately jump to conclusions and imagine the two of them standing in St Nicolas Church with bridal crowns held over their heads. He just hoped that she hadn't decided to invite a girl to lunch for his inspection as she sometimes did.

He was feeling so fed up that he couldn't face the Underground stairs and went by taxi to Victoria Station. He couldn't afford it but what the hell? He bought a ticket to Redhill which was only a thirty minute journey but, as often happened, the train crawled along and took fifty minutes. He passed the time looking out of the window, thinking about Katy. What he'd said about her being a romantic wasn't so terrible after all. Next time he saw her they'd carry on as usual and then one day he'd somehow find the courage to tell her how he felt. After all, he'd as much right to be happy as the next man.

The train had reached Redhill. Vladimir got out and made his way slowly down the steep steps to the station entrance where his mother, Magda Grodno, was waiting with the car. She was an attractive fair-haired woman in her late forties who bore a striking resemblance to him.

'Vladimir, darling, it's lovely to see you,' she said in Maloslavian, kissing him on both cheeks. 'It's been such a long time. You should come down more often.'

'I've been very busy,' he said getting into the car.

'You must tell me what you've been up to.' She put the key in the ignition and turned to him. 'I've invited Helen and Geoffrey Carter from No. 17 to lunch and they're bringing their daughter, Sally. I don't think you've met her but she's recently finished secretarial college and got a job with a firm of solicitors in London. She's sharing a flat with three other girls in Earls Court very near you so it would be good for her to get to know you.'

Vladimir didn't agree. 'I was hoping we'd have a nice lunch - just the three of us,' he said.

'It *will* be nice. You'll like Sally. She's a very sweet girl and you need to meet more people of your own age.'

He sighed. 'Mum, I do know people of my age.'

'Well, there's never any harm in widening your circle of friends.'

The Grodnos lived in a small detached house in Hillborough Close, a quiet cul-de-sac only five minutes walk from the station. While Magda put the car in the garage Vladimir went indoors. His father, Igor, a tall, bear-like man, came out of the kitchen and hugged him. He was proud of his son and of his decision to enter higher education. Although he'd tried to conceal it, he'd always found it hard to cope with his disappointment at his son's disability and the fact that he couldn't share his own passion for football and other sports. He'd also been worried that Vladimir would be content to go on working in the bookshop for the rest of his life when he was capable of so much more.

'Good to see you Vasya, come and have a drink,' he said.

They went into the sitting room where cocktail titbits were already laid out on the coffee table. Igor poured two dry Martinis and they sat down to discuss Vladimir's study plans but had hardly begun when the doorbell rang.

'The Carters are always punctual,' said Igor and the expression on his face made it clear that he had taken no part in inviting them.

Magda came in and introduced her three guests to Vladimir who rose to greet them.

'I think you've met Mr and Mrs Carter before haven't you?' she said.

'Oh, yes!' said Helen Carter, a plump florid-faced woman with wiry grey hair, 'I saw you when I came round to talk to your mother about the Women's Institute jumble sale. I've heard so much about you.'

Vladimir smiled and muttered something appropriate.

'And this is Sally who's just moved into a flat near you,' said Magda.

'Hullo,' said Sally, awkwardly shaking Vladimir's hand. She was plump like her mother - an insipid girl with round, pale blue eyes, a pink-and-white complexion and straggly blonde hair, wearing a full-skirted floral Liberty print dress that accentuated her rather large behind. In her mother's eyes Sally was a typical English rose but she knew this wasn't true and she was painfully shy with boys. She seemed embarrassed by Vladimir's crutches and carefully averted her gaze from his legs.

They all sat down and Helen Carter began relating to Magda the saga of the conservatory extension that they were having built.

'My dear, it's a nightmare! A friend of ours recommended this firm but they've been an absolute disaster. They started work three months ago and there's no sign of them finishing. They disappear for days on end and there's dust and rubble everywhere.'

Having exhausted the subject of the conservatory, she gossiped at considerable length about the other inhabitants of Hillborough Close until Magda escaped to the kitchen. In the meantime Igor was talking about his work for the BBC World Service with Geoffrey Carter, a man of few words and limited interests, who was in insurance in the City, but they had little in common and the conversation flagged.

Vladimir, half listening to what was being said, wondered how his parents could put up with such boring company. He knew that he had a tendency to be judgemental, but be couldn't help thinking the Carters banal and terribly middle class. He was trying to talk to Sally but it was hard work. He sensed that she felt uncomfortable with him because of his disability and although he was trying to put her at her ease it wasn't working. She spoke too quickly in nervous little gasps and seemed afraid of simply being herself. Like so many people, she had an irritating way of being extra careful of what she said to him, treating him as if he were different from the rest of humanity.

'Are you pleased with your flat?' he asked.

'Oh, yes! It's awfully nice. I couldn't have afforded a place like that on my own. There are four of us there - Jenny, Fiona, Charlotte and me. It's fun but we have a lot of arguments about housework and stuff. I'm the only one that seems to do the washing up!'

'Oh dear!'

'Mummy says it's very near where you live. You must come and see it. but...' she looked embarrassed, 'there's a few steps. Perhaps you couldn't manage...'

'I can manage steps if I take my time,' Vladimir said dryly. 'But I'm rather busy just now.'

'Oh, you've got a job then?' said Sally.

'Of course!' he snapped. 'There's nothing wrong with my brain. I work in a bookshop but in the autumn next year I'm going to Cambridge to study Orthodox theology.'

'Gosh! You must be clever. Are you very religious?'

'I have moments of doubt like most people but I do have faith.'

'I don't think I believe in God any more. I was confirmed at school but I've stopped going to church now.'

Vladimir didn't want to get involved in a religious discussion with Sally and was wondering how to change the subject when, to his relief, his mother came in and said that lunch was ready.

They went into the dining room where she had prepared a meal of Maloslavian specialities. The Carters commented politely on the food, saying it was 'delicious' and 'interesting' but they gave the impression that they would be happier with roast beef and Yorkshire pudding.

'Helen's a splendid cook,' said Geoffrey Carter, sliding the pieces of lamb off his kebab skewer, 'but she only does English dishes, don't you darling?'

'They're all recipes my mother taught me,' said Helen with a satisfied smile. 'I'm afraid I'm not really into foreign food, although of course,' she added hurriedly, 'it's absolutely delicious and I love trying new things.'

Vladimir was irritated. 'My mother's a great cook too. She likes giving guests specialities from Maloslavia but she also does English food brilliantly. She's taught me.'

'You can *cook*?' cried Helen in a patronizing tone and Geoffrey, who was sitting next to him, patted him on the shoulder and said 'You'll be a catch for any girl if you can cook. Most of them can't even boil an egg these days!'

Magda was embarrassed by the turn the conversation was taking. She collected the plates and went to fetch the dessert. While they were eating it, the Carters talked non-stop about their forthcoming holiday in Scotland and in the sitting room, over coffee, they showed the Grodnos their photos - many of them out of focus - of a trip the previous year to North Wales.

It was nearly four o'clock and Vladimir stood up. 'I'm afraid I'll have to be getting back to London.'

'Oh, Sally's got to go back too,' said Helen. 'You can travel together. It'll be nice for you to have company!'

Magda fetched the car keys. 'I'll drive you both to the station.'

Vladimir was dismayed. The thought of having to travel all the way to Earls Court with Sally was more than he could bear but he couldn't see any escape. He knew she was a nice enough girl, but she was desperately dull and rather silly and he was sure that she'd talk all the way to Victoria. He said goodbye to Mr and Mrs Carter and asked his father whether he could take the *The Sunday Times* with him. Igor put the various sections of the newspaper in a plastic bag and handed it to him. Hopefully this would stem the flow of chatter during the train journey.

'Sorry we didn't have more time to talk,' said his father at the front door giving him a meaning look.

'I'm sorry too, Dad. Let's meet for lunch one day next week.'

'That would be great. I'll ring you.' Igor gave his son a hug. 'I'm very proud of you. You know that don't you?'

Vladimir grinned. 'Of course I do! Thanks Dad.'

He got into the car where Sally was already waiting and they set off for the station, arriving on the platform just as the Victoria train pulled in. Magda kissed him goodbye.

'I wish I'd been able to hear more about your studies,' she said.

'Whose fault's that?' he thought, but aloud he said 'Goodbye Mum. Thanks for a lovely lunch.' He climbed into the train, turned and waved to her.

He sat down by the window, facing Sally and drew *The Sunday Times* out of the bag. He noticed that she hadn't brought any reading material with her and, so as to make it clear he didn't want to chatter, he quickly handed her the colour magazine and the travel supplement.

'Would you like a bit of *The Sunday Times* to read?' he said and buried himself in the Culture section.

Sally looked hurt. She took the papers and began half heartedly turning over the pages without really studying their contents. It wasn't that she particularly wanted to talk to Vladimir and anyway she couldn't think of anything interesting to say to him. It was simply that she realized that she bored him in the same way that she bored most of the men she met. She wished she could be like Jenny and Fiona who always had a flock of boyfriends hanging round the flat and who seemed able to flirt with them so easily. They wouldn't have been embarrassed by Vladimir's disability - they'd have laughed and joked and been perfectly comfortable with him.

She forced herself to read an article in the colour supplement about Bangladesh and then, as the train stopped at East Croydon, Vladimir looked up.

'I've finished with the Culture section. Shall we do a swop?'

'Oh yes,' she said quickly, handing him the supplements he'd given her and pretending she'd managed to finish them. She took the Culture section and scanned the ballet and theatre reviews, vowing that in future she would buy a quality Sunday newspaper and read some serious books. She wasn't much of a reader, but if she cultivated her mind men might find her less boring. She'd try to lose weight too and she'd get rid of the floral cotton dresses that Fiona said weren't sexy.

Although Vladimir appeared to be deep in his paper, he was in fact lost in thought. He knew that without actually being rude, he wasn't being particularly friendly towards Sally. The poor girl meant well but he sensed that she'd been stifled by an over-possessive mother and she didn't seem to have any personality of her own. He realized how lucky he was to have met someone like Katy even if, for the moment at any rate, she was just a friend. There was absolutely no comparison between her and Sally. Why on earth had his mother thought she would be a suitable girlfriend for him?

The train drew into Victoria and they got out and made their way to the Underground.

'Will you be all right on the stairs?' Sally asked timidly.

'Yes, I can manage. I've often done it before,' said Vladimir. It was sweet of her to be concerned about him even though, apart from Katy, he didn't like people fussing and wanting to help.

At Earls Court they shook hands and went their separate ways.

'Goodbye, it was nice meeting you,' said Sally. 'Perhaps you'd like to come round one evening. I'm sure the other girls would love to see you.'

Vladimir smiled politely. 'That's very kind of you but I'm afraid I'm rather busy at the moment. A friend of mine is organizing a project to raise money for an orphanage in Maloslavia and I'm helping her with it. We spend most of our free time on it.'

Sally's face fell. 'Oh, yes of course. Well never mind. Another time perhaps.'

Vladimir went home, thankful that Sunday was nearly over and hoping that he'd tactfully managed to give Sally the message that he wasn't interested in getting to know her better. He picked up the phone and rang Katy.

'Katy? I've had a brilliant idea for the posters. Can you come round to supper tomorrow?'

Chapter 14

Interest in the orphanage project exceeded Katy's and Vladimir's expectations and there was a large crowd for the opening meeting on the first Saturday in September. Although they'd made great efforts to publicize it, they hadn't expected that many people from outside the church would come but journalists and photographers from the local press turned up as well as a number of visitors from all over London. The church hall of St Nicolas was decorated with Maloslavian flags and handwoven kilims in vivid colours. and a large screen had been fixed on the wall behind the platform. Father Serge sat at a table in front of it with Katy, Vladimir and Dr Stenkovic. Every available seat was taken and latecomers had to stand.

Father Serge made a speech of welcome and introduced Katy who spoke about her visit to the orphanage and the bad conditions in which the children lived. She was followed by Vladimir who described how he had caught polio in Svyatograd at the age of two and, after receiving only very basic treatment, had been brought to England. Although he'd never spoken in public before, he knew instinctively how to hold the attention of his listeners and his eloquence and striking Slav features made a great impression.

Dr Stenkovic had agreed without hesitation to visit the orphanage at his own expense during August and had come back with a list of the equipment and drugs that were needed most urgently. After Vladimir finished talking, he made a short speech introducing the video that he had made covering a day in the life of St Paraskeva's. When it had finished, he appealed to the audience.

'I spoke to many of the children at the orphanage,' he said 'and I was moved by their courage and cheerfulness. I have made a list of the items that are most urgently needed and tonight we are launching our campaign to help them. Various fund-raising events are planned for this autumn and we are confident you will want to give them your support.'

Father Serge made a short closing speech and invited everyone to move into the adjoining room where there was a buffet supper and a box for donations to the orphanage. 'As members of the Maloslavian Orthodox Church,' he said, 'it is our duty to help relieve poverty and hardship in our Motherland in any way that we can. May God bless our endeavours.'

There was loud applause and people began to move towards the next room where a long table was laden with Maloslavian specialities. Marfa Andreevna stood behind a large urn distributing bowls of borsch and Kiril and Marina went round with plates of stuffed vine leaves and cabbage pies. Vladimir sat behind the table pouring out glasses of wine and Katy served the drinks from a tray, forcing her way through the crowd with difficulty. When she returned for another batch of glasses a slim girl with shoulder-length dark hair in an elegant black trouser suit was talking to Vladimir.

'Katy, this is Charlotte,' said Vladimir. 'She shares a flat with Sally who's the daughter of some friends of my parents.'

'Hullo,' said Charlotte with a patronizing smile.

'A lot of people haven't been served,' said Vladimir. 'Perhaps Charlotte can help with the drinks.'

'I'd love to,' said Charlotte. 'I'm used to this sort of thing.'

'Thank you,' said Katy trying not to sound reluctant. Charlotte had a condescending manner which made her feel awkward. She would have preferred to continue serving the drinks alone but Vladimir handed them each a tray of glasses and they circulated among the guests.

When everyone had been served and they had returned their empty trays to the table, Charlotte found two unoccupied chairs in a corner of the room and motioned Katy to sit down with her.

'I'm *so* glad I came,' she said. 'I hadn't intended to but Sally has a dreadful cold so I'm replacing her. She met Vladimir at his parents' house and heard all about your project. She wanted to be here very much. Poor Sally! Have you met her?'

'No, I'm afraid not.'

'We work in the same office. I'm a solicitor and Sally's a secretary - but not mine, fortunately! Actually, between you and me, she's not very good and I've rather taken her under my wing. She was looking for somewhere to live and we wanted a fourth girl to share our flat so she moved in with us.'

'How nice.'

'What about you?' asked Charlotte. 'After such an exciting time in Maloslavia it must seem very dull for you here but it's *so* good of you to want to help those poor children.'

'It isn't dull! I'm glad to have an opportunity to work for the children and Vladimir's been a great help.'

'He's so courageous isn't he? Standing up in front of an audience and talking about his disability! How did you get to know him?'

'We met when I was being received into the Orthodox Church.'

'Really? How interesting. I'm afraid I'm not religious but I'd love to hear more about it. You must both come round to dinner one evening and meet the other girls. Jenny and Fiona are art students and they're great fun.'

'That would be nice,' said Katy untruthfully. She knew she was probably being unfair but she had the impression that Charlotte was pushy and that she was interrogating her. Perhaps it was because of her permanent smile which failed to reach her inscrutable dark eyes. She rose and began collecting some empty glasses.

'People are leaving. I'd better start clearing up,' she said.

'Can I do anything else?' asked Charlotte.

'No, thanks. I can manage now. It was good to meet you. Thank you for coming.'

'It was a pleasure and I think your work for the orphanage is really *heroic*! I'll see you again soon I hope. I'll phone Vladimir and fix a date for you both to come round.'

Charlotte moved over to the buffet table where she remained deep in conversation with Vladimir for a few minutes, gazing at him intently. Katy saw her take his hand, holding it rather longer than for a formal handshake and then she went out, still smiling.

The evening was a great success. A considerable sum of money was raised and many people came forward offering to help with other fund-raising events. Katy and Vladimir sat down to count the takings which amounted to nearly five hundred pounds. The cheques and cash were locked away in the church safe and Katy said that on Monday she'd take the money to the bank and pay it into the special account which they'd set up for the orphanage. She knew she ought to be pleased at her success but instead she felt deflated. Vladimir, on the other hand, was exuberant.

As they walked towards Earls Court Underground, he said 'Wasn't it nice of Charlotte to turn up like that? I'd never met her before but I'm glad she came and not Sally! She reminds me of Sofia - she's got the same black hair and huge dark eyes. She wants us to come to dinner one evening.'

'Yes, she told me,' said Katy in a dull voice and they continued walking in silence. When they reached the station, Vladimir said,

'That was a great evening. You did jolly well, Katy!'

'Do you think so?' she said. He kissed her and she went down the steps of the Underground wondering why she felt so miserable.

* * *

Two weeks later she was having supper in Vladimir's flat when he suddenly said 'Charlotte phoned yesterday. She's invited us to dinner on Tuesday. Is that okay for you?'

'Yes, I suppose so,' said Katy trying to sound enthusiastic.

'The other girls will be there too - I don't know Jenny or Fiona but I met Sally at my parents. She's a bit silly but quite sweet.'

'Quite a hen party!'

'Don't be such a downer. It'll be fun!'

Katy wasn't so sure. On the way back, she thought about Charlotte and her supercilious ever-present smile. It was obvious that Vladimir found her attractive. He'd said that she reminded him of Sofia. Men often went for the same type of woman time after time, and he seemed to be drawn to black-haired, dark-eyed girls. Supposing he had an affair with Charlotte? She was extremely self-confident and probably wouldn't hesitate to make the first move, something that Katy was afraid to do. And yet perhaps that was what Vladimir needed. She sensed he was very conscious of his disability and maybe he wanted a girl to take the initiative.

Feeling thoroughly dissatisfied with herself, Katy reached home and went straight to the bathroom mirror. She studied herself critically. She wasn't bad-looking - her red hair was striking at any rate - but since her return to London she'd let herself go and started putting on weight again. It had been such a relief not to have to be well groomed at all times that she'd stopped dieting and begun eating all her favourite foods. Now her waistbands were too tight and once or twice she'd been embarrassed to discover that a blouse button had popped open revealing her bra. How could she compete with the elegant, sexy Charlotte?

'I may be the former heir to the Maloslavian throne, but I'm really just a slob,' she thought.

On Tuesday she felt more optimistic. At lunchtime she went to the hairdresser and on the way back to the office she noticed a striking emerald green linen tunic in the window of a small Italian boutique. She went in and tried it on. It suited her and although it was rather expensive she couldn't resist buying it. When she returned from the office, she put it on over a pair of well-cut black trousers and set off for the dinner party, her confidence restored.

Charlotte came to the door and greeted her effusively.

'Katy darling, how lovely to see you! I'm so glad you could make it.'

Katy handed her a bottle of wine.

'Thank you *so* much. You really shouldn't have!' cried Charlotte and led the way into the sitting room where a plump blond-haired girl was sitting on the sofa with Vladimir.

'This is Sally and, of course, I don't need to introduce Vladimir.'

Sally smiled nervously and Vladimir stood up and kissed Katy on the cheek.

'Jenny and Fiona will be joining us for the apéritif,' said Charlotte, 'but they can't stay for dinner because they're going to a party at the art school.' She handed Katy a Kir and disappeared into the kitchen leaving Katy, Vladimir and Sally sitting in an uncomfortable silence. Finally Sally broke the ice.

'I was so sorry I couldn't come to the launch of your orphanage project. I had an awful cold, but Charlotte says it was brilliant.'

'I don't know about that,' said Katy. 'But money's coming in and a lot of people have offered to help.'

'Gosh! You are clever!'

At this point Jenny and Fiona appeared and introduced themselves. They looked like art students. Jenny was a tall, rather buxom girl with long mousy hair in a multitude of thin African-style plaits and was dressed in a floor-length cotton patchwork skirt and a sloppy mohair sweater. Fiona was small, with cropped hair and a silver stud on her chin and was wearing a denim jacket and mini-skirt with thick black tights.

'Hi!' said Jenny. 'It's great to see you. What a shame we can't stay longer. We're going to a party at the St Martin's School of Art. We're students there.'

'We were talking to Vladimir before you arrived and he told us that you paint too,' said Fiona.

'I've never done a full-time art course, but I go to classes in oil painting at the Putney School of Art. I'm only an amateur though,' said Katy.

'It isn't important whether you're an amateur or a so-called professional,' said Jenny. 'All that matters is whether you've got talent and Vladimir says you have.'

Katy warmed to Jenny and Fiona and felt they were on the same wavelength. They chatted about painting classes and materials and Jenny was interested to learn that Katy worked for an art magazine.

After they had been talking for some time, Katy noticed out of the corner of her eye that Sally had gone into the kitchen and Charlotte was installed on the sofa next to Vladimir, deep in conversation. She was wearing black velvet jeans and a black silk jersey top with a plunging neckline and she leant towards him, giving him an enticing glimpse of her breasts. Katy's heart sank. Charlotte was laughing and devouring Vladimir with her eyes and he seemed to be enjoying the attention. Katy wondered what she was saying to him.

'Did you see that amazing exhibition of Russian art at the Royal Academy?' Fiona asked her.

'No, I don't think I was in London then,' said Katy distractedly. She had lost interest in the conversation and although she told herself it was silly to be jealous, her attention was fixed on Charlotte and Vladimir.

'There were some fabulous Kandinskys and Chagalls. Many of them hadn't ever left Russia before,' Fiona persisted.

'Really?'

'Well,' said Jenny looking at her watch, 'we'd better make a move. It was good to meet you and I'd love to see your paintings some time.'

''Bye, lovely to meet you,' said Fiona and went out with Jenny, nearly colliding with Sally who rushed in looking hot and flustered. Charlotte stood up and Sally whispered something in her ear.

'Oh God, what have you done now?' said Charlotte and the two of them went into the kitchen leaving Katy and Vladimir alone. He smiled sheepishly and they drifted into a stiff, formal conversation about her job and his work at the bookshop, interspersed with awkward silences. After a few minutes, to Katy's relief, Charlotte returned and said that dinner was served.

They went into a small adjoining room which was dominated by an over-large oval dining table covered by a white cutwork embroidered cloth and set with crystal glasses and an exquisite Crown Derby dinner service. There was a centre-piece consisting of a pewter bowl of pink and white roses.

'Vladimir brought the roses. Aren't they beautiful?' said Charlotte.

Katy suppressed the thought that Vladimir never bought her roses and tried to convince herself that flowers and gifts were unnecessary in a relationship such as theirs. Aloud she said,

'What a lovely dinner service!'

'My mother gave it to me when I moved here,' said Charlotte. 'It belonged to my grandmother and it's been in the family for years. And the glasses were a graduation present. I do like a dinner table to be civilized even if it's only for four people, don't you? Do sit down.'

She placed Vladimir at one of the long sides of the table and after bringing in the first course, she seated herself opposite him, indicating that Katy and Sally should sit at the far ends of the table.

'This is delicious,' said Vladimir, spreading chicken liver paté on thin slices of toast.

'I made it myself,' said Charlotte. 'I'm so glad you like it. I love cooking!'

'I enjoy it too!' said Vladimir and he and Charlotte launched into an enthusiastic discussion of recipes and cooking equipment. Katy tried to join in but they ignored her and as she was so far away from Sally that it was impossible to talk to her without shouting across the other two, she remained silent.

'Do you cook?' said Charlotte suddenly turning to Katy with one of her patronizing smiles.

'Yes. In fact I've been going to cookery classes since I returned from Maloslavia and Vladimir's taught me some recipes as well.'

'Katy made a jolly good Shepherd's Pie the other day,' said Vladimir.

'How nice,' said Charlotte as she collected the plates and went out. Sally smiled at Katy and said, 'I'm afraid I'm an awful fool in the kitchen. I burn things or let them boil over. I once tried to make a cake and it sank in the middle and my pastry's like leather.'

'You learn by experience,' said Vladimir.

Charlotte returned with a large Le Creuset casserole. '*Estouffade de Boeuf à la Provençale,*' she announced as she served the food, 'and I've made a simple *purée de pommes de terre* as an accompaniment. It sets off the richness of the beef. Vladimir could you take care of the wine for me?'

Vladimir opened a bottle of *Château Neuf du Pape* and they began to eat the stew.

There was no doubt that Charlotte was an accomplished cook. The meat in a thick red wine sauce was succulent and blended well with the mashed potatoes. It was followed by a green salad and a selection of French cheeses and then Charlotte rose, saying 'Now for the *pièce de resistance*!'

She returned from the kitchen with a moulded dessert - a shimmering frothy mountain of cream and eggs, over which flowed a stream of raspberry sauce.

'It's a *Bavarois à la vanille*,' she said. 'I made it yesterday because I was afraid it might not set, but luckily it did.'

'Gosh,' said Sally and Vladimir and Katy looked in silent admiration as Charlotte plunged a spoon into the dessert and divided it among the four of them.

'This is absolutely wonderful,' said Vladimir. 'You really are a Cordon Bleu chef!'

Charlotte accepted the praise with a satisfied smile. 'As a matter of fact, I worked in a restaurant for a time.'

'You did?'

'Yes, when I came down from Cambridge,. Although I had a First in Classics, I couldn't find any other job. I loved it but Mummy was furious, so I ended up going to law school to please her.'

' I'm going to Cambridge next year to study Orthodox theology.'

'Sally told me. It sounds absolutely fascinating. You'll love it there. And which university did you go to?' said Charlotte turning towards Katy.

'I didn't.'

'*Really*? That's rather unusual these days!'

'My A levels weren't good enough. I'm afraid I'm not very academic. I'm more interested in the arts. I enjoy painting and I write a bit in my present job.'

'Oh, so you do *have* a job in addition to collecting money for the orphans?'

'Well, I have to earn my living like everyone else,' said Katy coldly. 'I work for a magazine for amateur artists.'

'What fun! You must let me have a copy,' said Charlotte losing interest. She turned to face Vladimir again and began telling him how she could put him in touch with friends of hers in Cambridge.

Sally came in with a tray and served coffee. Then she drew up a chair and subjected Katy to a flood of office gossip. Sally was a bore, but at least she meant well and for a short time her banal chatter was a soothing antidote to Charlotte's patronizing behaviour. But when she had finished her coffee, Katy stood up and glanced at Charlotte and Vladimir who had moved back to the sofa and were laughing heartily at something. She looked at her watch and said 'It's getting late. I've got to make an early start in the morning.'

'You're not leaving already?' cried Charlotte getting up. Vladimir looked uncomfortable but made no move to go.

'I'm afraid so. I've got a deadline tomorrow. Thank you very much for a delicious dinner.'

'It was so nice to get to know you better. I'll fetch your things.'

Katy fixed Vladimir with a stony look. He blew her a kiss, but she turned away, went into the hall and put on her coat. Charlotte gave her a peck on the cheek and opened the door, saying 'Safe journey home! See you soon!'

'Not if I can help it,' thought Katy as she walked to the Underground, feeling angry that Charlotte had succeeded in humiliating her.

Chapter 15

Vladimir was unusually busy during the weeks following Charlotte's dinner. His boss at *The Bookworm*, Patrick Donovan, suddenly decided that he would hold some book signing events with promising young authors to take place after the shop closed for the evening. Planning the series involved Vladimir in a great deal of extra work and he had to stay late on several occasions and cancel arrangements he'd made with Katy. One evening, when he finally reached home after a lengthy discussion with Patrick, Charlotte phoned.

'Vladimir! I've been trying to ring you all evening.'

'I had to work late. We're organizing some events with new writers.'

'How exciting! I suppose you're very busy then?'

'I am at the moment.'

'What a pity. I was wondering whether you were free tomorrow night?'

Vladimir hesitated. What was she playing at? He knew that girls of Charlotte's sort were usually put off by the sight of his crutches and yet here she was asking if he was free tomorrow night! And he had to admit that since her dinner party, he'd been unable to forget the glimpse of her breasts peeping out from the low necked silk tee shirt when she'd leant towards him on the sofa. Why not accept? After all, it was just a pleasant evening out, nothing more, and he needn't mention it to Katy.

'Well, I suppose I could be free as I worked so late tonight,' he said.

'Great! One of Daddy's clients has given him two free tickets for *La Traviata* at Covent Garden for tomorrow. Daddy hates opera and he's let me have them. I wondered if you'd like to come.'

He caught his breath. He'd always wanted to go to Covent Garden but the prices were sky high and it was such a hassle trying to get tickets that he'd never got round to it. It was an opportunity not to be missed.

'I'd like to very much. Thank you.'

'They're really good seats in the front row of the Stalls Circle and Jonas Kaufmann and Anna Netrebko are singing. They're the great stars of opera at the moment.'

Vladimir thought quickly. If Charlotte was inviting him to Covent Garden, he ought to take her to a restaurant before the performance.

'Can I invite you to dinner before the opera?'

'That would be lovely,' said Charlotte in a tone that implied that she'd expected it. 'The best thing would be to eat at the Amphitheatre Restaurant in the Opera House. It's much the simplest solution and the food's good. Can you book a a table? Let's say for six o'clock because the performance starts at seven thirty. I'll meet you in the foyer.'

'Fine! I'll ring the restaurant in the morning.'

Vladimir put the phone down, still unable to believe what had happened. He would never have dreamt of asking Charlotte out because he would have been afraid she'd refuse like so many others and in any case he wouldn't want to hurt Katy. Now Charlotte had made the first move herself and although he felt a bit guilty, he'd accepted.

* * *

The following morning Vladimir had just reached *The Bookworm* when Katy rang.

'Hi Vladimir! You haven't forgotten about this evening I hope?'

Damn! He had forgotten. He'd been so busy at the shop that it had completely slipped his memory that it was Katy's birthday and she'd said she'd invite him for a special meal in her flat, cooking the new recipes she'd learnt at her cookery class. He hadn't even sent her a card or bought her a present.

'Happy birthday! I'm awfully sorry. I'm afraid I'd completely forgotten it was today. It's been so hectic at *The Bookworm* what with planning all these book signings.'

'Never mind. But you are coming?'

'I'm afraid I can't now.'

'But I've made a wonderful dessert. You're not working late again are you?'

'Sort of.' He wasn't in the habit of lying and he hated doing it. Quickly he said 'Look, I'll make it up to you on Saturday. I'll take you out to dinner. After all, it's *me* that should be treating *you*. And I'll bring your present. Am I forgiven?'

'I'll forgive you this once. Don't work too hard.'

He was thankful to have escaped so easily. He sent her an electronic birthday card and turned his mind to his work and the plans for the evening at the opera. In order to get to Covent Garden by six he would have to leave the shop promptly at five thirty. There would be no time to change and he had come to work wearing his one good dark grey suit with a white shirt and the crimson Dior tie his mother had given him for his birthday. When he went across the road to the pub for a sandwich lunch, Steve remarked on his appearance.

'I say! You're looking very elegant all of a sudden! New girl friend?'

Vladimir was embarrassed. 'Not exactly.'

'Well you've obviously got a date. Have a good time!'

Vladimir left the shop at five thirty and took the Piccadilly Line to Covent Garden. The first train that came was so crowded he couldn't get in it and he had to wait for the next one. Although there was a lift at Covent Garden station, there were also a few stairs to be negotiated and it was already ten past six when he reached the foyer of the Opera House. Charlotte was waiting for him, wearing an expensive looking scarlet cashmere coat over a black dress. She seemed agitated.

'I was beginning to get worried.'

'I'm sorry I'm a bit late but the Underground was packed and I couldn't get in the first train.'

'We haven't much time. We have to take the escalator to reach the Amphitheatre Restaurant. Do you think you can manage that or should we take the lift for the handicapped?'

Vladimir winced. He told himself Charlotte was showing concern for his well-being but she sounded so patronizing.

'Of course we can take the escalator,' he said. 'I do it all the time.'

A waiter showed them to their table and handed them each a menu. Vladimir's heart sank when he saw the prices. He couldn't afford to eat in a restaurant of this type.

'What would you like?' he asked nervously.

Charlotte had already decided.

'I'd like the "London cured smoked salmon with green olive tapenade" to start and then Beef Wellington with a side dish of creamed spinach. When they serve the desserts during the interval, I'll have the "Fresh cut fruit platter."'

Oh God! She'd chosen the most expensive items on the menu and the wine would undoubtedly cost the earth. Vladimir scanned the menu to find the cheapest things he could order for himself. 'Cream of spicy plum tomato soup' perhaps, followed by 'Goat's cheese and roast pepper tortellini'? He was tempted not to order a dessert but it would look bad in such an up-market place so he decided to spoil himself and have Sticky Toffee Pudding.

He gave the order and the waiter brought the wine list.

'They have an excellent *Crozes Hermitage* here,' Charlotte said, and Vladimir ordered a bottle, inwardly groaning at the astronomical price.

'Have you been here often?' he said.

'Oh yes. An ex-boyfriend of mine used to bring me here a lot. He was an investment banker in the City and a great opera fan so we always dined here before a performance. He was such a lovely man but unfortunately he's moved to Tokyo.' Charlotte smiled nostalgically and buttered a roll. Then she said in a condescending tone, 'Don't you work in a *bookshop*?'

'Well, I manage the shop for the owner actually,' said Vladimir. 'But it's only for a few more months because in the autumn next year I'll be going to study Orthodox theology in Cambridge.'

'Oh, of course! You told me. What a wonderful experience for you! I suppose you're going to be a priest?'

'No, but I hope to be a lecturer in Orthodox theology.'

'I'm not very religious I'm afraid. I was confirmed at boarding school but I don't go to church now. It must be rather difficult for you being Orthodox. The services last for about three hours don't they and you have to stand all the time?'

Vladimir was irritated. Why was it that whenever he told people he was Orthodox and was going to study theology they invariably said in a self-righteous way that they weren't really religious? And why did they automatically assume he couldn't do things because he was disabled? He said 'A lot of people don't stay for the full three hours you know and anyway I don't have to stand. There are seats round the walls for the handicapped or the elderly. The Church is for everyone.'

Charlotte was silent. She broke off a piece of her bread roll and ate it slowly. Vladimir looked at her. The evening was not going very well. She was glamorous, sophisticated, accustomed to rich boyfriends and obviously had an expensive lifestyle. He knew he wasn't in her league and he wondered why on earth she'd asked him to accompany her to the opera. He had an uncomfortable feeling that she pitied him but also that she could be hard and manipulative. But her sensuality was intoxicating - the luxuriant blue-black hair cascading on her bare shoulders, her slender fingers capped with long scarlet nails - and once again he was acutely aware of her firm well rounded breasts beneath the tight fitting strapless black dress. He tried to steer the conversation away from religion and get back to the flirtatious way of talking they'd had at her dinner party. The problem was that this kind of chat didn't come naturally to him; it was she who had initiated it at the dinner but tonight she was behaving quite differently.

'That's a lovely dress. It suits you,' he said.

She smiled. 'I'm glad you like it. It's from Prada. Daddy gave it to me for my birthday.'

Vladimir had no idea what Prada was but before he could ask, Charlotte continued, 'We went to Rome for the weekend recently and Daddy took me to this heavenly boutique and let me decide which dress I wanted. It was so sweet of him.'

He had never been to Italy and couldn't afford to go but before she could ask him, as he feared she would, whether he knew Rome, the waiter arrived with the first course.

'This looks good,' he said and tasted the soup. As the menu had said, it was 'spicy' but he liked hot, highly seasoned food. He looked at Charlotte's smoked salmon, served in accordance with the current fashion, on a plain white square plate. The portion seemed small to him but she said that it was 'exquisite.'

Conversation during dinner was strained. He tried asking her what she enjoyed doing in her spare time and felt discouraged when she told him that she played tennis a lot and often went jogging before breakfast. She loved dancing at an 'exclusive little club' she knew and on Sundays she usually had lunch with a group of friends at The Ivy. He was painfully aware that he was precluded from all these activities by his disability or his lack of funds and he hesitated when she wanted to know what his hobbies were.

'Well, I read a great deal, I like cooking and listening to music and I go to the cinema sometimes,' he said and added hurriedly, 'Of course, I'm spending a lot of time at the moment helping Katy with her orphanage project.' It was a perfectly reasonable answer but, although he knew it was silly of him, he couldn't help feeling inadequate.

'Of *course*!' said Charlotte. 'I'd forgotten about the orphanage. Dear Katy! It's so noble of her!'

He detected a note of sarcasm in her voice.

'Katy's an exceptional person,' he said curtly.

'I'm sure she is, but now I think we'd better go and take our places. I'm afraid we'll have to take the escalator again. We'll come back here in the interval for the dessert.'

It was a new experience for Vladimir to be sitting in the Stalls Circle at Covent Garden, and although Charlotte did make him feel slightly awkward he was very excited at the thought of seeing *La Traviata*. It was his favorite opera and he'd often listened to it on CDs but he'd never dreamt of actually watching it on the stage. The conductor arrived, the overture was played and the red velvet curtains rose on an animated gathering of men in tailcoats and women in the crinolines of the 1860s. Kaufmann as Alfredo, brandishing his champagne glass, sang his first aria with passion and then knelt adoringly at the feet of Violetta. He looked so young and vulnerable and his concern when she was seized with a fit of coughing was touching. Vladimir was gripped by his anger and despair when at the end of Act 2 he discovered that Violetta had left him and when the curtain fell for the interval he turned to Charlotte with shining eyes.

'It's wonderful isn't it? Kaufmann has a great voice but he's a splendid actor too and Violetta is really beautiful.'

Charlotte smiled condescendingly. 'I thought you'd enjoy it. *La Traviata* is a good choice for a first visit to the opera. Let's go back to the restaurant for our puds.'

They returned to their table and found the desserts they had ordered waiting for them A few minutes later the waiter appeared with coffee and the bill. Vladimir looked at it quickly and gave it back to him with his debit card. £115! He would have to live on rice and spaghetti until the end of the month if he wasn't going to be overdrawn. And how could he afford to take Katy out on Saturday as he'd promised? He'd have to try and cook something for her at home.

'You look worried,' said Charlotte. 'What's wrong?'

'Nothing,' said Vladimir quickly. 'I was just thinking about Alfredo and Violetta. What a tragic story.'

'Most operas *are* tragic. We must hurry. That was the bell for the second half.'

Vladimir found it difficult to concentrate during Act 3. He was sorry he'd had to let Katy down on her birthday and he was beginning to wish he hadn't accepted Charlotte's invitation. She was so patronizing and he realized that she'd probably asked him to the opera at the last minute because she couldn't find anyone else but he pushed the idea out of his mind, telling himself firmly that he was fortunate to be at Covent Garden with an attractive girl.

In Act 4 his thoughts ceased to wander and he was deeply moved when Alfredo and the dying Violetta were reunited. Instinctively he took Charlotte's hand and was humiliated when she quickly snatched it away. He stared blankly at the stage until the curtain fell and the opera house was drowned in wave after wave of applause. Although he felt completely deflated, he forced himself to clap and even to call 'Bravo!' when Jonas Kaufmann and Anna Netrebko appeared. Charlotte applauded in a ladylike fashion and smiled indulgently at his display of enthusiasm.

'I'm glad you enjoyed it,' she said. 'It was quite the best *Traviata* I've seen. Kaufmann is the perfect Latin lover isn't he?'

'I suppose so,' said Vladimir, bending to retrieve his crutches from under his seat.

They made their way out of the Opera House and Charlotte pushed her way through the crowds looking for a taxi.

'We can take the Underground from Covent Garden. It's a direct line to Earls Court,' said Vladimir. He didn't want to end up paying a fortune for a taxi.

'No, a cab will be much easier for you. I don't often take the Underground. It's *so* sordid.'

He was tired and he didn't have the courage to disagree with her. After a few minutes Charlotte succeeded in hailing a taxi and they got in. The traffic wasn't too bad but practically every light they came to was red and Vladimir listened gloomily to the meter's frantic whirring. When they reached Charlotte's flat, he said 'Thank you very much for the opera. It was a wonderful experience.'

'Yes, it *was* fun wasn't it? Thanks for dinner. 'Bye.'

Charlotte gave him a quick kiss on the cheek, got out and hurried up the steps to her front door. The taxi continued to Vladimir's building two streets away and he paid the driver. Twenty-one pounds! And on top of that he had to give a two pound tip. He didn't know how he'd get through the rest of the month. Perhaps Patrick would give him an advance on his salary. After all, he'd been working late for the book signing events without any overtime pay. He decided to phone him in the morning.

* * *

The dinner Vladimir had cooked for Katy was going remarkably well and she hadn't reproached him for standing her up on her birthday. They were eating the *canard à l'orange* that he'd prepared from a complicated recipe in *Mastering the Art of French Cooking* and she gave him a radiant smile and told him it was delicious. Looking at her, he thought how beautiful she was this evening - like a Burne Jones painting, with her mane of red-gold hair, pale skin and a green dress that matched her eyes. Why not ask her to spend the night with him? But he was afraid any such attempt would be disastrous and destroy their precious friendship.

Katy was laughing and telling him about a visit she'd paid the day before to her old office at *The English Countrywoman*.

'Can you imagine it? Mrs Cartwright actually rang me and asked to see me! She'd read an article in the paper about our project to help the orphanage and said she wanted to make a donation on behalf of *The Countrywoman*. She received me like royalty.'

'Well, you *are* royalty don't forget!'

'I *was*. I'd almost forgotten! Mrs Cartwright was all smiles and she said "I'm afraid I misjudged you, Miss Brennan. I had no idea what your plans were when you left *The Countrywoman* and it was such a pleasant surprise to learn that you are devoting your life to the service of those less fortunate than yourself!" I felt as though I was being given a good conduct prize by the Headmistress! Anyway, the important thing is that she's given us a cheque for five hundred pounds.'

'That's fantastic! The biggest donation we've had so far! I'll go and make coffee.'

Vladimir went into the kitchen. Katy sat down on the sofa and picked up *The Times* which was on the drinks table in front of her. She glanced at it and her eye fell on the programme of *La Traviata* which had been concealed by the newspaper. She looked at the date on it - the twenty-fifth October, her birthday! So he'd lied to her!

He limped back into the room, laden with cups, coffee pot, milk, sugar and chocolate biscuits but she made no move to take the tray from him as she usually did. He put it on the table and sat beside her. She looked at him and he saw the hurt disbelief in her eyes.

'So you went to the opera on my birthday? That must have been nice for you!'

'I'm sorry. I should have told you. It was a last minute thing. You see, Charlotte had been given these tickets and she asked me to go with her. It was difficult to refuse.'

'*Charlotte!* But it was my birthday! I'd prepared a meal for you.'

'I know. I feel really ashamed. But it was a chance to go to Covent Garden and *La Traviata* is my favourite opera. I'm afraid I was tempted. And I have tried to make it up to you tonight.'

'If you'd explained all that to me I'd have done my best to understand but you lied to me! You can keep your present!'

Katy got up and threw her birthday present - a copy of *A Hero of Our Time* - on the floor. She picked up her coat and bag.

'Please don't go,' said Vladimir. He tried to stand up but his crutches were on the other side of the room and his legs refused to obey him. He flopped back on the sofa and helplessly watched her go, slamming the front door behind her.

* * *

He spent a wretched Sunday trying every few minutes to phone Katy but only got her answering machine. In the end he left her a message saying how sorry he was that he'd hurt her, that he should never have lied to her but he hoped they were still friends. She didn't ring back.

He couldn't bring himself to go to church and hobbled around in his pyjamas, not bothering to wash or shave. For lunch, he toyed with the remaining scraps of duck, sitting amidst the remains of last night's dinner and drank a bottle of beer which lulled him into a doze. When he woke it was four o'clock and he made himself some tea and tried to think logically about what had happened. The real mistake he'd made was not to tell Katy at the outset that he'd had an invitation to the opera. If he'd told her the truth, and at the same time invited her to dinner on Saturday, she would probably have understood. She might not have liked it but she was a reasonable person and, after all, he was perfectly entitled to go out with other girls. He wasn't engaged to her. It was cowardly to have lied to her but he'd done it to avoid hurting her and he couldn't help feeling that she'd over-reacted. She'd thrown his present on the floor like a spoilt child and hadn't even thanked him for the elaborate dinner which he'd spent all day preparing. Although, because of his disability, he found it difficult to believe that anybody could be in love with him, it seemed that she was, which explained her jealous outburst. He began to feel more optimistic; after a few days she'd forgive and forget and in any case she couldn't do without his help on her orphanage project. He got dressed and went out to buy *The Observer*.

On Monday evening he was shopping in his local supermarket when he noticed Charlotte at the cheese counter. She was testing a Camembert for ripeness and had her back to him. He came up behind her and touched her on the arm.

'Hullo,' he said smiling.

She turned round with a look that unnerved him. Was that repulsion in her eyes? No, he told himself firmly; he was just being hyper-sensitive about his disability again.

'Oh, hullo,' she said in an off-hand voice. 'They don't know how to store cheeses here. They're at quite the wrong temperature. How can they ripen in these conditions?'

'I've no idea. I suppose they don't have enough space,' Vladimir said not knowing what answer to give.

'Well it's the last time I buy cheese here. In future I'll go to Harrods.'

Vladimir hurriedly changed the subject. 'Thank you again for the opera. I did enjoy it.'

'Yes, it was good wasn't it? I'm glad you were able to help me out. It's practically impossible to find anyone who's free at the last minute isn't it?'

It was the ultimate put-down, but in spite of it he had a sudden irrational urge to invite her out. He knew she wasn't interested in him but for a brief moment he wanted to *make* her interested.

'It was such fun the other evening,' he said. 'We should do it again. Would you like to have dinner with me next week?'

Charlotte gave him a supercilious smile. 'It's very sweet of you but I'm afraid that won't be possible. I had a lovely surprise this morning. My old boyfriend rang me from Tokyo. He's coming back to London and he wants us to get back together again. I won't have a minute to myself! 'Bye!'

She replaced the Camembert on the counter and pushed her heavily laden trolley towards the checkout, balancing precariously on her six-inch heels.

Vladimir watched her go. The bitch! It was unlike him, but he hoped she'd sprain her ankle.

Chapter 16

Katy was swamped in paperwork. Since the meeting to launch the orphanage project there had been a continuous stream of letters and she usually spent two nights a week and Sunday afternoons with Vladimir at his flat dealing with correspondence and doing the accounts. Various fund raising events were held at St Nicolas - a bring and buy sale, concerts, coffee mornings and a Maloslavian dinner - and although Katy and Vladimir were not actually responsible for running these activities, they had to oversee the arrangements which involved a good deal of work. Moreover, because it had leaked out that she was the former heir to the throne of Maloslavia, she was interviewed on local radio and this took up more time.

. As a result of the opera incident, their friendship had gone back to a rather formal working relationship. Two or three days after Vladimir's message apologizing, Katy decided she would phone him because she had previously arranged to meet him to work on the accounts. She was sorry she'd thrown his birthday present on the floor and although she was hurt that he'd lied to her, because she was in love with him she'd forgiven him. But when she rang him, her pride prevented her showing her real feelings and she simply thanked him in a cold voice for his message, saying that she appreciated his help with the orphanage. Now when they met they talked about nothing but the project and although they still ate supper after they'd finished their work the atmosphere was distinctly chilly.

Vladimir's encounter with Charlotte in the supermarket had reawakened the feelings of rejection that he'd struggled against all his life. He knew she'd never been interested in him and cursed himself for accepting her invitation to the opera. What an idiot he'd been to invite her to have dinner! He hadn't really wanted to go out with her and he ought to have known she'd refuse. Women never wanted to be with him, but he had at least been under the impression that Katy was attracted to him. Now he'd blown that as well. He felt she was only staying in touch with him because she needed his help with the orphanage and he was too discouraged to try to get back to their former comfortable relationship.

One Sunday towards the end of November they had finished sorting a pile of letters in silence and Katy looked at him, searching for something to say.

'Before we know where we are it'll be Christmas again,' she said, aware that it was a banal remark.

'Yes. This year I'll have to go to my parents. They're expecting me and I can't let them down but it'll be pretty awful. They've invited the Carters from next door and Sally will be staying with them over the holiday too.'

'Will Charlotte be there?' said Katy on a sudden impulse.

'No, of course not,' said Vladimir. 'If you must know, she's back with her rich banker boyfriend from Tokyo and she's going to live with him. I bumped into Sally the other day and she told me Charlotte was moving out.'

'Good!' thought Katy. With Charlotte out of the picture perhaps Vladimir would invite her for Christmas with his parents. Her hopes were soon dashed.

'What are *you* doing for Christmas this year?' he said. 'You don't want to spend it by yourself.'

'Oh, I expect I'll think of something,' she said trying to hide her disappointment. Christmas in Vladimir's flat had been great fun, but this year, as so often in the past, it promised to be a dismal event.

* * *

At the beginning of December Katy received a letter from Emma who had been transferred to the Paris branch of the bank for which she worked. She wrote enthusiastically about her new job and the flat she'd rented in the Marais and invited Katy to stay with her over Christmas. Katy hesitated. She was upset that Vladimir wouldn't be spending the holiday with her and didn't much care what she did. Then she told herself not to be silly - the way things were she had no reason to expect that he'd invite her to meet his parents. Besides, it would be nice to see Paris again - she hadn't been there since she was an *au pair*. She wrote to Emma telling her she'd take Eurostar to the Gare du Nord on the twenty-third December, returning on the twenty-seventh. Emma replied suggesting that she bring Vladimir; she had a big flat and there was plenty of room. Although she knew that he wouldn't come, Katy couldn't resist asking him.

The day after she received Emma's reply, she broached the subject while she and Vladimir were having a break from the orphanage project accounts.

Trying to sound casual as she stirred her Nescafé, she said 'Emma's invited me to Paris for Christmas.'

'How nice! You should go.'

'I *am* going. On the twenty-third.'

'Well, I hope you have a lovely time.'

Nervously she said, 'Emma suggested you come with me. It would be fun.'

'You know I'm not free. I have to go to my parents.'

'Couldn't you see them after Christmas? You could go for the New Year.'

'Katy, I've told you that's not possible. And what would I do in Paris? There would be a lot of walking and I couldn't cope.'

'It wouldn't be any worse than London. You manage very well here. We'd take buses and go on a *bâteau mouche*. And Emma lives right in the centre of the city. We needn't walk a lot and there are cafés everywhere where you can sit if you're tired.'

'No!' said Vladimir. 'It's not going to happen. Now we must get on with the accounts.'

* * *

The twenty-second December was a Sunday and Katy went to the liturgy at St Nicolas. It was the last time she'd see Vladimir before she went to Paris the following day and when the service was over she looked at him, trying to gauge his mood. He smiled at her and suggested they went for coffee and a sandwich at their usual café.

'So you're off tomorrow?' he said.

'Yes, I'm taking Eurostar in the morning but I'll be back on the twenty-seventh.'

'Where does Emma live?'

'In the Marais. It's a lovely historic district right in the centre of the city.'

'Sounds interesting. I must see it some time,' he said.

Was he regretting his decision not to go with her?

'Well, you could have come with me,' she said.

'I know. But my parents would be so disappointed if I spent a second Christmas away from them.'

He sounded as if he were apologizing.

'I understand. It's difficult for you,' she said.

He took a small packet out of his pocket and gave it to her.

'This is my Christmas present. Why don't you open it now as you're going away?'

Katy removed the red and gold wrapping paper. Instead of the book she'd expected to find, there was a box containing a spray bottle of Nina Ricci's *l'Air du Temps*. She'd been sure that he'd opt for an impersonal present like a volume of poetry, but instead he'd given her perfume! She felt sorry that, confused by his recent attitude, she'd played for safety and bought him another book - Vladimir Nabokov's *Lectures on Russian Literature*. But she could always bring him back something more personal from Paris.

'Thank you so much,' she said. 'It was a lovely idea and it's my favourite perfume.'

She gave him his present. 'I'm afraid it's not as exciting as yours. I wasn't sure what to get you.'

But Vladimir was very pleased with the book.

'Nabokov is rather amusing on Dostoievsky. I'm going to enjoy this,' he said, smiling at her with his old warmth.

When they left the café, he took her hand and kissed her lightly on the lips - something he hadn't done for a while.

'Have a wonderful time, Katy, and I'll see you soon.'

'I hope you have a good Christmas with your parents,' she said and went down into the Underground feeling she could go to Paris with a light heart.

* * *

Katy arrived at the Gare du Nord at lunchtime. Emma was waiting on the platform and Katy suggested they have a meal at the brasserie *Terminus Nord* opposite the station. 'My treat,' she said.

They hadn't seen each other since Katy's departure for Maloslavia and Emma wanted to hear about her adventures in Svyatograd. She was horrified to learn of the attempted poisoning and the shooting.

'Thank goodness you lost the referendum!' she said.

'I couldn't wait to get back to England. But I want to know why you decided to come to Paris?'

'I was fed up with the rat race in London and when I got the chance of a transfer here I took it. So far everything's fine. You'll love my flat. It's only two minutes from the Place des Vosges. Why didn't Vladimir want to come?'

'He's got to spend Christmas with his parents.'

'Couldn't he have seen them at the New Year?'

'Apparently not. Things are a bit complicated. Now, what are we going to eat?'

They looked at the menu and gave the order. Then Emma said 'Is Vladimir going to be a monk?'

'No. The monastery wouldn't accept him because of his disability. But he'd realized anyway that it wasn't the right path for him.'

'Good! So are things going the way you want now?'

'Not really. We're working together to raise money for an orphanage I visited in Maloslavia but apart from that it's all rather confusing. I think we were more comfortable when he wanted to be a monk.'

'Oh, come on! It ought to be easier now.'

'No, it's not. I never know where I am with him. He seemed so happy to see me when I returned, but then sometimes he'd become cold and remote,' said Katy and she went on to tell Emma how on her birthday Vladimir had gone to Covent Garden with Charlotte.

'What a creep!' said Emma when she'd finished.

'What really made me angry was the fact that he'd lied. The next day he left a phone message apologizing and after a few days I rang him and we arranged to meet as usual to work on the orphanage project. I realized he'd been flattered by Charlotte's attention and the opportunity to go to Covent Garden but she'd only asked him at the last minute because she couldn't find anyone else. She isn't the slightest bit interested in him and she's moving in with a rich boyfriend who's just come back from Tokyo.'

'So where are you now?' asked Emma.

'We've got a good working relationship. That's all. Although yesterday when I saw him, he was more like his old self and I think he regretted not coming to Paris. He even gave me perfume for a Christmas present!'

'Well, that's something. But it sounds as if he doesn't know what he wants.'

'He doesn't show it but he's got a hang-up about his disability. I've tried to let him see it isn't a problem for me but he doesn't seem to understand.'

'I'm sure he does unless he's completely blind. You love him don't you?'

'He's the only man I've ever really loved.'

'Then you must try to bring things to a head soon. There's no point in wasting time on something that isn't going anywhere,' said Emma. 'If he can't make up his mind, you can come and work in Paris. That'll wake him up!'

'What would I do here?'

'A friend of mine, Jean-Paul, runs an art gallery on the Left Bank and his assistant will be leaving in May next year. You could take her place. You'll meet Jean-Paul tomorrow night because he's invited us for the *Reveillon*. You can ask him about it.'

Emma's flat in the rue de Béarn dated from the eighteenth century and had oak-beamed ceilings, a large fireplace and red tiled floors. The bathroom was small and there was only an 'American' kitchen, separated from the living room by a bar counter, but Emma, like Katy, wasn't much of a cook and wasn't bothered by the lack of space.

On Christmas Eve, they went food shopping in the rue Saint Antoine. They bought *foie gras* to take to Jean-Paul's dinner and Katy looked for a more personal gift for Vladimir. She didn't want to buy after-shave lotion or cologne because she felt they were too similar to the present he'd given her. Emma suggested a tie but Katy said she'd never seen Vladimir wear one and she thought that a leather wallet might be a good choice as the one he had was very shabby. In the Bazar de l'Hôtel de Ville they found an elegant black leather wallet with plenty of room for cards and identity papers and a zipped section for coins. It was rather expensive and although Katy could afford it, she wondered whether Vladimir would be embarrassed by such a gift, especially as she had already given him a book.

'Nonsense!' said Emma. 'After all, people bring back presents from trips abroad don't they?'

After lunch at a Jewish restaurant in the rue des Rosiers and a visit to the Musée Carnavalet they returned to the flat exhausted. They had tea and rested until it was time to change for the festivities which began with midnight mass at Saint Eustache. It seemed strange to Katy to be in a Catholic church again. She wished she could have been at St Nicolas with Vladimir but the choir and organ were magnificent and even Emma, who never went near a church, was impressed.

'I forgot to tell you that Jean-Paul is gay,' said Emma as they walked the short distance to his flat in the rue Montorgeuil after the mass.

'Where did you meet him?'

'He's the boyfriend of a colleague of mine and they've got an amazing flat crammed full of antiques. He's a wonderful cook.'

'Will there be many people there?'

'Just eight - Jean-Paul and Hervé, his boyfriend, you and me and two other couples - one straight and one gay.'

They had arrived at Jean-Paul's building and climbed four steep flights of stairs to reach his flat. The door was open and the smell of roasting turkey drifted on to the landing. Jean-Paul came out to greet them. He was about thirty, tall and thin, with long black hair in a pony tail and was dressed in a scarlet satin Russian shirt and tight black jeans. He hugged Katy and Emma enthusiastically.

'Emma *chérie* it is wonderful to see you. And this is Katy? I have heard a lot about you. Come and meet my friends.'

He led them into a large living room with silk-panelled walls and long gilt mirrors. The ancient parquet floor was highly polished and the ceiling was painted in *trompe l'oeil* giving the effect of a summer sky with delicate pink-tinged clouds. The floor-length curtains were of powder blue silk and antique vases and Grecian statues of young men were crammed into every available space. A table was laid at the far end of the room with an antique Sèvres porcelain dinner service and eighteenth century silver.

Jean-Paul introduced them to the other guests who were seated round a small table near the window drinking champagne. Hervé, his partner, was small and fair-haired with a huge moustache and wore a formal dark grey suit with a white shirt and a pink tie. Guy and François, dressed in silk brocade waistcoats and Byronic shirts, ran an antique shop and Marvin and Mary Beth were overweight ageing hippies from California on a year's sabbatical leave. Marvin was a poet who also taught creative writing and his wife was a romantic novelist. They both had shoulder length-grey hair and were dressed in flowing African kaftans and sandals.

'Hi there!' said Mary Beth as Emma and Katy sat down. 'I've met Emma before but I'm so happy to know *you*,' and she smiled at Katy, displaying a set of large nicotine stained teeth.

'How come you two lovely ladies aren't with your boyfriends at Christmas?' said Marvin.

'Because they have to be with their families,' snapped Emma and Katy thought, not for the first time, that some Americans had a disconcerting habit of asking personal questions to people they'd only just met.

'Is your boyfriend in England?' asked Mary Beth.

'Yes,' said Katy, deciding it was best to let Mary Beth think Vladimir was her boyfriend, even though 'friend' would be a more accurate description.

'Well, I think it's a real shame to let a beautiful girl like you come to Paris alone at Christmas. What's the guy thinking of?' said Marvin.

'I know just the right man for you,' said Mary Beth. 'I could introduce you to him.'

'The cheek of the woman! Why can't she mind her own business?' thought Katy but she managed to smile and say 'Thank you but I'm not looking for another relationship at present.'

Fortunately they were interrupted by the entry of Jean-Paul who asked them to take their places at the dinner table. They sat down and he brought in a large platter of oysters on a bed of crushed ice and seaweed.

Katy didn't like oysters: she knew that they were traditional Christmas fare in France but to her they were like lumps of jelly in seawater and she had once been ill after eating them. She swallowed them resolutely and had to admit they were better than she had expected. The roast turkey with chestnut purée which followed was more to her taste but the real highlight of the meal was the *bûche de Noel* - a delicious confection of meringue filled with chocolate mousse and decorated with thin chocolate leaves.

'Did you make the *bûche?*' she asked Jean-Paul who had seated her on his right. He laughed.

'*Mais non!* This kind of *bûche* is very complicated to make. I ordered it from Le Nôtre. You know Le Nôtre.'

'Yes, I know they are one of the best *patissiers* in Paris. When I was an *au pair* here the family I worked for sometimes ordered desserts from them for dinner parties. Unfortunately I never got to eat them because I had to have my meals with the children.'

'Such people are snobs. I expect their apartment was in the *seizième,* yes? But you should try living in Paris again. I think you would enjoy it. Emma told me that you paint?'

'Yes, but only in my spare time.'

'Perhaps Emma told you that I am looking for someone to work in my gallery?'

'She did say something about it.'

'Agnès, my assistant, is expecting her first child and she will be leaving at the end of May. She does not intend to return and I need a replacement. You would be ideal. You work for an art magazine and know about painting. And you are so charming and beautiful. You have that English *je ne sais quoi*. You would be an adornment to my gallery.'

Katy laughed. 'Flattery doesn't work with me.'

'But you will consider my proposal? I have friends in the Marais who could let you have a delightful apartment for a reasonable rent.'

'At present I'm very busy organizing a project to help an orphanage in Maloslavia but your offer is tempting. I'll think about it.'

'Well don't think about it too long. I need an answer by the end of March at the latest.'

* * *

On Christmas Day Katy and Emma woke at eleven o'clock feeling weak and tired. Katy had a bad headache and toyed with her breakfast. Then she was violently sick and went back to bed. She spent the rest of the day there, occasionally trying to swallow tea and toast and vowing that she would never touch oysters again. On the twenty-sixth, which was a normal working day in Paris, she felt much better and did some shopping before visiting the Rodin museum and on the twenty-seventh she was once again on Eurostar, returning to London.

'Do think about Jean-Paul's offer,' said Emma when they parted at the Gare du Nord. 'It would be fun if you came to live here.'

'I'm not making any promises. I don't feel up to making such an important decision at the moment,' said Katy.

She boarded the train and waved goodbye. She'd decided to spoil herself and travel first class but her pleasure at having an individual seat and being served a good lunch was marred by thoughts about the job in Paris. Should she leave London again? It was less than a year since she'd gone to Maloslavia and the idea of another move didn't appeal to her. She only wanted one thing - an intimate loving relationship with Vladimir. But if this didn't happen, what point was there in staying? If she told him about Jean-Paul's offer perhaps he would be afraid of losing her and try to stop her leaving. But it was more likely that he would be discouraged and let her go. She decided not to say anything to him for the time being and see how things progressed. After all, they planned to drive to Maloslavia in March with the equipment for the orphanage and a great deal could happen before then.

Two days later she met him for coffee and gave him the wallet she'd bought in Paris. He was touched.

'Katy, it's beautiful! You shouldn't have bought me such an expensive present. You'd already given me a book! I don't deserve it,' he said.

'Nonsense! I wanted to give it to you. Your old wallet was falling to bits.'

'Well, thank you so much. It's cheered me up after a ghastly Christmas.'

'Was it that bad?'

'It would have been all right if I could have just spent it with my parents but the Carters are dreadful bores and they monopolized the conversation. And Sally's sweet but rather silly. How was your Christmas?'

'All right. Paris was as beautiful as ever but the Christmas dinner was terribly rich and the oysters made me ill. Your dinner last year was much better.'

Vladimir beamed. 'Do you really think so?'

'Of course I do,' said Katy. 'Give me an English Christmas every time!'

Chapter 17

It seemed as if the Great Hungarian Plain would go on for ever. Katy had been driving in heavy rain along a muddy pot-holed road for two hours and apart from the occasional isolated farm or the odd flock of geese there were few signs of life. It was the beginning of April and, with Kiril as co-driver and Vladimir and Marina as navigators, she was at last on her way back to Maloslavia to deliver the equipment for the orphanage in a hired van crammed with medicines, toys, walking frames and lightweight wheelchairs. Vladimir was pouring over the map and grumbling because Marina, who had been navigating before lunch, had directed them on to a secondary country road which had taken them miles out of their way.

'Mezöhegyes is near the Romanian border,' said Vladimir. 'We must be nearly there but I can't see any turning that'll get us back on to the right road.'

'Well, I've got to have a rest,' said Katy. 'I'm fed up with driving in this rain.'

She pulled over to the side of the road and changed places with Kiril. 'You've landed us in a bloody awful mess,' he said to Marina. 'It'll be dark soon and we haven't the faintest idea where we are.'

'Mezöhegyes can't be far,' said Vladimir. 'Once we're back on the main road we'll be there in no time.'

Nobody felt like arguing with him and they drove on in silence. It was early evening and the many sweep-pole wells used for watering the herds of long-horned cattle loomed eerily in the rapidly fading light. Katy was dozing and woke with a start when Vladimir gave a shout.

'There's a turning to a place called Totkomlos. If we take it, we'll be able to join the main road after about ten kilometres and we'll be almost there'.

In less than half-an-hour they were in Mezöhegyes and began looking for somewhere to stay. They'd spent the two previous nights at cheap guesthouses but this little town appeared to have only one hotel in an old converted manor house attached to a farm which, according to the guidebook, had bred horses for the Hapsburgs.

'It's probably expensive,' said Vladimir.

'We're exhausted. We've been travelling for three days and I think we should spoil ourselves tonight,' said Katy. 'Our accommodation at the orphanage will be free and in Svyatograd the Hotel Franz Joseph will give us a discount because they know me.'

They parked their van in the courtyard of the pink and white stone manor and went in. The tourist season hadn't begun and the place was nearly empty. They were given two single rooms and one double on the first floor, each with a balcony, and when they'd showered and changed they went down to dinner. They were alone in the large dining room and the waiter treated them as honoured guests. Following his advice, they ordered goulash and apricot tart accompanied by a Hungarian red wine.

'You look very nice tonight,' said Vladimir smiling at Katy.

'Thank you,' she said, surprised at the compliment. She was wearing a low-necked Austrian dirndl dress made of dark green wool which she'd bought in Svyatograd, and she knew she looked her best in it but Vladimir didn't usually notice her clothes.

'Thank God we'll be in Maloslavia tomorrow,' said Kiril. 'It's been a hell of a slog hasn't it? Three solid days driving that bloody van!'

' Katy's never even driven a van before,' said Vladimir. 'She's done a great job. Kiril too. Let's drink their health.'

Marina and Vladimir raised their glasses. Katy blushed and looked down at her plate. When she raised her head she saw that Vladimir's eyes were fixed on her with a tender expression she hadn't seen for a long time. She returned his glance and said quickly,

'It's fun driving the van. I never thought I'd be capable of handling such a monster.'

'You're doing brilliantly,' said Kiril, helping himself to the goulash.

'Do you remember Maloslavia?' asked Marina, turning to Vladimir.

'Not really. I left when I was two. I've a vague memory of lying in a hospital bed in a darkened room with a lot of other children. I was crying because I wanted my mother.'

'I suppose you were too young to understand what was happening to you?' said Katy.

'I understood very well what was happening to me,' said Vladimir. 'The only positive thing about having polio was that I was able to come to England. If I hadn't caught it, I'd probably still be stuck in Maloslavia.'

He turned to Kiril. 'I must learn to drive,' he said. 'It would be good if I could have a car in Cambridge and I think my father would lend me the money.'

'It would make all the difference to your life,' said Kiril.

Katy's heart sank at the mention of Cambridge. In six months time Vladimir would be leaving London and she would hardly ever see him. She found it hard to join in the conversation during the rest of the meal and when the waiter brought coffee she drank hers quickly and got up.

'I'm tired. I'm going to bed,' she said.

Vladimir caught her by the arm and kissed her. 'It's wonderful what you're doing. This whole trip is due to your hard work.'

'Not really,' she said abruptly and went out.

* * *

When she reached her room she didn't feel like going to bed. It was only ten o'clock and she went out on to her white-columned balcony which overlooked a garden with apricot trees in full blossom. The rain had stopped and the sky was clear with a full moon. It wasn't cold and she sat at a small table admiring the view and wishing that Vladimir was sharing it with her. It had been hard for her on the two previous nights to say goodnight to him and see him go to his room while she went to hers.

Since her return from Christmas in Paris they'd slipped back into their old comfortable friendship. They'd been out several times to concerts and films but, apart from occasionally holding her hand in the cinema, things never went any further. She was beginning to wonder if they ever would, although tonight he'd been more attentive and affectionate than usual. Jean-Paul had written to her recently, asking if she intended to accept the offer of a job in his gallery as he needed to have an answer as soon as possible. She'd replied, saying she'd let him have her decision as soon as she returned from Maloslavia. She had never mentioned the possibility of working in Paris to Vladimir and she was hoping that this trip together would bring them closer. If when it was over there was no sign of their relationship developing, there was really nothing to keep her in London.

She thought about the plans they'd had when they first met. She'd said they were Quixotic and it was true - they'd been tilting at windmills. It had been unrealistic to think of being a monk on Mount Athos or Queen of Maloslavia! They'd both failed in their attempts but because of that they'd met up again. That was what was important. And whatever might happen, they'd done something worthwhile together helping the orphanage.

* * *

'We've made it!' said Kiril, as Katy drove up the bumpy, winding track that led to the orphanage. A few minutes later Sister Athanasia with a crowd of children ran out to greet them.

'You have arrived safely! The children have been looking forward to your coming and they have been asking about you, Your Royal Highness. They wanted so much to see you again.'

'I'm no longer a Royal Highness,' said Katy laughing. 'I'm just plain Katy Brennan and these are the other members of our team.'

She introduced Vladimir, Kiril and Marina and explained how they'd all been involved in the fund raising project.

'So, you left Maloslavia when you were two?' said Sister Athanasia to Vladimir.

'Yes, I left because I'd had polio and there was a scheme to bring disabled children to England for treatment.'

'But you speak Maloslavian?'

'Yes, I always used to speak it with my parents.'

'That is good. You will be able to talk to the children. Now I will show you your rooms in the guesthouse while the van is being unloaded. We have brought some helpers from the village to do that.'

Four young men began emptying the van and carrying the goods into the orphanage while Sister Athanasia led her visitors to a small building behind the convent. The rooms, on the first floor, were small and simply furnished. Each had one or two narrow beds, a chair, a table, a cupboard and an icon of the Virgin.

'There are toilets and showers at the end of the corridor,' said Sister Athanasia, 'but I am afraid there is only cold water.'

'That's fine,' said Marina, although she didn't relish the idea of a cold shower in the chilly spring weather.

'I hope you will be comfortable here,' said Sister Athanasia. 'Vespers will be celebrated in the chapel in half-an-hour if you would like to attend and afterwards there will be supper in the refectory. Tomorrow morning you will be able to see the children and they are going to sing for you.'

'I'm looking forward to that very much,' said Katy, going into her room. She flopped on the bed, exhausted after so much driving, but after about ten minutes decided she'd go to Vespers after all. She went down to the chapel where the nuns, in their black robes, were already assembled. Marina and Kiril were resting but Vladimir was there, sitting by the wall. Katy went over to him and he looked up and smiled. Towards the end of the service she sat down beside him and he took her hand. The nuns were singing the vesperal hymn and she thought how beautiful it was and how good it was to be there beside him.

When Vespers were over, they walked towards the refectory. Neither of them spoke, but it was a new kind of silence, warm and compatible, unlike the uncomfortable silences of the last few months.

* * *

A little girl with blonde plaits hurtled towards Katy in a wheelchair. She struggled to say something and Katy recognized Maria, who had cerebral palsy and had been bedridden on her previous visit.

Sister Athanasia came up to her. 'Maria is so pleased to have her own wheelchair for the first time. Until now she has had to spend most of her time in bed.'

Maria was trying hard to speak but she was too excited and the syllables tumbled out incoherently.

'Breathe deeply,' said Sister Athanasia in Maloslavian. 'Remember the words I taught you in English and try to say them slowly.'

Maria filled her lungs, puffing out her chest. As she expelled the air, she forced out the words 'Tank you for the chair!' and gave a triumphant smile. Tears welled up in Katy's eyes and she bent down and kissed her.

Several small boys surrounded Katy and Vladimir and talking excitedly, they led them to the oak panelled refectory on the ground floor of the orphanage where the tables had been removed and rows of chairs arranged. They were greeted by the Superior, Mother Ioanna, who invited them to take their seats on the platform at the far end of the room. After asking Vladimir if he would act as interpreter, she rose to speak to the assembled children and nuns.

'Nearly a year ago, Her Royal Highness, Princess Katerina visited our orphanage and was shocked that the medical equipment the children required was lacking. She vowed to do something to help us and although she lost the referendum to become Queen and gave up her rights to the throne, she never gave up on *us*. She launched a fund to aid St Paraskeva's, bought what was required and, with her friends, has driven here with a van loaded with materials. Thanks to her efforts there are now wheelchairs for all those who need them and we also have the medecines and vitamins necessary to control a variety of disorders. But that is not all: each child has been given a doll or a teddy bear because our generous guests have also brought a large box of toys. Think what this means to a little girl who has never had a doll and possibly never even seen one. I do not want to say anything more - only to thank Katy, as we must now call her, and also Vladimir, Marina and Kiril for everything they have done for us. May God bless you all.'

There was loud applause and a boy of about twelve came forward and handed bouquets of flowers from the convent garden to Katy and Marina. They smiled their thanks and then a group of the youngest children mounted the platform. A nun sat at the piano and the little choir sang three Maloslavian folk songs. They kept in tune surprisingly well, although two very small girls didn't appear to understand why they were there and remained silent, smiling at the audience and clutching their teddy bears. They were followed by the older children who were more ambitious and gave a moving performance of Tchakovsky's *Hymn to the Trinity* and Gounod's *Ave Maria*. When it was over, Katy and Vladimir congratulated the singers while Marina and Kiril talked to some boys who had discovered a train set in the box of toys and wanted to know how to set it up.

'It's time for us to go,' Vladimir whispered to Katy. 'It's half-past eleven already.'

Katy went up to Mother Ioanna. 'Thank you so much, Mother, for your kindness and hospitality. We're glad to see the children using all the things we brought.'

'You have given us exactly what we needed,' said Mother Ioanna. 'Do you really have to leave now?'

'I'm afraid we must. We're going to Svyatograd and we want to get there before it's dark as the roads aren't very good.'

'Very well, but remember you can come back to see us whenever you wish. You will always be welcome. May God guide you and keep you safe on your journey.'

The four of them walked back to the van accompanied by Sister Athanasia and followed by a crowd of children, all clamouring for them to stay.

Sister Athanasia kissed Katy on the forehead.

'You have done so much for us,' she said.

Katy looked at the others, smiling. 'I could never have done it without Vladimir. He's been my support all the way and Marina and Kiril have been a great help too.'

They climbed into the van and Kiril started the engine. The children followed them to the gate and waved until they were out of sight.

* * *

'It feels strange eating a buffet breakfast in the dining room,' said Katy. 'When I was in the Franz Josef last year I had to eat breakfast in my private suite. This is much nicer.'

'No regrets?' asked Marina.

'Absolutely none! Now what are we all going to do on our one day in Svyatograd?' said Katy.

'Marina and I have to visit the head office of our paper,' said Kiril. 'We're taking Vladimir with us because after that we'll give him a tour of the city and he also wants to try and find the block of flats where he lived with his parents and the hospital where he had polio. Are you coming with us?'

'I'd love to but I'm going to visit Janko in prison - the boy who tried to assassinate me.' said Katy.

'You must be crazy!' said Marina.

'No! The boy was foolish. He joined the Pioneers and they made fun of him because he was smaller and weaker than they were. They talked him into the shooting and he gave in because he was frightened of them and wanted to prove himself. He's sorry for what he did.'

'I should jolly well hope so!' said Marina. 'I can't understand why on earth you want to see him.'

'I can,' said Vladimir. 'If Katy meets him she can show him that she's forgiven him and that may help him put the past behind him and start a new life.'

'When are you going to see the boy?' asked Kiril.

'I phoned Dimitar and I'm meeting him outside the Central Prison at three o'clock.'

'Good!' said Kiril. 'You can come with us now, we'll visit our newspaper, do the tour of the city, find Vladimir's flat and hospital and then drop you at the prison at three.'

They left the dining room and as they came out into the foyer they nearly collided with Boyana, dressed in a starched white overall and chef's hat. When she saw them, she flung her arms round Katy's neck and kissed her to the surprise of several guests standing at the reception desk.

'I learn to be chef,' she said in English.

'That's wonderful. I'm very glad,' said Katy. 'Do you have any news of Yurek?'

' He got new girlfriend. They will have baby. He very happy,' said Boyana. 'And you? Are *you* happy?'

'Yes, I think so,' said Katy, smiling.

* * *

'What number is it?' asked Kiril as they drove down Frederick Engels Boulevard.

'A hundred-and-six,' said Vladimir.

'This road was my first glimpse of Svyatograd on the way from the airport last year,' said Katy. 'All these suburbs look alike.'

'There it is!' shouted Marina.

Kiril stopped and parked the van half on the pavement. They got out and looked. Number a hundred-and-six resembled all the other buildings on the Boulevard - a shabby Soviet-style apartment block covered in graffiti and adorned with lines of washing. There were cracks in the facade - a sure sign of subsidence - and the balconies' iron railings were rusty.

'Thank God my parents managed to take me to England. Imagine living there!' said Vladimir.

'It might have been better when your parents were there. The building was probably new then. It's been badly maintained,' said Katy.

'Or not maintained at all! And the hospital where I was taken looked just as bad didn't it? I shouldn't think anything's been done to it since the Second World War!'

'We'd better go,' said Kiril. 'I can't stay parked here and we've got to take Katy to the Central Prison. It's not far but it's nearly three o'clock already.'

Five minutes later they were at the prison gates.

'Are you sure you'll be all right?' asked Vladimir. 'Would you like me to come with you?'

'No, I must do this on my own,' said Katy. 'Janko's hardly going to assassinate me in prison is he?'

She waved goodbye and went over to a diplomatic car where Dimitar was sitting waiting for her. He got out and greeted her, bowing and kissing her hand.

'How nice to see you Katy! I suppose I have to call you Katy now?'

'That's right!' she said.

'It is good that you have asked to see Janko. He regrets very much what he did and he wants to meet you to tell you he is sorry. He is studying hard so that when he leaves the prison he can return to school and take his final exams.'

'How long will he have to be here?'

'He has a three year sentence, but because he has repented and his behaviour is good it is possible that he will be released in a year.'

A warder led them down a dark stone corridor with cells on each side and stopped at one at the far end. He unlocked the door and said in Maloslavian 'Make it short. I'll be waiting outside.'

Katy and Dimitar went in and the door was locked behind them. The cell contained a narrow bed, a metal cupboard, two chairs and a table piled with school books. Light came from a small barred window high up in the far wall. Janko was sitting at the table writing. His head was shaved and he wore an overall and trousers made of some coarse grey material. He looked at them with a sullen expression.

'*Vot knageena Katerina*,' said Dimitar. '*Na tyeper ona ne knageena. Ona zavoot Katy.*'

Janko said timidly 'Hullo. I can speak English. I learn English in the school.'

'Hullo Janko,' said Katy. 'It's good you can speak English. My

223

Maloslavian is very bad. Were you studying when we came in?'

'Yes, I study. I work hard and I like to read English book but it is difficult.' He handed her a copy of *David Copperfield*. She looked at it.

'That must be quite hard for you and it's very long too. Perhaps you should try something shorter and easier. If you like, I could send you some English books from London.'

Janko beamed. 'You would do that? I would like that very much. Thank you!' Then his face fell.

'I am very sorry for what I did. I did not want to kill you. They made me do it. You are good woman. Do you forgive me?'

'I understand what happened and I forgave you a long time ago,' she said. 'Now you must work hard so that when you get out of here you can go to university. They tell me that you used to have very good marks at school.'

'I will work hard! Will you write to me?'

'Of course I will,' said Katy and was about to give him a hug when the warder appeared, looking at his watch. 'Goodbye,' she said and hurried out with tears in her eyes, followed by Dimitar.

* * *

'How did your visit go?' asked Vladimir. He was sitting on the hotel terrace with Katy, having a drink before dinner.

'It went very well. Janko's a nice kid really and he's sorry for what he did. He was bullied into it by those Pioneer thugs. I think he's quite bright and he's studying hard in the prison. If he could get to university when he came out it would be the making of him.'

'Your visit must have meant a lot to him. University would be good for him if only they let him go there. And by the way, in six months' time I'll be in Cambridge starting *my* university studies!'

'I know,' said Katy. Then, on the spur of the moment, she said 'I might be leaving London too.'

Vladimir looked at her, surprised.'

'Oh, why?'

Katy told him about the Paris job. There was a long silence and then Vladimir said 'You never mentioned this before. Are you going to accept?'

'I don't know. What is there to keep me in London?'

His voice was cold. He said 'You've got an interesting job that you're good at. You're well on the way to becoming a journalist now that you're working on that magazine. In that art gallery you'd just be a glorified receptionist. What future is there in that?'

He hadn't said what she'd hoped to hear. There was no indication that he'd miss her. She had no idea what he felt about her and she was sorry she'd mentioned Paris.

'I haven't reached a decision yet, but I'll have to when I get back,' she said. 'Of course, it would be hard to leave London and I do like my job.'

* * *

The return journey was difficult because, once again, the rain came down in sheets and the narrow, badly maintained Balkan roads made driving treacherous. Kiril gripped the wheel and kept his attention glued to the highway. They were all tired and irritable and Katy was feeling depressed. Since she mentioned the possibility of moving to Paris Vladimir had hardly spoken to her.

'Have I done anything to upset you,' she'd asked him as they loaded their luggage into the van.

'What could you possibly do to upset me?' he'd replied, refusing to look at her.

After they crossed the frontier into Austria, the road conditions improved considerably. The rain had almost stopped but darkness was falling and when a small inn came into view not far from the Czech border, they decided to spend the night there. It was a pleasant looking place and as they entered delicious smells drifted in from the kitchen.

The innkeeper said he had rooms available and he could also give them some supper. They went into the dining room where a log fire was burning and sat on a bench at a long wooden table. A waiter brought them liver dumpling soup and apple strudel which they washed down with local white wine.

'That was good,' said Marina. 'I feel a lot better now. Let's have coffee.'

Kiril yawned. 'I don't want coffee. I've done most of the driving today and I'm whacked. I'm going to bed.'

He left and then Vladimir got up. 'I've got to ring my parents,' he said and went out in search of a phone.

Katy and Marina remained at the table and the innkeeper served them coffee with whipped cream. They talked for a while about the trip and then Marina, who had noticed Katy's sombre mood, said 'You love Vladimir don't you?'

'Yes,' said Katy and her hand shook as she stirred the mountain of cream into her coffee.

'Then you must show him that you love him.'

'I've tried so often to let him know how I feel but he doesn't seem to understand and now I've messed things up by telling him about the possibility of a job in Paris. I hoped it would spur him on but it's had the reverse effect.'

'I'm sure he loves you but he's afraid of being a burden and he doesn't want pity, so he hides his feelings. He's very proud. He'll never make the first move. That has to come from you.'

'I don't pity him! I love him! He's the only man I've ever really loved.'

'Then you must show him that. Don't tell him! Show him!'

She stopped talking abruptly because Vladimir had come back and was looking at them. Katy sensed that he knew they'd been talking about him. Embarrassed, she said 'Are your parents all right?'

'Yes, they're fine, thanks.'

'I'm going to bed,' said Marina and went out. Katy looked at Vladimir, trying to find something to say.

'I think it's stopped raining.'

'Yes.'

'The driving will be easier tomorrow if the weather's fine.'

They were silent. Then Vladimir said 'Well, I think I'll go up now.'

'So will I.'

There was no lift and he began laboriously to climb the steep flight of stairs. When they reached the landing they stood looking at one another.

'Good night,' he said abruptly. Forcing back tears, she went into her room, had a shower, and got into bed.

An hour later she was still awake, turning over the events of the day in her mind. She remembered Marina's words: 'Show him!' 'What have I got to lose?' she thought. She got up and went into the corridor. Vladimir's door was opposite hers. It was unlocked and she opened it gently and crept in. Some light filtered into the room from a street lamp and she saw a massive oak double bed. He was asleep under a heavy feather quilt and she slipped in beside him. He stirred as though half aware of her presence and it seemed to her that he smiled but he didn't wake up. She laid her head on his chest and snuggled up against him contentedly. The warmth of his body made her drowsy and she soon fell asleep.

Some hours later, she woke to find him smiling at her as though it was the most natural thing in the world to discover her in his bed. He took her in his arms and kissed her. 'It's so good you're here,' he whispered. 'I love you,' she said, stroking his hair and running her fingers lightly over his face. She sensed the thrill of pleasure that ran through him and felt her own body respond to it. They made love passionately but with a deep tenderness, discovering in each other a joy and fulfilment they had never known before. Afterwards, entwined in a close embrace, they slept, happy to be together at last, feeling they had come home.

In the morning, when she opened her eyes, she saw that he'd already left and she returned to her room, after checking that there was nobody in the corridor. She washed, dressed and went down to breakfast, afraid that he might have become cold and remote again but he was sitting at a table talking happily to Marina and Kiril. She sat down opposite him, poured herself some coffee and concentrated on spreading butter and jam on a roll. Then she forced herself to look up at him and he gave her a conspiratorial smile. The conversation flowed easily between the four of them and when they had finished eating, Vladimir said to her 'Let's go outside for a bit. It's a lovely day.'

They sat side by side on the terrace in the early spring sunshine looking at the river. The trees were coming into leaf and there were splashes of fresh green on the hills. He took her hand and for a long time they were silent, feeling so comfortable with each other that there was no need for words. Then he turned to her.

'It was a wonderful surprise last night when I woke and found you beside me. I've loved you for a very long time you know - even when I thought it was my vocation to become a monk - and when you told me you might go to Paris I couldn't bear the thought of losing you.'

'But I never knew what you were thinking and sometimes you've been really cold and unpleasant .'

'I'm sorry. I felt I'd got no right to show you my real feelings because I'm crippled. I was afraid you'd reject me.'

She ruffled his hair affectionately and said 'You can be very silly sometimes! Are you blind as well as crippled? Couldn't you see that I was trying as hard as I could to show you how much I cared for you?'

'Of course I saw you cared for me,' he said apologetically, 'But I wouldn't let myself believe it and I didn't want you to be with me out of pity and then regret it and feel I was a burden on you.'

She leaned over and gently kissed his legs. Looking into his eyes, she said 'But I love you just as you are and I love everything that makes you what you are! How could I possibly pity you? You make me happy and I want to be with you!'

He took her in his arms and their lips met in a long, tender kiss. Then, as she laid her head on his shoulder, he said 'I'll be moving to Cambridge in the autumn and I want you to come with me but,' he hesitated, 'I'm going to be studying at the Institute for Orthodox Christian Studies, and they might disapprove of us living together.'

She was surprised.

'Why, for heaven's sake?'

'Anyway I've got a much better idea!' He smiled. 'Katy, I'm afraid I can't go down on one knee, but will you marry me?'

Her face was radiant with happiness. 'Of course I will!' she said. 'You really mean it?'

'You know I do. I've waited so long to hear you say that!'

He held her close and kissed her forehead, her eyelids, her lips. Then he became serious and said 'You know it won't be easy at first. I'll have a student loan and also a grant because of my disability. My parents will assist me a bit but we won't have much to live on.'

'I'll get a job and that will help.' She smiled at him. 'The only thing that matters is that I'll be with you!'

'Then let's go and tell the others our news,' he said.

He took her arm and laughing and talking they went back to the inn.

Lightning Source UK Ltd.
Milton Keynes UK
UKOW031200040313

207100UK00012B/352/P